DENNY'S LAW

Recent Titles by Elizabeth Gunn from Severn House

The Sarah Burke Series

COOL IN TUCSON
NEW RIVER BLUES
KISSING ARIZONA
THE MAGIC LINE
RED MAN DOWN
DENNY'S LAW

The Jake Hines Series

McCAFFERTY'S NINE
THE TEN MILE TRIALS
ELEVEN LITTLE PIGGIES
NOONTIME FOLLIES

DENNY'S LAW

Elizabeth Gunn

Severn House Large Print
London & New York

This first large print edition published 2017
in Great Britain and the USA by
SEVERN HOUSE PUBLISHERS LTD of
19 Cedar Road, Sutton, Surrey, England, SM2 5DA.
First world regular print edition published 2016 by
Severn House Publishers Ltd.

Copyright © 2016 by Elizabeth Gunn.

British Library Cataloguing in Publication Data
A CIP catalogue record for this title is available from the British Library.

ISBN-13: 9780727895622

Severn House Publishers support the Forest Stewardship Council™
[FSC™], the leading international forest certification organisation. All
our titles that are printed on FSC certified paper carry the FSC logo.

MIX
Paper from
responsible sources
FSC® C013056

Typeset by Palimpsest Book Production Ltd.,
Falkirk, Stirlingshire, Scotland.
Printed and bound in Great Britain by
T J International, Padstow, Cornwall.

One

Martina didn't hear the fight until the yelling started. Five pre-school kids in one small house, a telenovela on the TV and a swamp cooler in the window, she had plenty of noise going on even before the parade started.

Sofia was the one who heard something and ran to the front window. 'Hey, there's a parade going by,' she said and pressed her face to the glass to look down the street. 'There's a school band and then cowboys on paint horses. So pretty, come and see!'

'I can't look,' Martina said. 'I got the twins up in the sink.' She could hear the crackle of snare drums, though, and feet keeping time on the pavement.

The twin girls were making the most of their bath, laughing and squealing while she doused them with the little bit of water they hadn't already splashed all over the kitchen. Then Sofia said, 'Oh, Ma, the drummer in this band is juggling his sticks – hoo! Is that cool or what?'

'Just what I needed,' Martina muttered, 'one more noise in here.'

'Aw, lighten up, Ma. Can't we have a little fun out of the Fourth like everybody else? Look, there's a mariachi band coming.' She giggled. 'With little American flags stuck on their instruments. I never seen that before, did you? Ooh,

1

la, that trumpet player gets his pants any tighter he won't be able to blow!'

'Figures you'd notice the one with the tightest pants,' Martina said.

But how could you not love that music? The mariachis must have paused right in front of her house; she could hear the trumpet plainly, high and sweet like notes straight out of heaven.

Then the singer came in with the first words of *Por Un Amor*, a lament about a man with pain in his poor *corazon*. His heart hurt very much because his lover was leaving. When he reached the climax the singer held one wonderful clear note till you were sure he would die from lack of oxygen. But no, he took a breath just in time to save his life and the song soared on as the band resumed its march.

'That's funny,' Sofia said, 'I never seen a mariachi band with a clown at the back, did you?'

'A clown? No. He must belong to some other float,' Martina said.

'He's lame, too – ain't that odd in a parade?'

'How you coming with the snacks? Sofia, will you watch what those boys are doing?'

'I see 'em, don't have a spazz.' She went back to her job at the dinette table, doling out apple slices to the two Anglo boys they called the Talibans. They were brothers, three and four years old. 'Sooo competitive,' their mother always said with a fond laugh.

About ready to kill somebody was more like it, Martina thought. But Mama paid in cash and on time, so what could you do but watch out for teeth and kicking? Sofia had them strapped into

2

high chairs at opposite sides of the table so they couldn't get at her or each other. They watched her cut up the apple, arguing like judges over who got bigger bites.

And now Sofia's baby was waking up, starting to whimper for her ten o'clock feeding.

'Let Juana cry a while,' Martina said. 'Good for her lungs.' Sofia was still providing the baby's milk so Juana would have to wait until Martina got the twins dressed and took over the Talibans. She reached for the big brown towel and shook it out one-handed over the counter by the sink, keeping a grip with her other hand on an arm apiece from the twins.

She said, 'Sit still now, my little beauties, here we go,' and hoisted Isabella, her fat brown body smooth and slippery as a seal, onto the towel. As she turned to pick up Yvette, she heard a man's howl of pain, a drawn-out 'No-o-o!' and yelling close by. Then a crash, like something heavy hitting a wall.

'Holy mother,' she said, 'what was that?'

'Sounds like it's next door,' Sofia said, getting up from the table again and moving toward the side window this time. They heard another yell and the sound of breaking glass. Craning her neck to see into the yard over the swamp cooler, Sofia said, 'Hey, there's a fight going on next door. Where that old guy lives? Wow, they gonna come right out through that window if they don't—' There was more yelling and pounding, then Sofia said, 'Ma, there's blood all over the glass now.'

'Well, what'm I s'posed to do about *that*?'

Martina said. But she lifted the two naked girls, towel and all, and carried them to the playpen in the hall. Diverted and happy, they waved and crowed while their hair curled into golden brown halos.

Martina hurried back to look. She was two inches taller than Sofia – she didn't have to stand on tiptoe – and after one quick glance she said, 'Oh, Jesus.'

There was indeed a terrific fight going on in the house next door. She heard the pounding sounds again and saw the window bulge when something collided with it. But the street was full of marching bands and floats, colorful and noisy. All the people who had come out of their houses were watching the parade, paying no attention to the fight.

The bystanders along the street pointed and waved at the next float, a shiny red convertible carrying a homecoming queen and her attendants. The queen waved back at the crowd and smiled, while the tubas in the band behind her brayed 'Oom-pah, oom-pah-pah.' Nobody noticed as a body hit the window again and more blood leaked out through the crack in the glass.

'Listen, I'll call the cops,' Martina told her daughter. 'You get back to the Talibans before they get their hands on that knife.' Both boys were stretching out of their seat restraints, cracking their shoulder joints in an effort to reach the knife Sofia had been using on the apple.

Martina hurried past the naked twins who were contentedly babbling to each other as they threw blocks and action figures out of the playpen.

4

They'd be yelling to get them all back in a minute. She hurried into her bedroom and fished her cell phone out of the folded quilt on the highest closet shelf.

She was hiding it up there so Sofia couldn't sneak phone calls to her new worthless boyfriend. It was uncanny – did Sofia have some dog-whistle thing only dropout losers could hear? This latest deadbeat had plenty of tattoos but no job, of course. So he had time to hang around, to slip into Sofia's futon, the sheets not even cooled off yet from when Juana's no-good father slipped out of them. Martina didn't think Juana needed a baby sister just yet.

As her hand felt the phone, Martina heard a sound outside her bedroom window, somewhere nearby, a quiet *thunk* that was somehow familiar but she didn't have time to think about it now.

Cursing the rotten luck that brought her all these distractions – as if day-care money wasn't still hard to collect, dependent children money always tough to get and donations from the Food Bank shrinking – didn't she have *Dios mia*, plenty to think about already? Last thing she needed was to get involved in this trouble next door.

She had schooled herself to always speak English but when she got excited her thoughts slid back into some of her mother's expressions. She warned herself now, *No vale la pena llamar!* The police always questioned the one who called. But the blood was on the glass, the window was broken – somebody had to do something.

Martina dialed 911.

Two

'Lotta blood inside, I hear, Detective,' the young patrolman said, holding the posse box steady so Sarah could sign in. 'You got plenty of gum?'

'Yeah, Delaney told me,' Sarah said.

'You think we got a slasher?'

The new kids always like to punch up the story a little. She hunched over the sign-in sheet, trying to shield the paper from the wind. A fine line of stinging grit slid under her arm, her pen hit a pebble and her signature wobbled.

'Stupid wind,' she said. 'When is it ever going to bring that monsoon?' She put the pen back in its slot and squinted at the young patrolman's name tag. 'Tobin? Oh, you're Leo's son, aren't you? I watched you graduate not too long ago. I'm Sarah Burke.' She shook his hand. 'Is it Tom?'

'Yes. Just please don't call me Tommy like my dad does.'

She laughed. 'Go easy on your dad. He's so proud of you; he's ready to bust a gut. How's the career going?'

'So far I've mostly been doing fun rides with my FTO.' He made a face and she chuckled obligingly. To head off horror stories about field training officers she pulled out her phone and scrolled for messages.

But Tom Tobin had been alone too long; he wanted to chat. 'I been standing here half an hour

6

and you're the first detective I've seen,' he said. 'I know where my dad is – on his wimpy little motorbike in the Shriner parade. But where's everybody else?'

'Doing what most people do on Sunday the Fourth of July, I guess – enjoying themselves. Weekends and holidays, Delaney has to find us before he can send us. I was a little slow getting out of the house so he found me first.'

She was in full working gear, the good shirt, pressed slacks, badge on her belt and Glock on her hip. Her off-duty clothes were in the car, so if the case didn't keep her all day she could still make the family picnic at the ranch – her watch said not quite ten.

'Has the neighborhood been this quiet ever since you got here? I don't see anybody around.' Behind Tom Tobin a cracked sidewalk led across a few feet of thin gravel to a tan stucco house with two narrow windows flanking a peeling wooden door.

Dust and trash blew across the yard and a bigger gust brought the faint smell of hay and horse manure. Menlo Park had been partially gentrified but the stables must be still there on Spruce Street, she realized with satisfaction. The birthday parties of her childhood had often included a trail ride into the desert, starting from this neighborhood.

'Quiet as a church,' Tom said as she stepped around him. 'Only ones here are the ME and a couple of techies that came in that van behind you. And watch out for that pushy black lady with the dyed red hair.'

7

'You mean Gloria? From the crime lab? What about her?'

'She came back out here about two minutes after she signed in and said she was locking the front door so I should tell everybody to go around to the back.'

'Oh? OK.'

Tom cleared his throat and said, 'Boy, she really knows how to say what she wants, huh?'

'Yup. Better not argue with Gloria.' *And if you think I'm going to discuss her with a rookie you still need a few more rides with that training officer.*

Thinking about the scene she was walking toward, she put two fresh sticks of gum in her mouth and followed the walk to the front door. 'Looks like a home invasion that found somebody home and turned into a murder,' Delaney had said. She turned right along a faint path that ran along the front of the house and then left along the side wall to the back. The path didn't exactly stand out since the rest of the yard was almost bare of gravel too. But there was no danger she'd get lost. The rear of the house was just ahead.

She took note of the shattered glass and blood smears on the side window as she passed it. This must be from the fight that got the neighbors' attention, she thought. Delaney had said the call came from the house next door. She stayed close to the side of the victim's house, not wanting to disturb the scene outside.

'Jason's the only other detective I've found so far,' Delaney had told her, 'so he'll take the scene on this one, but he's at some pageant with his nephew so it'll be a while before he gets there.'

Good, maybe I'll get a few minutes by myself in here after the scene techs get done, Sarah thought. First impressions could tell you a lot sometimes, if there wasn't too much commotion to think.

Standing by the rear corner of the house on Alameda Avenue, she looked around her as she pulled on plastic booties and gloved up. Hard to believe she was only about a mile and a half from her office on South Stone. It was just a scoot under the highway and then down Congress past the Mercado, no more than ten minutes in any weather, but Menlo Park felt like a different world.

Headquarters building was downtown, on the edge of the constantly shifting power centers that ran the city. But this neighborhood below Signal Mountain was in the oldest part of Tucson. Prehistoric people had grown corn and beans here for thousands of years before the first Spanish soldiers showed up, looking for a route to the California coast.

Before you put down footings in this neighborhood, a builder had once told Sarah, you should consider the risk of digging up the bones and artifacts of people who were making pots here ten thousand years ago. Then the paleontologists would come out of their classrooms at the university, conveniently located nearby. An exploration might soon be organized, and later a photo spread would run in the *Tucson Daily Star*, crowing happily about another historic find in the Old

Pueblo. The dig might continue for months, even years, while your banker found a way to weasel out of your loan.

Anglo merchants had moved in behind the soldiers at the end of the nineteenth century. They built brick-and-stucco bungalows on top of the ancient fire pits with covenants forbidding any sales to Hispanics. As they prospered, though, they moved out to bigger houses on pricier lots. This section was more than half Hispanic now, many houses occupied for four or five generations by the same family.

Jason would have no trouble searching this backyard, Sarah saw – it was small and simple, graveled like its neighbors, with a couple of mesquite trees and a small bench.

There were two substantial items back here, though – a good dirt bike tethered to the bench with a padlocked chain and a white Ford Ranger pickup, five or six years old but in good shape with new-looking tires. Few houses in this part of town had garages – people just parked in their yards.

Many of the yards in this block of Alameda had fences or walls, but this one was marked off from its neighbors only by a row of river stones that followed the depression, not quite a ditch, that marked its edges along both sides. The house had a deeper overhang on the roof in back. At each end of the overhang vines in brick planters climbed lattices staked upright in the planter and fastened to the roof edge at the top. Pretty smart, actually, Sarah thought, walking around it. The vines created an area of cooler privacy, like a

10

patio but without a floor. A small, cheap outdoor table and two chairs sheltered in the vines' shade on the other side of the door.

She stepped under the overhang and walked five paces to the exact middle of the rear wall where a stone slab served as the rear stoop. When she opened the back door a gust of super-cool air came out, smelling like blood and feces, sweat and black powder. And bacon? She stuck her head in and said, 'How's it going, Gloria?'

'Hey, Sarah. Not quite ready to let you at it,' Gloria said, not pausing, her camera flash blazing away. 'Be about ten minutes longer.' Her bright curls, a shade or two more coppery than her skin, bobbed above the camera. 'You can come in if you promise to stand on one of those pads I put down.'

'Gotcha.' Sarah hopped onto a Styrofoam pad and looked around for the next safety zone. She didn't expect any more guidance from Gloria, who continued working steadily, hitting the flash twice in each spot before she moved three inches and lit up again.

I suppose she did startle poor Tom a little, she thought. Gloria Jackson had learned the hard way how to defend her turf – she'd survived public schools in Watts and held onto a basketball scholarship at UCLA for two years before she gave up her dreams of world pro touring and got serious about her forensic science degree.

Moving into the room, Sarah took shallow breaths and chewed her gum energetically for a couple of minutes. It didn't take much time – her brain had learned to accept gross sights and disgusting smells as part of the job. After that first two minutes of careful breathing she would stay focused on the body and its surroundings, sorting the rich bouquet of odors like a K-9, retaining the useful information it brought her.

First, the sharp smells of urine and feces. Then cooking smells, still strong in here, especially bacon. And the sweet, slightly metallic aroma of blood. But looking around she saw less blood than she'd expected. Spatters on the tile floor and two area rugs, and the smears on the broken side window she'd seen from outside. Part of a bloody handprint gleamed on the round wood dining table by the window, and a little blood had pooled and clotted in the carpet five feet inside the front door, where the ME knelt beside the body.

Two other crime-scene technicians were at work in the room. The older one, Sandy, was swabbing bloodstains onto slides for DNA identification. The younger criminalist, whom Sarah didn't know, was spreading black powder over every surface that might yield latent fingerprints.

Neither technician looked up from her work so Sarah just said, 'Morning,' and read the new one's name, Jody, off her ID tag as she hopped past them. She followed a line of white safety pads until she reached a spot where most of the body was visible between her and Dr Cameron.

Safe on her clean spot, Sarah pulled her electronic tablet out of its slot in her day-pack and began to type in details about the scene and the victim in random order as they occurred to her. No use trying to hurry criminalists at a crime scene; they were tasked with being thorough, not fast. Anyway, some quiet time in a corner was not a bad way to start.

So, now, what have we got here?

The victim was spread-eagled on his back in a sleeveless T-shirt and khaki shorts. He'd been described to her as 'an old guy' but he looked surprisingly solid and fit. His arms and legs were smoothly muscled and strong as if he'd spent a lot of time riding the bike in the backyard.

No way to judge how his face might have impressed her before this morning. Now it looked pretty much like dog meat. This must have been a helluva fight, she thought. I wonder what the other guy looks like? Besides the battered face and broken window she could see broken pieces of a chair and smashed crockery scattered around.

The attacker had used a club of some kind – fists alone could not have done that much damage to a face. He must have carried the weapon away with him; she scanned the room twice and saw nothing that would have broken the victim's nose and cheekbones and put that bloody hole in the right side of his forehead. A broken tooth hung by a glistening thread out of the remnants of his mouth.

The dead man's sparse summer clothing had been reduced to shreds – the T-shirt was ripped almost off and the top button of his shorts was missing. He had been wearing flip-flops till the fight started – one was under the table now, the other beneath the cracked window. He wore threadbare but surprisingly clean boxers under the ruined shorts, and no jewelry but a drugstore watch.

Sarah typed in a description of the clothing and added, *Vic fit for his age, prob late 60s.*

Then she added thoughtfully, *Can't see defen wounds on arms/hands. Not alarmed at first?*

In fact – 'Gloria?'

'Mmm?'

'You take pictures of the front door yet?'

'Yup. Got a bunch.' She looked up. 'Nothing broken, is that what you're wondering? Here, you want to see?' She reached out a long arm, twisted the latch and swung it open. The door and its latch were both intact. 'Looks like the invader got in without a fight.'

''K. Thanks.'

Gloria closed the door again quickly and locked it.

Doctor Cameron, the till-now silent man who had not paused to greet Sarah, almost startled her when he said, 'Gloria, will you help me roll the body, please?'

Gloria put her camera down on the floor, said, 'Sure,' and worked her way carefully to a spot beside the body, where she stooped to help him. Gloria had once told Sarah that Dr Cameron was the coolest dude on the ME's staff. 'So polite and nice,' she said. 'It's a pleasure to work with a guy like that.'

Sarah had been amused to learn that noisy Gloria, the most assertive of the scene techs, admired the awkward, bony Scot who rarely spoke. But after she'd seen them work together a couple of times she realized that, unlikely or not, she was watching a demonstration of perfect rapport in the workplace.

Sarah paid close attention as the doctor laid the shreds of T-shirt aside and pulled the pants down. 'Some lividity has started, in the shoulders and buttocks.' He looked at his watch. 'Little over two hours since this was called in. Seems about right.'

Gloria said, 'Doc, can you hold his clothes like that while I get some shots? Careful now, don't let me blind you.' While Gloria stood over him, shooting one picture after another, Sarah took a couple with her cell phone too. She liked having her own pictures to review while she worked a case.

'Rigor's just getting started in the hands and feet,' Cameron said as they laid the body back in its original position. 'Usually it starts in the jaw, but for this guy, of course . . .' He touched a section of pulpy flesh and shrugged.

'Doc,' Sarah said, 'I think I saw a wallet in his left pocket – OK if I fish it out of there?'

'Sure, go ahead.'

She stooped, reached carefully between the doctor's raised hands and stood up holding the wallet just as Delaney walked into the room. A pale redhead whose skin was ill-suited to summer on the Mexican border, the chief of homicide was burned to a high pink color, skin peeling on his nose and chin. He was in booties and gloved up but still wore the striped shirt and black pants of the baseball game he'd been umpiring at his son's school when he took the call. It might have looked comical in this setting but Delaney's aloof seriousness forestalled comment. He could probably walk in wearing a tutu, Sarah thought, and nobody would say a word.

15

'Ah, you found ID, good,' he said. 'Who've we got?'

'Driver's license says Calvin Springer.'

'Good, that matches what I found for this house.'

'Same name on everything else in here – two credit cards, gas card, ATM, discount cards for groceries and the drug store, library card—' She looked up. 'Library card? Didn't expect that.'

Delaney said, 'So your victim could read, so what? Well, you might want to check out what he's been reading. What else?'

'Hundred and forty-three dollars – he wasn't robbed. Monthly pass on the streetcar. Couple of winning chits from the slots at the Indian Casino. Numbers taped in an inside pocket, looks like bank accounts, or maybe a safety deposit drawer? So far,' she folded the wallet and dropped it in an evidence bag, 'the records of the model citizen.'

'Except no Medicare card? Looks old enough, doesn't he?'

'Yes. Come to think of it no social security card either – most people don't carry that with them, though. Probably find a drawer full of records here someplace.'

'Yeah.' He scanned the house. 'Place looks pretty straightforward, doesn't it? No frills. Don't see any signs of high life.'

'Nope. Good bike out there tied to an old bench. Decent pickup. Everything says quiet habits, lower middle class. But he sure made somebody cross, didn't he?' The signs of rage in the fight scene were so strong they were beginning to make Sarah's stomach hurt. This man had waged all-out war in his house, the stakes plainly life or death from the start. Although how could they know who started it? 'The other guy must have some marks on him too.'

'Guy or guys? We don't know there was only one invader, do we?'

'No. But it doesn't look like a gang. The door lock's not broken – nobody broke in. Will you show him, Gloria?' Delaney moved carefully to look. 'And he doesn't have defensive marks on his hands and arms, see? He wasn't alarmed until they started to fight.'

'The center panel on the front door's dented, though.'

'From the inside. Must have happened during the fight.'

'So maybe they knew each other? One of them's gotta be pretty strong,' Delaney said, 'to throw a grown man against a door like that.'

'Probably both. This victim doesn't look like any pushover, does he?' Sarah said. 'The woman who called it in said he was "an old guy." But he sure looks able-bodied to me.'

'I agree,' Delaney said. 'And we don't actually know which man got thrown against the door, do we?'

'Good point.' There was silence in the room for a couple of minutes while they both scrutinized the muddle of broken furniture and dishes in the middle of the room.

The victim must have been eating breakfast when the killer arrived. Shards of his breakfast plate were on the floor near the table, a fork nearby holding the drying remnant of a fried egg. Sarah was thinking, did the attacker knock? Maybe. Because the victim got up out of his chair, pushed it back toward the wall . . . opened the door? Let the visitor in and then . . . what? The visitor said something. Or did something?

Then the fight started and one of them . . . maybe grabbed the chair that's broken over there. They had a big skirmish by the side window, broke the glass . . . looks like the victim broke free at some point and ran toward the front door. Trying to get outside?

Or . . . scanning again, she saw something – a shadow? – underneath the string of dried red peppers that hung by the front door. She hadn't thought about it before because a string of drying peppers was so ubiquitous in Tucson houses it was no more noticeable than windows and doors.

'Gloria, can you reach that *ristra*? Just move it a few . . . Yeah, there. That's what I thought.' There was a leather belt hanging beneath the peppers, its buckle hooked over the same wooden peg. A holster hung from the belt with the butt of a handgun showing.

'Ooo-*eeee*,' Gloria said. 'Ain't that a hole in the boat?' She had been packing up by the front door where she shot the last pictures. Now she stooped to her bags, muttering, 'Damn, gotta get all my stuff back out . . .'

Delaney held the string of peppers up so Gloria could photograph the weapon from both sides where it hung.

A soft leather belt and matching holster, dark oxblood finish, tooled in a quietly elegant geometric pattern, held a stainless-steel Smith & Wesson revolver with a rubber stock.

Delaney pulled the gun out, said, 'Hmm, very nice weapon.' He swung the cylinder out. 'A .22 10-shot. Cylinder's full, though.' He sniffed. 'Nice and clean. Didn't get used in this fight, apparently. Might as well disarm it right away, get pictures and bag it, hmm?'

'Here,' Gloria said. 'I'll put a drop cloth on the kitchen counter.' They passed the revolver from one gloved hand to another. As Gloria laid it out, Delaney dictated the description while Sarah took notes. 'Smith and Wesson revolver, Model 617, K-22 Masterpiece, has a four-inch barrel with a satin stainless-steel finish and a Hogue Rubber stock. Ammo is .22 Long Rifle, rim-fire, of course. Let's see, what else?'

'Well, it doesn't need to go in this description,' Sarah said, 'but I'll put in my report that this is a surprisingly luxurious item to find in the bare-bones dwelling of a threadbare man.'

'Agreed. Now where did I put—' Delaney was patting his pockets with his left hand.

'Here,' Sarah said, passing him an evidence bag.

'Thanks. Ah, the number's not filed, that's nice. The lab will tell us if this weapon's been to any other crime scenes we have on record.'

'Sure. But it's not going to help us with this case, is it? You seen any evidence of gunfire, Doc?'

'Not so far.' Cameron stood up, massaged his knees and sighed. 'But I can't say what killed him yet, either. You're going to have to wait for the autopsy on this one.'

19

'Getting his head reduced to cat food wasn't enough?' Delaney said. 'Don't think I've ever seen anybody beat up this bad.'

'I know. But . . . well, I don't want to say more until after I get him on the table. Be patient.'

Delaney said, 'OK. But so far the evidence matches what the caller said. She heard a big fight with yelling but she didn't hear any gunfire.'

'All that blood over there by the window, Doc,' Sarah said. 'Isn't that evidence of a horrendous beating?'

'Spatters,' the doctor said. 'Might have been a fairly even fight there for a while, so we got a lot of streaks and spatters. But look, this guy's head is beat to a *pulp*. Seems like there should be more blood here around the body.'

'So what are you saying? That maybe he was already dead before the last blows landed? That's pretty weird.'

'Unusual, too,' Cameron said. 'Ordinarily it takes time to die from a beating, no matter how severe.'

'You think maybe the killer went on beating a dead man? I don't like that at all,' Sarah said. 'That means we're looking for a crazy guy.'

'Or somebody so mad he's out of control,' Gloria said.

'Not sure I buy that,' Delaney said. 'He wasn't too looney to sneak out of here, was he? Nobody's reported seeing him go, have they? He must have had blood all over himself, too.'

'Yeah – how did he do that? A helper, maybe,' Sarah said. 'Somebody waiting with a car?'

'Or he lives right here in the neighborhood,' Gloria suggested, zipping lids on her bags.

20

'And he's probably watching us now? I like that even less,' Sarah said.

'Before you go scaring yourselves to death,' Cameron said, 'you might consider waiting for the lab reports.'

'You're the one who started this,' Sarah said, 'saying there's not enough blood.'

Cameron rolled his eyes up and said, 'When will I learn to be silent?'

Oh, now I've done it, Sarah thought. If Cameron gets any quieter than he's been so far, we'll be working with a mute.

A message squawked into the coil in the doctor's ear as he did a full-body stretch, groaning after too much time on his knees.

Delaney, watching his angular body reach for the ceiling, said, 'You finished for now, Doc?'

'Yes,' the doctor said, 'and the pick-up team's just arrived. This must be the driver now.' Somebody was rattling the front-door latch.

But when Delaney unlocked it Jason Peete stuck his head in and said, 'The meat wagon's right behind me – you ready for them?' Even for Jason, he looked unusually animated in skin-tight biking shorts and a wife-beater shirt. 'Better be close because the mother of all rainstorms is right behind *them*.'

'Ready to go,' Cameron said, gimping toward the door, still stiff. 'Wait, though, I better tell those drivers to come in the back . . .'

'They can't get the ambulance back there,' Delaney said. 'Tell them to park at the curb in front and come to the front door. We'll work it out somehow.'

'I'll do it,' Jason said and streaked across the yard.

When he knocked on the front door a couple of minutes later, Gloria opened it, letting in a gust of wind filled with dirt and trash. On the doorstep, Jason stood with two storm-buffeted men who were struggling to set up the legs on a gurney.

Delaney said, 'Now, you can't bring that thing in here. You'll have to carry the body out on a stretcher.'

Grumbling, the ambulance drivers ran back to their vehicle and returned with a stretcher. They fumbled with the assembly, looking up anxiously at the sky. Big drops of water had begun plinking into the dusty yard and lightning flashed along the horizon.

In the house, they bagged the body, lifted it onto the stretcher and carried it quickly outside, not paying much attention to Gloria's pleas about where to put their feet.

The doctor gathered his own tools and ran to his car, saying he'd better get to the morgue before the streets in the low end of town flooded.

Jason helped the ambulance crew get the body shifted onto the gurney in the yard. Grunting, they heaved it into the van. As soon as the ambulance was rolling Jason ran full tilt for the house and threw open the door. As he jumped back inside he was lit from behind by a dazzling bolt of lightning that split the blackening sky and gleamed off his shaved head. 'Holy shit, guys, that was close!' His words were drowned in thunder as a gale-force wind shook the house.

Delaney stuck his head out to look, pulled it back in completely disheveled and said, 'Highway Ten is disappearing into a dust cloud.'

'I am *out* of here,' Gloria said, zipping up her gear bags one last time. She bolted out to her car, running with the bags clutched close to her chest.

The house was briefly quiet inside. Small puddles began to form as rain and grit blew in through the cracked side window. Delaney, on his phone, began begging the repair team he'd called earlier to come right away. 'It's essential we seal this window before the storm blows it out entirely!' Sounds of protest came over the phone. 'I know you can't handle plywood in this wind but we can't let the house get flooded either. Bring some plastic sheeting and we'll seal it on the inside.'

The two remaining technicians, relieved of the need to work around a body, put on fresh gloves and went right back to their chores, chattering as cheerfully as sparrows about a TV series whose back seasons they were both binge-watching on TV.

Delaney's phone chirped. He answered and then launched into what Sarah called 'one of his phoning fits,' texting and talking rapid-fire to one person after another. He was always multi-tasking and now, with the storm, had to rearrange several work sites.

Sarah and Jason moved too, hopping together from one clean spot to the next while she filled him in on the details about the table, the cracked window and the broken chair. When they came to a standstill near the back door they put their heads together and talked softly over Delaney's ongoing phone conversations.

'This victim,' Jason said, 'you got a read on him yet?'

She showed him the contents of the wallet, adding, 'I still need to talk to the neighbor who called it in. She told the first responders he was a quiet old guy who never caused any trouble. He looks quite a bit more agile than I expected but the house matches what she said – plain but decent.'

'See what you mean,' Jason said, peering around. 'One set of dishes in the cupboard by the table. Bed's made in the bedroom.' They were standing where he could see through the open door. 'Cheap bedspread. No frills, for sure. One straight chair in there, clip-on light on the bed.'

'But a reader, you see that?' Sarah said. 'Library card in the wallet, and besides the books in there he had, uh . . .' squinting, '. . . *Sports Illustrated* and a couple of boating magazines.'

'Funny, though, I don't see any pictures.' Jason went on scanning. 'No family photos, none of the usual clutter. He live here long?'

'Don't know yet. The other thing we don't know,' Sarah said, 'is how the attacker got here and left. I was hoping you'd find some vehicle tracks when you did the crime-scene report. But now, with this storm . . .' She shrugged.

Another gust shook the house, followed by the rattle of hail against the roof and front windows. Lightning lit the room and thunder crashed, so loud they all jumped.

'Wow, it came up fast, didn't it?' Sarah said.

24

'Standard monsoon schedule, first storm on the Fourth of July,' Jason said. 'Now we got us a body we can go right ahead with our holiday thriller movie. But where's Tony Soprano when we need him?'

'Actually I don't think we do need him; I think you'll do fine,' Sarah said, suddenly vastly amused by how bizarre he looked, mud-spattered and soaked in his skin-tight speedos with wet leaves plastered to his calves. 'How come you're turning up to work in bike jammies?'

'Delaney caught me helping out at my nephew's day-care Fourth of July pageant,' Jason said. 'I was in stars and stripes and a tall hat, the whole nine yards. I asked the boss if I should come as Uncle Sam or go home and change and he said, "Just find something decent to put on and get over there, Sarah's all alone." This is what I wear under my Uncle Sam costume and when I saw the weather report I thought it might be just the ticket. Turned out I was right about *that*.'

Tom Tobin burst in the back door, hugging his posse box, letting in a great gust filled with dirty rain. 'Hoo,' he said, 'I gotta get in outta that.'

'My God, I forgot about you,' Delaney said. 'Where have you been?'

'I jumped in my car when the lightning started,' Tom said. 'I figured it would let up pretty soon and the rest of the crew would be along, but . . .'

The lights went out. Momentarily shocked into silence, everybody stood still, looking around. The air conditioner sighed once and died. Tom rolled his eyes toward Delaney along a darkening wall. 'I guess this kind of wraps it up, doesn't it?'

25

'We'll see,' Delaney said, out of the gloom. 'After the carpenters get here to seal up that window and secure the doors, if it clears up a little maybe we can start the canvass, hmm?' Ignoring the dubious looks he was getting from his detectives, he said, 'But you can go check out, Tom. You can't stand out here in this weather. The crime scene's already fucked and we can time ourselves out when we get back to the station.'

'You got it,' Tom said and fought his way out the door into the worsening storm.

'Well, I've got a couple of LED lights in the van,' Jody said, 'but I honestly don't think it's worth the trouble to set them up. Really, I've got about all the prints I'm going to get here.'

'I was just about to say I got all my DNA swabs too,' Sandy said. 'And have you thought about how hot it's going to get in here in a few minutes?'

'The storm will cool it off a little. But let's see,' Delaney said. 'Is the whole neighborhood dark or is it just—'

They all peered out the windows. Sarah said, 'No light anywhere. Lightning must have hit a transformer.'

'Damn. That's not going to get fixed right away.' Delaney took a breath. 'OK, Sandy, Jody, guess you better go. You need any help getting your gear out to the van?'

'No, we can manage,' Sandy said, anxious to leave before Delaney thought of some jobs they might be able to do in the dark. Jason insisted on helping, though, as they struggled out the door and into the van. Sarah watched through a front window as their van lit up and rolled away and

26

Jason made another heroic dash for the door through the crashing storm.

Then it was just the three of them hunkered in the dark, bloody room, listening as the storm battered the house.

'Well, I suppose we could get some of the scene work done while we wait,' Delaney said. 'Try to find an address book. Measure and sketch this room. You got a tape with you, Jason?'

'In the car,' Jason said. He looked out the window at the chaos, raised his eyebrows at Delaney and asked, 'You don't have one?' With an ugly cracking sound a branch split off a nearby mesquite tree and went tumbling down the street.

'But listen, I've been thinking,' Sarah said. 'You haven't found any more records on this victim so far, have you, boss?'

'Just what I already told you, what I got in the initial complaint,' Delaney said, looking resentfully at the phone he was holding. 'And I think the first responders got that off Google. Fourth of July, the support staff isn't working and I can't seem to get any of my messages returned. Looks like I won't get much till tomorrow.'

'What if the body we just sent to the morgue isn't Calvin Springer?'

'What? Why would you think it wasn't? He had this wallet in his pocket in his own house.'

'Right. But if the homeowner won the fight and didn't want to talk about the man he just killed . . . I'm just saying, it wouldn't take long to switch wallets. And it might give him a whole day's head start.'

'That's pretty far-fetched, Sarah. Haven't we

got trouble enough right here with this broken window and no lights? What are you suggesting?'

'The only picture we've found here is in this wallet. On his driver's license. Pretty miserable picture, as usual' – she showed him – 'but I took a couple of pictures of the body with my phone while Gloria was shooting hers, see? And surely the neighbor who phoned in the complaint could say if they look like the man who lives here.'

'Is that worth going out in this storm?'

'She might know other stuff about him. The neighbors are really all we've got right now, aren't they? And didn't you say the person who called this in is next door?'

'Well, yes . . . let's see. Martina Ybarra. Runs a day-care center here on Alameda – must be this stucco bungalow with the swing set, right across the little ditch with the river stones.' He peered out through the water and grit leaking through the broken window beside him. 'Ah, but that ditch is a little river now.'

'Still,' Sarah said, 'I could run to my car. I've got my camera out there and my Glock.'

'I don't want you to go alone, it's too crazy out there. And Jason can't go to a door dressed like that; nobody'll believe he's a cop.'

'That's right, Sarah,' Jason said quickly. 'I'd be *inappropriate*.'

'No problem. I've got a slicker in the car – you can put that over your biker suit and look like all-weather police. Come on, it beats squatting in here watching trees fall apart, doesn't it?'

'Aw, hell, I guess. And they're sure to be home,

huh? Not going out in the rain with all those babies.'

Three

They stood on the front porch under Sarah's big umbrella, holding up their badges. The door was opened by a pretty girl holding a baby.

'Good afternoon,' Sarah said. 'We're from the Tucson Police Department.' People sometimes freaked if she said homicide; she'd learned to ease into it. 'We need to ask you some questions about the complaint you called in—'

The girl turned away and yelled across the baby's head, 'Mama!' Naked except for a diaper, the baby waved its arms and smiled, looking pleased to have company.

A dark-haired woman looked up from a round table at the back where she was minding several children. 'What?'

'These people say they police!' the girl yelled.

'What?' The woman peered toward the open door, said something to the children and came forward, carrying a lighted candle in a small glass holder. The flame wavered in wind from the door and she protected it with her hand. Peering over it at the two of them huddled under the dripping umbrella, she said, 'Your car break down or something?' Then she saw their badges and said, 'Oh.'

'Tucson Police,' Sarah said again and explained that they were detectives investigating 'the

29

problem' next door. 'Was it you who called in the report about the fight?'

'Yes. But I don't know nothing more,' the woman said firmly. 'That man never talked to me; I don't know him at all.'

'I understand. Could we just come in a minute so I can ask you a couple of questions?' The wind blew her hair across her face and she scrabbled at it with her free hand, feeling disadvantaged. She tried to stay tidy so people would know she was trustworthy.

But windblown worked for her this time. The dark woman took pity on her, standing there getting pelted by the storm. 'Oh, sure, come in . . .' She clucked. 'Such weather.'

They edged in and closed the door. In the sudden silence they wiped their feet on the aged doormat and looked around them at the crowded room. Then Jason reopened the door and leaned out to close the umbrella and leave it. Before he got the door closed, lightning flashed again, very close, followed quickly by a roll of thunder. Jason flinched as he pulled the door closed and turned to face the two women. Water dripped off his naked skull onto his shoulders.

The girl with the baby handed Jason the towel she had slung over her shoulder. Smiling, she said matter-of-factly, 'Here, you wanna wipe off?'

Jason was so dumbfounded he took it and dried his head. Handing it back, he said, 'Thanks,' and smiled into her lovely dark eyes. She smiled back, watching him attentively, as if he were some exotic life form in a museum she was visiting for the first time.

30

Sarah said, 'We need to ask you a few questions about the trouble you reported next door.'

'I made the call,' the older woman said, 'but I don't know nothing else. Only it sounded like a big fight. They broke the window.'

'Do you know the man who lives there? Your neighbor?'

'Know what he looks like. We don't talk much at all.' She was apprehensive and careful again. 'He's an old Anglo guy – quiet.'

'Is his name Calvin Springer?'

'Don't know his name. He probably don't know mine either.' They saw her making a decision, getting firmer. 'And I got all I can manage here – I don't think I can help you anymore.' She cleared her throat and then, carefully respectful, added, 'Officers.'

Jason said sympathetically, 'We can sure see got your hands full here, um, Martina. Have I got that right? You're Martina Ybarra?'

'That's right. This is my daughter, Sofia.' She pointed to his name on his shield and said, 'That's how you spell Peete, with all those e's?'

'Well, Peete's my last name, see. My first name's Jason. That is a little confusing, I guess. And this is Detective Sarah Burke – she's the lead detective on this case. We've got just a, you know, a few questions.'

'Well . . . I'd like to help if I could, but . . .' The woman looked from one of them to the other. 'But I don't *know* him,' she said again.

'You're very alert and observant, though, aren't you? You did such a terrific thing already, using your head and calling us so promptly in

31

spite of this awful storm.' He leaned a little toward the older woman, oozing respect. 'And all these children . . . how many babies you got in here?'

'Oh, just five today. I got more clients than this but some people kept theirs home today because of the holiday.'

'Oh, sure, the Fourth,' Jason said. 'Celebrations all over town, I guess. I got called away from my nephew's school pageant.' For one dizzy instant he grew an antic expression and Sarah was afraid he was going to show her what he was wearing under the slicker. But he stifled the impulse and went back to smiling kindly at the two women.

Sofia said, 'Yeah, we even had a mariachi band go by here. With little US flags stuck to their instruments – ain't that crazy? And something else different – a clown with a limp.'

'Still not sure I believe that part,' Martina muttered.

'You weren't looking. I *saw* him,' Sofia said. She had a sweet face but resentment seethed in her when her mother put her down.

'A band went by during the fight?' Sarah looked dubious.

'Yes,' the mother said. 'It was a parade.'

'At the same time as the fight? But no connection, right?' Sarah had her tablet out, typing. People like to see their words noted down but this story seemed so unlikely. 'When did you notice the fight – you saw something, or . . .?'

'No, it was a noise. Like a thump.' She looked at the girl. 'And then Sofia ran to look.' They took turns, then, telling the story – the noises, the broken glass and blood on the window.

'Could you hear sounds? Did they say anything, yell anything?'

'Once I heard . . . high voices, like screaming,' Martina said. 'But there was so much noise here then, with the bands and a queen outside.'

'A queen? Like a homecoming queen?' She was typing fast.

'This is so great,' Jason said, spreading his hands out as if getting ready to give them a prize for passing the memory test. 'Ain't they terrific? Giving us all the details.'

'Yes, great.' *How the hell do you write this in a report?* 'So it all happened at once – the fight and the parade, right? And you had the children to take care of so you never left the house, is that right?'

'Yes. I mean no. I never went outside so I still don't know what started it or any of that. We're too busy in here to be spying on the neighbors.'

'I hear you. But when they broke the window and you could see blood—'

'And we heard the yelling,' Sofia said.

'That's when you called us – is that about it?'

Mother and daughter nodded, yes, yes – agreeing for once.

Then Martina added, 'But we don't know him really.' Her face was growing that set-in-cement look again.

'But you know what he looks like,' Sarah said. 'You've seen him plenty of times? How long has he lived there?'

33

'As long as I can remember,' Martina said.

Sofia, nodding again, said, 'All my life.'

'Do you know if he has relatives here in town?'

'No idea,' Martina said. 'Never seen any.'

'But you could identify the, uh, the body?'

'The body? Mother of God, you saying he's dead?'

'Well . . . we think so.'

'You ain't sure? Shouldn't you take him to the hospital then?'

'No, I mean, we'd like to ask you to look at this picture we've got here on the driver's license we found over there. And just . . . tell us if that looks like the man who lives there – lived.'

Jason pulled the little plastic card, nice and dry, out of an inside pocket of the slicker and held it out to Martina, smiling. She took it from him reluctantly, held it at arm's length and gave it one quick peek. Seeing nothing alarming, she looked again, shrugged and said, 'I think so. Them driver's license pictures . . . hard to tell, huh?'

'Well, take a look at this picture on my camera, will you?' Sarah said. 'And tell us if that looks like the same man to you?' The woman, who had been getting quite friendly, began shaking her head. 'Is this a picture of a body? Please don't ask me to look at no body.'

'I'll do it,' the pretty girl said quickly. 'I know what he looks like.'

'Sofia,' Martina said, speaking very softly, '*ya basta.*' The girl gave her back an impudent stare and shrugged.

34

'Well, now, Martina,' Jason said, 'you did such a great job of calling us right away, I'm sure you're strong enough to do this one more thing, which is take a good look at the picture on Detective Burke's camera. Because, see, we need to be sure that was actually the homeowner that we sent to the morgue.'

Martina did not want to look at a picture of a dead body. It would give her nightmares, she thought. But people so seldom gave her the respect she knew she was entitled to for all the hard jobs she did. Here was her chance. Not to mention that Jason Peete had looked kind of cute with rainwater dripping off his skull. And Sofia was right there poking her nose in, determined to get her some of that. Martina, suddenly looking solid as a rock, reached out to Sarah and said, 'Lessee that camera.'

Sarah brought the photo up on her phone and handed it over. Martina made one small sound, like a child's whimper, at her first sight of the abused corpse. Then she took a deep breath, squared her shoulders and looked at it long and hard while Jason peppered her with questions.

'I know his face is messed up, but . . . you see anything familiar? The shape of his arms, his haircut? Any of the clothes? I know they're pretty torn, but—'

'The arms,' she said. 'He always wore them sleeveless shirts. Liked to show off his muscles, I think.'

'He *was* in good shape for his age, wasn't he?'

'Oh, yeah. Rode that bike every day.'

'He have a lot of girlfriends?'

'I never saw one over there. He was always alone.'

'Anything else?'

'Um . . . his feet. He always wore flip-flops or sandals but he never took care of his toenails so his feet were always ugly like that – long toenails with dirt underneath. Yes, now that I get a good look I'm sure this is the old guy from next door.'

One of the children she had left at the table in the back began to cry and Sofia said, 'Ma, the Talibans are biting one of the twins.'

'Well, make them stop,' Martina said. But to Sarah, she said, 'I better fix lunch before they eat each other.'

'Yes. Thank you for taking the time to talk to us.' They gave her their cards.

Jason pointed at his card as he gave it her, and said, 'You call this number, any time, if you feel you need some help. Anything bothers you, you call, OK?'

Looking alarmed, Martina said, 'You think we're going to have more trouble around here?'

'Oh, no, I didn't mean anything like that.' He leaned toward her and put his hand out as if to touch her but then didn't quite. His fingertips hovered there, two inches from her shoulder as he said, 'I just want to tell you, don't worry. If you need help we're here to help you.'

'Well.' Martina blinked, tucked the cards carefully in the pocket of her jeans and gave him a small, quick smile. 'Thanks. That's . . . good to know.'

'All right!' Sarah said, hearty as a camp counselor. Seized by an anxious desire to be gone from this room, where emotions seemed to turn on a dime, she said, 'Bye, Sofia. Thanks for your help too!' She waved, reached for the door and opened it just as another blazing streak of lightning split the sky. To hell with the umbrella, she decided; she grabbed it up still folded and jumped off the step into a front yard so flooded it didn't matter whether you stayed on the walkway or not. They splashed like heedless children to her car, wrenched open a door apiece and then, groaning against the power of the wind, heaved them shut.

Panting and soaking her car seat, Sarah got the motor started and the wipers on. They thumped aggressively but made scant difference otherwise; the deluge all around the car reduced visibility to near zero. She enlisted Jason to squint through the storm; told him to call out if he saw she was about to hit something. They backed slowly along the curb till Jason told her she was even with the front walk on the crime scene.

Not even hurrying much anymore since all her clothing was already ruined, she jumped out and followed Jason along the twig-and-trash-strewn walk and through the front door that Delaney was holding open for them.

Another terrifying bolt of lightning blazed as she stepped inside. She didn't even flinch, just pushed the door shut and leaned against it, dripping. Peering through the wet hair hanging in front her eyes, she asked Delaney, 'Whose stupid idea was it to go out in this typhoon?'

'Yeah, boss, after Sarah begged you not to make us go.' Jason cracked up over his own wit. Sarah began to chuckle too and soon they were leaning on each other, soaked and helpless with laughter as the storm shook the house.

But before long Sarah realized that Delaney, not amused, was watching them impatiently, trying to say something. Sarah stopped laughing and said, 'What?'

'I looked around some more after you left. Found a couple of things.' He showed them a shoe box on the kitchen counter. Holding up one end of the lid, he said, 'Look but don't touch, huh? Almost all jewelry. Two gold rings, look like matched wedding rings. Some jade earrings and one woman's ring that might be pretty valuable, that pear-shaped diamond. Heavy silver ring with a jade stone – that's the only thing for a man.'

'And the paper?'

'A bike license and the deed to this house.'

'Funny. Where'd you find it?'

'Behind the one cupboard door that wouldn't open, by the stove there. I couldn't see any reason why it would be stuck so I turned my flashlight on it and found this one thin screw in the bottom corner.'

'Oh, cool,' Jason said softly.

'Yeah. But still no social security or Medicare card, so remember you're still looking for those. They must be here somewhere.'

'We're probably going to find another hidey-hole,' Jason said. 'People who like to hide things usually have several.'

'Yes. And we might get prints or DNA off these.'

38

'Yeah,' Sarah said, 'the guy can't have worn gloves every waking hour, can he? Nice find, boss.'

'Yeah, well, the other thing is even better.' He unzipped one of the many pockets in his jacket, pulled out a paper evidence bag and shook the contents into his gloved hand. Even in the near-dark, the brass had a glamorous glint.

Sarah leaned over it, wishing she could pick it up. Jason, behind her, said, 'Whatcha got?'

'A casing.'

'Where'd you find it?'

'Right here in the cupboard.' He showed them the little paint scrape on the shelf in the open dish cupboard between the front door and the window. 'Damnedest thing. I'm sure the scene techs worked all around it. But it had wedged in tight behind this stack of plates and they never saw it.'

Sarah squinted. 'It's a .22, isn't it?'

Delaney nodded. 'Yup.'

'And Long Rifle. Probably out of this revolver we found here, right? Although why would he take a casing out of his own gun and then wedge it in behind his plates? But . . . so, maybe – what do you think?'

'It's not out of the Masterpiece,' Delaney said. 'It's rim-fire, all right, but a different firing pin mark, and besides, this casing has an extractor mark. You can't see it here in this light but I turned my flashlight on it when I found it and it's there. This ammo wasn't fired by a revolver.'

'So maybe our attacker had a pistol?'

'And the bullet's still in the victim – that's what I'm thinking.'

39

'I'm trying to get my head around this. The ME complains there's not enough blood for the beating he took but now it turns out there's a bullet in him too?'

'You'll find out tomorrow. Cameron phoned while you were over there. He's got first dibs on an autopsy room in the morning.'

Sarah's cell phone rang as she was zipping her day-pack, getting ready to leave the crime scene. 'I hope I'm in time to head you off,' her mother said. 'This storm wrecked Howard's plans for fireworks so we're leaving the ranch now. Got lots of picnic leftovers – can you come home pretty soon?'

'I'm just heading back,' Sarah said. 'Be careful on the road; I think you'll see a lot of downed trees.'

She called Will to tell him not to cook anything. 'Mom says the neighbors didn't come to the picnic because they saw the storm coming, so she's got more food in the car than she started out with.'

'That I have to see,' he said. 'She looked like she was mounting a relief expedition when she left.'

Sarah had to detour around a couple of collisions and a downed power line on the way but she still beat Aggie home. Will was enjoying a major league baseball game on TV, having been chased off his back-door repair job by the storm.

'Go back and watch your game – don't touch me,' she said. 'I have to shower off a murder scene.'

When she came out of their room in seersucker cutoffs and sandals his game had gone into extra innings and he didn't even hear her walk past. She went into their small kitchen and began stacking things in the refrigerator to make space. Aggie came in the house a few minutes later, exclaiming about all the trash in the yard.

'I'm glad you're home safe,' Sarah said, helping her unload an armload of plastic containers. 'Look, I cleared out a whole shelf.'

'Wonderful. It won't hold it all but we'll prioritize. I'm not that crazy about sweet pickles, are you? And the bread and cake can stay out, of course, and – what have you got there, Denny?'

'Deviled eggs and potato salad. Don't throw any of these away, will you, Grandma? I can eat them all myself if necessary.'

'I know you could but then you'd be sick. I believe we can all help you eat the eggs, Denny. Just bring in one more load of food and then you're free to go in your room and play that awful game I wouldn't let you turn on at the ranch.' Denny had blown some of her allowance to put a game called Cookie Clicker on her phone. She had only had it two days and already Aggie had threatened to destroy her phone if she played it in the kitchen.

Denny giggled and told Sarah, 'Turns out Grandma can't stand freaky noises.'

'It's not just the noises it makes,' Aggie said. 'It's the idiotic behavior you indulge in while you play it.'

'I can't help myself, it's so exciting. Anyway, it's better than hearing what the Evil Trolls say

41

about their stupid Barbie dolls, isn't it?' Denny's relationship with her cousins had never recovered from the times when she'd been stranded at the ranch by her runaway mother. Howard's daughters had made no secret about not wanting her there.

'It's a hard pick,' Aggie said, 'but I believe I hate Cookie Clicker even more than those obscene dolls. I love all my granddaughters,' she told Sarah, 'but their toys may yet drive me to distraction.'

'You hated the Hula Hoop too, Ma,' Sarah said, 'and think how fast we grew out of that. I'll come help you with the rest of the food,' she told Denny. In the yard she plucked a blowing trash sack out of a cactus and began stuffing it full of the trash that was still flying across lots. 'Too bad about the fireworks.'

'Uncle Howard says he'll shoot them off later. Whee, isn't this wild?' Denny grabbed wet newsprint out of a palo verde. 'You went to a crime scene but you're home early? How come?'

'The storm obligingly blew a transmitter so we had to quit.'

'Fantastic. You want to play a game of Cookie Clicker with me?'

Surprised, Sarah laughed out loud. After the crazy stress of the crime scene and the storm, it felt good to her cheeks. 'Sure,' she said, 'let's get all this food put away and go play.'

Will's ball game ended in a noisy pile-up of bodies just as they went through the living room. When he turned off the sound, she asked him, 'You want to come along and play Denny's new game with us?'

42

He grinned and said, 'Why not? Can't be much rowdier than what I just watched.'

'You want to bet? Aggie really hates this game so it must be pretty loud.'

'I'll play the first game and show you how,' Denny said. 'Let's each play for two minutes, OK? Highest score wins all the cookies.' She held the phone in front of her with her left hand and twitched her right middle finger up and down rapidly, clicking the cookie hundreds of times in two minutes. It did make a very annoying sound, but the striking factor of the game was Denny's posture while she played – she became rigid with concentration, only her right hand moving as the device clicked madly on. Was she having an epileptic seizure? But she stopped abruptly, noted down her impressive score and handed the phone to Sarah, saying, 'Now you try.'

Sarah expected to tolerate one whole game if she could, but soon found herself yelling like a banshee as her agreed-upon two minutes sped by before her score was even close to Denny's. When she relinquished the phone, she said, 'Well, there must be a steep learning curve,' and handed it to Will.

To her annoyance Will's score soon dwarfed her own, but she felt better when she saw it still came nowhere near Denny's.

After two games, Will said, 'I think I have to stop – my heart won't take any more.'

'Don't you just love it?' Denny said.

'Yes. But I need to calm down a little before supper.' Aggie tapped on the door then and when they opened it, said, 'Please tell me the two of

43

you have not become addicted to this horrible game too.'

'No,' Sarah said, 'but we'd better stop right now or I may never stop.'

In the kitchen, pulling picnic food back out of the refrigerator, Sarah said, 'So what will you do with all those cookies you just won, Denny? Are there prizes?'

'Just games.'

'What?'

'The more cookies you win the more games you can play. I figure I've got enough in the bank right now to last me till I'm about thirty.'

'You see what I mean? It's a game for idiots. I'm afraid it's going to rot her brain.'

'We'll watch her closely but I'm sure it won't. That was fun, Will. We should play games more often, not be always so *busy*.'

Will said, 'Well, you know there's something I've wanted to do with the two of you and we never seem to have time. After we finish this picnic could we try it for a few minutes?'

'Great. Better than fireworks,' Sarah said.

Cleanup was easy because they'd brought along the paper plates. When the food was put away again, Sarah said, 'What's your game?'

'Remember when we moved into this house you gave Denny that smart phone?'

'You're not going to take it back, are you?' Denny turned her patented pleading look on him. 'I love my phone.'

'The phone's yours; we need you to have it. I'm just saying your aunt was very proud of herself when she installed that tracker app on all

44

our phones so we could always find each other. But I don't think we've ever used it, have we?'

'I tried it out when I first installed it,' Sarah said, 'because that was right after Denny was . . . you know, lost that time.' They never talked about the terrible day when her sister Denice left the motor running while she went after beer and cigarettes and the car got stolen with Denny in it. 'But she's never been lost again, I'm happy to say.' She reached across her chairback and touched her niece on the arm. Denny patted her hand. 'I always know where she is and I just forgot about the app.'

'Fine. But right now we've got an evening with nothing to do so why don't we try working the thing? Because I can't remember how.'

Ten minutes later they were sitting knee-to-knee, all talking at once and pointing at the phones they were holding.

'I wish it wasn't so wild out on the street,' Denny said, 'so I could see this thing actually working.'

'Oh, well,' Will said, 'it isn't that bad, is it?' He got up and peered out the window. 'Nah. There's a lot of trash around but the wind's gone down. I'll go out and drive a mile or so and come back. You two get a fix on me and make notes, so when I come back you can tell me where I've been.'

Will turned his lights on, braved the windy sprinkles left from the storm and came back all excited again – a big acacia tree had fallen on a house near the end of his mile-long drive.

'So that's why you took that big detour,' Denny

said. 'We've been wondering what you saw.' She crowed happily as she identified the locations he'd been to and heard his praise.

Sarah did a run in her car so Will could see the tracker at work. When she came back, she said, 'Well, this was kind of fun. Any more games we could play before bedtime?'

'Well, if you mean that,' Will said, 'I'd like to add one more thing.'

'Will, now,' Sarah said. 'You're not going to start teaching her the old ten-code, are you?'

'No. When would she ever use it?' Will said. 'But I think it might be fun to pick one or two numbers for our own family code.'

Denny lit up. 'Hey, I'd love that. Like, I could send you a number that means "Come at once, I'm being strangled by aliens?"'

'Or eaten by alligators? Probably better to keep it kind of general. What do we call now for help?'

'Nine-one-one.'

'Right. But among ourselves we don't need three numbers, do we? Why not pick one number that means, "Help"?'

'Oh, I see.' She thought with her mouth puckered. 'I don't know why but three seems about right.'

'Maybe because I just said it, but fine, let's make it three.' They all did fist bumps to endorse number three.

'So let's review,' Will said, striking a professorial pose, index finger in the air. 'My phone chirps, I say, "Great Scott! Someone has sent me a text message!"' Really into it now, he morphed into a faux Dick Tracy, staring at the phone in his hand.

Sarah giggled and said, 'Where's your yellow fedora?'

'Must have mislaid it. I see the message is from Denny. All it says is, "Three." But that's all it needs to say, isn't it? Because the next thing I'm going to do is—'

'Switch to your locator app and find me,' Denny crowed. 'Ho ho! Will Dietz has got you, you rotten bandido!'

She considered for a few seconds with her head on one side. 'Does anybody ever use happy codes?'

'For what?'

'Like right now I could send one that says "Come at once, the devil's food cake isn't getting any younger"?'

'Oh, damn,' Sarah said, belting on a plastic lab coat on the morning of the fifth, 'I had some phone calls I had to take so I couldn't come sooner. And now you're already half done, aren't you?'

'We've got three more autopsies scheduled in here today,' Cameron said. 'I couldn't wait.'

'Sure. Push comes to shove all the time down here, doesn't it?' Illegal immigration had slowed a little from last year but now that medicinal marijuana was eroding some revenue streams, new drug wars kept popping up – dealers fighting to grab a slot as the heroin or meth dealer of choice – so the Pima County morgue was still a lively place. At nine o'clock in the morning all its exam rooms were in use.

'Well, the only surprise so far,' Cameron said, 'is that this old bird looks even better on the inside than he did on the surface.' The big V-cut had been made and the corpse opened, all the organs in dishes alongside. 'See here? Lungs, heart, kidneys, liver – the average man twenty years younger would be glad to have any of these.'

Glad you like them, Sarah thought. To her they just looked like guts. 'So he took care of himself,' she said. 'But did you get Delaney's message about the casing he found?'

'Yes. No sign of a slug yet, though. Be good to find one – it would explain why he didn't bleed more when his attacker did all that whaling on him. I thought I might find a big cancer in here, eating him up, but au contraire, this guy was good for another thirty years easy. So I'm going to go ahead now and look at his brain.'

He got out the big saw and went to work. Sarah had seen her share of autopsies but she still had to set her jaw to keep from wincing as the saw screamed through bone. When the doctor had the cranium opened he folded the scalp down over the face, made another diagonal cut to create a wedge of skull and lifted it out.

'Hmmm. Well. Plenty of blood in here, huh?' He suctioned the area dry, cut the arteries and nerves that connected the brain to the body and called a young assistant named Blake to help him lift it out. Even with four hands they had a hard time moving it – the brain was badly damaged and disintegrating into pulp. Looking down at it in the lab dish, Cameron said, 'Yeah, here's your answer, I guess.'

48

'You think there's a bullet in this brain?'

'Sure looks like it,' Cameron said. 'Wow, it is so messed up. Yes, this is a portion of a wound track across the top here. And see, something broke the surface here and then veered off.'

'And ends up where, do you think?'

'Can't tell yet. It probably made a couple of circuits, ricocheting off bone. I'll have to slice this whole mass up carefully to find—'

'I don't think so, Doc,' his assistant said. 'Isn't this it, here' – he was pointing inside the empty skull – 'in the brain stem?'

'Well . . . by damn, I think you're right.' The dark-pewter edge of a misshapen bullet poked out through a red-brown mound of protoplasm. 'Hang on, now,' Cameron said. His gleaming tweezer flashed and a bloody lump of metal dropped onto a clean tissue by the bowl.

'Pretty badly mangled,' Sarah said. 'You think Banjo can make anything of that?'

'Well, we're sure going to give him a chance to try.' He wiggled his shoulders. His coral plastic lab gown crackled and his rimless eyeglasses gleamed. The air in the lab actually seemed to effervesce. Cameron might not talk much but it was easy to tell when he was pleased.

He said, 'Very well done, Blake.' His assistant's cheeks bloomed a nice shade of pink. 'Now let's see if I can find an entry wound.' He adjusted a light and began cleaning the bloody left ear. He swabbed, stooped, squinted, tilted the light again and said something like *Schmerz.* More wiping and muttering till finally he said, 'Ah.'

Satisfied again, he showed her a little dike of

49

tissue inside the outer ear mounded aside to make room for the entering bullet. The hole was surprisingly small, hardly more than a pinprick.

'You see it? Good. Now we'll look inside.' He cleaned up some more inside the empty crater of the braincase and said, 'Ooh, yeah.' He moved over three inches and told Sarah, 'Stand here. Look right here.' He pointed with a probe.

'I see it,' Sarah said, looking at the ragged hole inside the ear, bigger than the hole outside.

'Went right on into the brain here.' He pointed to the left side of the oozing mass. 'Yeah, about here, I think. The attacker's almost certainly right-handed, you might want to know.'

'Thanks,' Sarah said, and made a note.

'The bullet entered the brain on the left side, just about in the hearing area. Probably made him deaf, then bounced around the cranium a couple of times and buried itself down here in the medulla. By then he didn't care about being deaf – he was dead. Whole thing took about a second. Maybe two.'

'And happened by the door where we found him?'

'Yes. Trust me, he didn't do any more walking after the shot.'

'A fatal shot just inside the door, yet the people in the house next door say they never heard gunfire.'

'But how much else was going on? Let's see, the storm didn't start till later, did it?'

'No,' Sarah said, 'but there was a parade earlier. A marching band and mariachis. And a clown with a limp, they said.'

50

Cameron shrugged. 'Well, there you go,' he said. 'A clown with a limp, plenty of squealing.'

'Maybe. In my experience, a gunshot is easy to distinguish from other noises.'

'Because you're trained to identify it. But how many times have you heard witnesses say, "We thought it was a car backfiring"?'

Four

Working her way through phone messages the day after the autopsy, Sarah saw one from Firearms Identification and Toolmarks Comparison and skipped ahead to it. Waiting through canned music for a fast-talking techie to answer the phone, Sarah thought, the wait's longer now than it was when we just called it Ballistics.

But she didn't waste any time sighing over the good old days. The state-of-the-art equipment at the new crime lab held the promise of better law enforcement, and who didn't love that? It was fascinating, though, how quickly criminals found ways around any new edge law enforcement devised. If a section of border ever got closed off completely they brought the drugs for that area in by boat. If there were no ports they'd get airplanes. Or ATVs or camels. Oh, now you like drones, Mr Policeman? Zap, so do we.

Obviously the word *fun* had no place in a crime file, but Sarah privately thought the ongoing arms race was what made her job the best game in town. And in that contest Banjo Bailey was a good man to have on your side.

The firearms' division's head chemist and firearms expert got his nickname moonlighting in a bluegrass band. On the stage, Banjo's costume of red sleeve garters, blue suspenders and white spats took on added authenticity when he let his abundant curly white hair grow. Gradually he added a goatee and a generous mustache curled and waxed on the ends, plus a long white braid that hung down his back under his farmer's straw hat. None of his costume came with him to his day job, of course, but the hair couldn't be grown in a day so he wore it matter-of-factly with Dockers and a polo shirt, and his fellow scientists eventually got used to his shtick and quit ragging him about it.

Getting applauded at night for his funky plucking seemed to relieve whatever stress he encountered in his day job. Banjo Bailey at work in a forensics lab was benevolent and generous, never appearing impatient or overworked. He greeted each new search you brought him with the air of an unusually agreeable child getting handed a shiny new toy.

'We examined that slug the doc took out of your victim,' he told her when he came on the line, 'and got some quite good results. You want to come up and talk?'

She looked at the clock: three o'clock. It wasn't as handy as when she used to just run upstairs, but the new lab was only ten minutes away in normal traffic.

Which unfortunately we never have anymore,

she thought five minutes later as she took her life in her hands and plunged into the hectic flow on I-10. None of the eighteen-wheelers crushed her as she merged so she got in line and practiced her yoga breaths for four miles. She exhaled happily at the Miracle Mile exit, which she always thought of as making good her escape into Pothole City.

In two minutes she tensed again to make the tricky U-turn onto the big parking lot full of benches and outdoor art that fronted the West Side station and crime lab.

'OK, lessee now,' Banjo said, patting his way around his big, crowded bench till he found the work order for her search. 'Here it is: a slug from the head of that victim you found during the storm, right? Fourth of July must have been quite a day. Did you ever get to the ice cream and sparklers?'

'Missed all the fun – I nearly drowned at the crime scene. Was that a storm or what? I ruined a good pair of shoes and my dry cleaner's not sure she can save my pants.'

'You got a cleaner who actually cares about your clothes? Lucky Sarah. I got the slug in the scope over here.'

She followed him to a work stand where he waved her onto a comfortable high stool.

Using a pointer, he directed her attention to the ugly remains of a .22 slug that had bounced around a skull several times. Despite its beat-up condition, he had been able to discern lands and grooves, had test-fired a number of weapons from the lab's supply and was ready to make a fairly firm ID of the bullet as having been fired by a Taurus semi-auto pistol.

'You familiar with this weapon, Sarah?'

'No.'

'Often called "the Dolly's Gun." It's manufactured in Brazil and is a popular choice among wives and girlfriends of big-time macho guys who always carry guns, usually concealed, and want their sweeties to learn to shoot so they'll be safe when the Big Kahuna's out of town. I guess I won't comment on what I think of that idea.'

'What's the use?'

'Precisely. Anyway, these women often have difficulty trying to rack the slide on a semi-auto and the Taurus solves that by having a tilt-up barrel so you can chamber the first round from the front. Here, I brought one out so you can see it.'

He showed her the action on a PT-22.

'Easy on the wrist, maybe,' Sarah said, 'but no opponent's going to stand around while you load it. So you have to carry it ready to fire?'

'I would certainly suggest that course of action, yes.'

'Where's the safety?'

'Doesn't have one. It's a semi-auto, same as your Glock.' He showed her how the first half of the trigger pull cocked the hammer and the second half fired the bullet.

'Well, so . . . it has to use .22 Long Rifles?'

'Yeah, the auto-load mechanism won't work with shorter ammo. But the tilt-up barrel makes it very attractive to old guys with arthritis who find it hard to rack the slide on the usual semi-auto, and to juveniles just learning to shoot. Also to women – especially the ones with small hands. Any chance your victim was attacked by a woman?'

'It would have to be a most unusual female. They staged a hellacious fight in the house before he got shot.'

'I see. Well, for some reason this tough guy opted for a Taurus. Maybe just because it's reasonably priced.'

'Are there a lot of them around?'

'It's a popular weapon but they still all have their anomalies,' Banjo said. 'If you find the right gun I'll be able to ID it.'

'Good, I'll look forward to that.' She stared into space briefly, came back and said, 'A cheap weapon with no criminal record, and all the other signs in the room say that rage was a factor. Doesn't that sound personal?'

'Or like a really serious grudge fight. Guys in gangs can rub each other the wrong way some-times, as you know. Remember the Ortegas? The brother who got his dick bit off?'

'Oh, please, now, Banjo . . .'

'OK, I'm just saying. Let's not jump to any conclusions yet. Anyway, you haven't found any next of kin so far, have you?'

'Gossip's already reaching the lab, huh?'

'It's what we have to talk about, Sarah.'

'Yup. You heard right, too. We've had two detectives canvassing the neighborhood for two days and we can't find anybody he was even close to. The man lived alone in that house and when he came out of it he rode his bike or drove away in his pickup. Alone, the neighbors say. Nobody reports seeing buddies, girlfriends – no grandkids stopping by to hug grandad's legs.'

'Well . . .' Banjo turned toward the stand where he had the handsome Smith & Wesson revolver clamped under the microscope. 'On the other hand, this weapon you found . . . hanging under a string of peppers, was that it? I bet that brightened up the scene for a while, didn't it?'

'Sure did. Hanging there fully loaded, ready to go to war. Made the victim seem a little less . . . victimized, for sure.' She moved over to stand by him. 'How do you like it?'

'Oh, I like it a lot. But unfortunately it didn't fire that bullet we were just looking at. Well, of course you know that.' Head cocked, Banjo regarded the revolver the way a hen looks at a fresh handful of grain. 'This is really quite an elegant weapon, Sarah.'

'Surprisingly upmarket for the wall it was hanging on,' Sarah said. 'And for its presumptive owner. Everything else on the premises was plain and cheap.'

'Nothing cheap about this item,' Banjo said. 'Well over eight hundred dollars new, plus tax. If you include the cost of this very nice belt and holster you're looking at close to a thousand. Worth it, of course, if you value first-rate accuracy and reliability.'

'But not exactly a first-choice weapon for a pro, would you say?'

'Depends what he wants to do. A .22 is not the high-powered weapon most thugs would want but it's ideally suited for a head shot like the one you've been looking at.'

'The shot that didn't come from this weapon.'

'Kind of curls your toes, doesn't it? I keep coming back to that, too – the perfect gun hanging right there but it's not the one this bullet came from. What you said about a pro, though – is that how you're thinking about this victim now? Delaney said he was a quiet older guy in that old residential neighborhood under Signal Mountain, and you're saying plain and cheap. Where does pro fit into that?'

'Something about the way he conducted himself – such a loner. And if he owned this gun he must have been a serious shooter, wouldn't you say?'

'Serious on some level. Some people just enter contests, remember. Belong to clubs and go to meets at well-groomed firing ranges.'

'Yeah. In a way this weapon does make you think about an elitist shooter like that. It's been very well treated, hasn't it?'

'Indeed. Pristine clean, hasn't been fired since it was oiled. Nothing to tie it to the crime you're working on, Sarah, but Delaney asked me to find out if it's been involved in any other interesting scenes so I'm searching NIBIN, the ATF database.'

'Anything so far?'

He shook his head. 'I just put the search online.'

'Isn't this the twenty-first century? How long can it take for an electronic search?'

'After it gets out of the queue, about thirty seconds.'

'Oh, crap. How many in the queue?'

'Depends on the day and time. If you're lucky maybe only a few thousand but possibly gazillions. Think about the drive-by shootings, the gang-bangers' shoot-outs in cities like Baltimore and LA. There are a lot of casings out there – an endless stream of evidence being submitted, often with no suspects in mind but just entered for future reference. They can prioritize, however, when a murder and a suspect need to be tied to each other. I'm not sure I have all the elements I need to get us moved up in the queue but I'm going to try.'

'What would we do without you?'

'You don't need to worry about that. Where else could I work to have this much fun? I'll be in touch.'

Sarah rode along with Oscar Cifuentes for a couple of hours the next day to see if she could figure out why he wasn't coming back with more skinny.

'I thought you said you knew this area well,' she said.

'I do,' Oscar said, 'like the back of my hand. My nana lived in that house all her life,' he said, pointing. 'She passed away last year and two of her grandsons live there now. My cousins.' He sighed. 'Well, only Miguel is there right now; Chuy is in Pima County. But he'll be back in a few months.'

'Your cousin's in jail?' Sarah was shocked. Oscar always spoke of his family as proud and upright perfect examples of establishment Mexican values.

'It's a sad thing,' he said. 'He can't break his meth habit and it always gets him in trouble.'

'How does your family feel about that?'

He shrugged. 'Well, not happy, but . . . drug trafficking in the Tucson school system is so well established that it has come to be accepted that most families will lose one or two out of each generation into that sucking swamp.'

'God. Actually, I guess that's not so far out of line with the national average, is it? I suppose I should be keeping an eye on Denny pretty soon.'

'Your niece that you adopted? How old is she?'

'Eleven. Well, nearly twelve.'

'Well then, it's not pretty soon, Sarah, it's already happening with her classmates. Better talk to her.'

'Damn. I was just getting going on menstruation.'

'Menstruation?' He threw his head back and laughed, enjoying himself. 'Really, Sarah, where did you grow up?'

'Right here. Well, on a ranch, south of town – east of Sahuarita.'

'I should have guessed that.'

'Why?'

'Some of your attitudes are surprisingly . . . optimistic, for a Tucson cop.'

'Why? Because I expect the best of everybody till they show me otherwise?'

'Yes. Now I've offended you and I'm sorry.' A courteous and rather formal man by nature, always immaculately dressed, Cifuentes had got crosswise with Delaney when he first came into the squad, had barely salvaged his job and since

59

then was so careful and correct he almost made Sarah's teeth ache. But when she'd asked Leo Tobin if there was some way to put him at ease, he'd said, 'I wouldn't try that if I were you, Sarah. I think Delaney enjoys having one person in the section who's always trying hard to please him.'

'I guess. It just gives me the itch the way he's always apologizing.'

But now, suddenly, he didn't look sorry at all – he was pointing across the street and smiling. 'There's where I grew up, that brick house on the corner. That's my dad in the yard.' He tapped the horn once and the man trimming the hedge waved his clipper and smiled.

'Not hard to see he's your father,' Sarah said.

'I guess we do look alike.'

'Also, his hair stays perfect even while he does yard work.'

Oscar pulled over to the curb on the wrong side of the street, ran his window down and said, 'I thought we agreed I would do this job for you on Saturday.'

'After that big rain it's growing so fast, I couldn't wait.' He patted his clipper and said, 'I'll just do this front part and leave the back for you, Curro.'

'OK. You promise? And drink plenty of water.' Oscar pulled back to the legal side of the street and shook his head as they drove away. 'Six months ago he had his heart attack. All the men in my family have one the year after they retire.'

'Oh, dear. And cops retire so early. Better be thinking about it, Oscar.'

'I already made a deal with my sister. I help her in the shop now on my days off and we expand into our own retail line the week after Tucson PD punches my ticket.'

'Ah, the Tucson solution: don't retire, keep working. What's that he called you? A nickname?'

'Curro. It means . . .' Oscar looked embarrassed. 'He thinks I look handsome. You know how parents are.'

'Oh, yes.' Papa Cifuentes was not alone in that opinion, she knew. Oscar had a well-earned reputation as a ladies' man which he had been trying to soft-pedal since he realized it made Delaney question his suitability for the homicide squad.

Anyway, Oscar was the best detective on the crew to canvass this neighborhood, Sarah thought, and she was pleased when he got the assignment. But he wasn't coming up with much information about Calvin Springer. The victim had evidently led an incredibly solitary life.

'He's been right here in plain sight but he has no buds that I can find,' Oscar said. 'Didn't even have coffee dates or go to ball games with anybody. It isn't that they didn't like him, they just didn't *notice* him. He didn't mingle.' He added thoughtfully, 'Of course, he was Anglo, and the Mexican community down here is pretty . . . tight knit. Maybe Ollie will have better luck.'

Working off property tax rolls and picking their targets according to the names, the two detectives had divided the task. It wasn't a hundred percent, but since Ollie's Spanish was pretty sketchy he had been knocking on the doors with non-Hispanic names, working a widening spiral around the crime scene.

They talked about it in Delaney's office. 'Found more black people than I knew we had,' Ollie said, 'and a few Muslims, a few Mormons. Interesting part of town, actually.' His good-humored face reflected amusement. A gregarious man, he enjoyed canvassing and was proud of his reputation for getting the most out of interviews. But he hadn't done any better than Oscar on this job.

'Two days of canvassing and I kept at it,' Oscar said. 'I'm sure I got all there is to get out of his immediate neighborhood, and believe me, there's no use going beyond it. You get two blocks away from Springer's house in any direction and all anybody knows about Calvin Springer is what they've heard on the news.'

'Yeah, same here,' Ollie said. 'The few people around his own block who noticed him at all say he came out of his house every day, got on his bike and rode off.'

'That's all?' Delaney said. 'He rode his bike?'

Ollie shrugged. 'Some days, after he came back and chained up the bike, he got in his pickup and drove away without talking to anybody.'

'But they don't know where he went?'

'Sarah, I didn't find anybody who gave a fiddler's fart where he went. Calvin Springer seems to have spent every day minding his own business – I believe he was the most private man in the city of Tucson.' He flipped through his notes. 'I did find one woman two doors west across the street who thinks that once or twice a month he drove away and was gone for two or three days. But she's quite wobbly about that information. It's just an impression she got and she doesn't want to swear to it.'

'Swell,' Sarah said. 'Just what I like – wobbly witnesses.'

'I did talk to one guy, Mitch Somebody – it's in my notes – who said he saw Calvin a couple of times at the Indian casino on South Nogales Highway. Mitch said he nodded and waved but Springer didn't respond – acted like he couldn't even see him.'

The three of them had been waiting outside Delaney's office for some time while he talked non-stop on the phone. He waved them in during a sudden break and they stood by his desk delivering a quick rant about how little they knew about the dead man. With Delaney you always felt you had to talk fast.

'Sarah,' Delaney said, 'are you sure you've found all his bank records?'

'No. I just found all I could. I only found one Calvin Springer in Tucson. There's a few other Springers but they don't claim to know him. He's been getting three thousand a month, bi-monthly checks from a wealth management firm in Nogales. Direct deposit into his credit union account here and he spent it all, just about, every month. Almost all that's on his credit cards is groceries and gas. Occasionally tires, tools and some clothes from Wal-Mart.'

'Three thousand. Doesn't seem like quite enough, does it?'

'Well, he had no house or car payments.'

'How could he pay off a house and truck on three thousand a month?'

'I don't know about the vehicle yet but I was able to find the realtor who sold him the house. Told me Calvin paid cash for it when he moved in eighteen years ago.'

'Isn't that odd? Where does an ordinary guy get that kind of money?'

'Yes, it's odd, like so many things about this man. He's lived very frugally ever since he bought the house – wrote his occasional checks by hand. Very lo-tech. No computer. Calvin was not a swinger.'

'You still haven't found anything from social security or Medicare?'

'No. Nor any doctor's bills, for that matter.'

'What about lab reports,' Delaney said, 'are we close to getting anything?'

'No match on his fingerprints. He doesn't have a criminal history. And it'll probably be weeks before we get anything back on his DNA.'

'Did you try the military?'

'Well, no – he's way too old to . . . well, I suppose maybe Vietnam, is that what you're thinking? OK, I'll try the military.' She turned a page and found a note. 'Oh, I was going to ask you, have you still got Springer's house keys?'

Delaney gave her a pop-eyed look. 'Come to think of it, I have. I meant to sign them into the evidence room this morning and forgot.'

'Before you put them away can I take them for a couple of hours?'

'Sure, if you want to. But I gave that house a

pretty thorough going over while you and Jason were out in the storm.'

'I know. I just want to do one more crawl-through before I give up on the place. Common sense says there has to be more about this man than we've found and the most natural place for it to be is that house and yard.'

'Take plenty of water. And somebody has to go with you. It's an open crime scene – you can't be there alone.'

'Can I take Ollie? He's good with houses.'

'Sure, I'll go,' Ollie Greenaway said when she asked him. 'My skills are all fresh – I spent half the spring in my crawl spaces fixing leaks in my A/C.' He had three children and lived in a sprawling fifties-era house somewhat like the one she had bought with Will Dietz. She loved her big, cool bedrooms and fully-grown trees, but then she didn't have to do the house main-tenance – Will did that more or less continually. She thought, as usual when her lover's name surfaced, how was I ever lucky enough to find that man?

He had come along soon after the angry divorce that she'd thought left her unfit to ever risk loving another man. Sometimes, still, when she thought of him she stopped what she was doing for a few seconds and willed herself to believe: I can have this happiness; it's real and I can keep it.

'Better go now before it gets any hotter,' Delaney said. 'The power's back on out there but the A/C's been turned off. You're going to be good and hot till you get it going. You want to take a crime-scene van? You'd have a ladder then, some fans and extra lights.'

'Sounds like a plan.' Sarah looked at Ollie. 'You free now?'

'Ten minutes to check my emails and I'm ready.'

The crime-scene tape around the house lot had been mostly destroyed by the storm. Delaney's crew had cleaned it up but hadn't replaced it. There was still a crime-scene lock on the front and back doors. The house hadn't been cleaned yet and smelled terrible. They put big fans in the front and back doors to get fresh air in. But the fresh air was well over ninety degrees, so as soon as the A/C blew cool air they closed up the doors.

'You'll be cool pretty soon,' Ollie said, 'and I'll take the outside. Anything you need help with in here before I start?'

'Help me take the bed apart. I'll come and find you if there's anything else.'

There were no pictures hanging. The place had shades, not drapes, so she finished the windows fast. The one dresser had held sparse clothing, which Jody had taken out in a box on the day of the storm. There was nothing on the undersides of the drawers which lay upside down on the bedroom floor. *Funny, I thought she put those drawers back. And that little bedside table – did Jody leave it upside down like that? Have to ask her when I'm done here.*

The kitchen was the hardest. Delaney had pulled the stove and refrigerator out of their spaces and left them open. Sarah took the few pans and groceries out of the tiny cupboard, inspected the roach hotels and took a box of trash sacks apart.

An hour later Ollie found her in the bathroom, wedged into a space between the toilet and the wall, shining her light at the underside of the toilet tank. He squatted by her feet and said, 'I found something in the soffit above the back door. You want to come out and look?'

'Sure.' She slithered partway out of her space and stopped. 'Damn, damn.'

'You hurt yourself?'

'Yeah, I bumped my head.' She slid the rest of the way out, sat up and rubbed her head. 'What's a soffit?'

'It's like a floor under the overhang.'

'Oh.' She rubbed her head a few seconds longer, blinked her eyes and surprised him with a sudden, brilliant smile. 'Hey, I'll see your something in a soffit and raise you a trifle behind a toilet.'

'What? Sarah, did you find something, too?'

'I think so.' She reached behind her and pulled it out – a flat oblong wrapped in a blue plastic sack trailing ragged strands of duct tape.

They unrolled the plastic sack on the kitchen counter and found a business-size envelope, unsealed, with the flap tucked inside. Money fell out when Sarah opened the flap.

'Hundreds,' Ollie said. 'Aren't they the prettiest?'

'Nice new ones.' Sarah counted. 'A hundred of them.'

They looked at each other. 'Getaway money,' Ollie said.

'Yup. Why didn't Delaney find this, I wonder?'

'He couldn't get into that space you were in so I suppose he assumed Springer wouldn't be able to hide anything there.'

'How did he, do you think?'

'My guess? He took the tank off the wall, taped the money on the back of the tank and replaced it. He could do all that standing up.' He pondered. 'Man, it took strength, though. How he managed *that* at his age . . . This guy sure ate up all his grits like a good boy.'

Sarah laughed. 'Is that your mother's expression?'

'My grandmother Bratvold. She was from Norway and had some very distinct ideas on the care and feeding of boys. My mother used to roll her eyes up and walk out of the room. Fun to watch.'

We should all be blessed with Ollie Greenaway's temperament, Sarah thought – in his eyes, even family conflict was amusing.

'OK, here goes this pretty money into the evidence bag. We're both going to sign this label, right? Wait, I have to dry myself off or I'll smear it. Man, I almost melted under that toilet.'

'I noticed that before – the bathroom duct doesn't work as well as the rest of the house.'

'Never mind,' Sarah said, seeing his face take on the speculative gleam of the do-it-yourselfer. 'Somebody else can figure that one out.' She had found paper towels and was drying her hands. She signed the evidence slip and said, 'There. Now show me your soffit.'

They went out into the punishing heat of the backyard and stood in the shade of the overhang where the air was maybe five degrees cooler than out in the sun. The vines climbing the lattices on either end looked about ready to let go and slump to earth.

'That was a good idea the boss had about bringing a crime-scene van,' Ollie said. 'Look at this top-of-the-line ladder we've got to use.'

'Nice. And you're going to climb it because? Oh, I see,' she said as his feet appeared at her eye level. 'There's a seam in this end section of the soffit, isn't there?' It had overhung the little metal table which he'd now set out in the yard with the chairs.

'Yes, there is. The only section in the whole house to have a seam. So isn't it logical to think there might be a . . . yes, there it is. A sweet little latch painted to match the wood. Right there where the wood facing almost covers it. Isn't that clever?'

'And you think maybe there's a hinge on the inside of that seam . . .'

'I do. Because otherwise why does this one section *have* a seam? Now if I can just get this little hummer to *move* . . .' He hurt himself, swore, sucked on a knuckle briefly and tried again. Sarah heard a small metallic screech, a bolt slid back and the end of the section dropped down. The hinges inside squeaked a little but they stayed put; the section didn't fall.

While it hung swaying, Ollie climbed another rung on the ladder, stuck his head in the hole and crammed his lit flashlight in beside his ear.

'Ah.' His voice became quieter, muffled by the space inside the hole. 'Well, look at that.' He pulled his head back out and looked down to make sure Sarah was still beside him. Smiling into her upturned face, he said, 'Can I hand you down a few things?'

Five

'Sarah, it's not my fault he kept all his records in a crawl space,' Ollie said. 'It's just a backache. You'll get over it.'

'Not if I lift those stinking boxes again,' Sarah said. 'Don't we have a maintenance crew in this building?'

'Hang on while I find the janitor,' Ollie said. 'He's got that wheeled pallet thing . . .'

They set up a long table alongside their workstations and the janitor brought in the boxes on his wheeled luggage cart. All the detectives dragged chairs around the table and began to remark that these filthy boxes were full of spiders and the overhead lights weren't even close to being bright enough to see . . . And one after another said, 'Are these handwritten records? Really?'

Delaney said, 'You're detectives, for Christ's sake. Find what you need.'

So Jason and Ollie ran around the building borrowing, or sometimes simply stealing, extra lights, power cords and file boxes. Oscar, concerned as always about his clothes, raided the janitors' cupboard for wipes and cleaned dust and cobwebs off the boxes.

70

Soon the table was littered with all the loot Sarah kept bringing from desks – pens, paper clips, staple guns and Scotch tape. Little islands of coffee cups, tissues and eyeglasses formed among the boxes. The clattering and complaining died down gradually and a kind of permanent buzzing murmur formed as the team opened the boxes and examined what they came to call 'the big honking puzzle.'

Delaney took a couple of pieces of paper out of each box for the lab, saying, 'We can never test all of this – we'll just do a sampling. Go ahead now and see what you can make of the rest.'

The first thing they made of it was that Calvin Springer had been a busy man. He worked for – or perhaps owned? – a company called Argos Inc., which, judging by its cash flow, was quite successful. In fact, Leo told Delaney after an hour, it must be one of the biggest accounts in this little credit union branch.

'Doing what?'

'A little of everything, it looks like,' Sarah said. 'But so far we can't see how it all fits together.'

After another paper-rustling hour with a lot of dusty sneezing, she sat back in her chair and said, 'Well, if this is big-time vice it's a lot less fun than I always imagined.'

'What,' Delaney said, stopping by again as he did every time his phone stopped ringing for a minute, 'no prostitution?'

'Nor anything else the least bit titillating. Just day after day of Calvin sending orders and payments around, delivering mounds of something called "product" and then back home adding stuff up on the stupid little adding machine, then more donkey labor, heaving plastic boxes up into crawl spaces—'

'And then down again before long,' Ollie said. 'Because all this paper's dated after March of this year. So he must have emptied this stash often.'

'And done what with it, I wonder?' Jason said.

'Loaded up that sturdy six-year-old Ford pickup and driven the whole load out on his good solid tires to . . . someplace else,' Ollie said.

'Yeah,' Sarah said, 'on one of those three-day trips the wobbly lady thinks she might have noticed.'

'You're right,' Delaney said. 'That doesn't sound much like Bogie in Casablanca with his nice white coat.'

'And the whole thing's so damn quaint,' Leo Tobin said, shaking his head in wonder.

Tobin had been working a desk in the cold-case section where Delaney had put him in May, saying, 'I'd like to see him start drawing retirement before his blood pressure spikes again.' He was a happy Leo Tobin today because Sarah had begged permission to get him back on his regular crew, helping them paw through these dusty records.

Sitting in a widening circle of spreadsheets, courthouse records and adding machine tapes, he said, 'I feel like I'm strolling down memory lane. One little Casio adding machine, for Pete's sake. Not even a cheap computer? Handwritten spreadsheets – do you know how long it takes to set one of these up?'

'Don't you just love adding machine tapes?' Ollie said, waving a fistful. 'How long has it been since you saw anybody operating this way?'

'If they weren't all dated in the last four months,' Leo said, 'I'd think we'd found an archive from thirty years ago.'

'Maybe that's the genius part, though,' Sarah said. 'Everything low tech. He's not putting anything on a computer so he can't get hacked.'

'What a great plan for the future,' Jason said. 'Back to pencils and carbon paper, right? How far do you suppose he was going with this? We gonna be finding buggy whips in another crawl space?'

'Maybe we should all start riding mules to work,' Ray Menendez said. 'We get in sync with this guy's zeitgeist and we might be able to sniff our way to the money pile.'

Leo Tobin began to speculate about finding a still out in the desert somewhere.

Jason said, 'Oh, and you'll know what it is right away?'

'Sure,' Leo said. 'Didn't I ever tell you about my years with Eliot Ness?'

Then Delaney came out of his office, fresh from another round of phoning, and introduced the man with him as, 'Don Belgrave, from the Phoenix ICE office. I heard he was coming to town today and I asked him to stop in and take a look at what we've got here.'

Don Belgrave was quietly dressed and barbered, presentable but not flashy, and had, Sarah thought, that edgy patina that well-placed Feds tended to get – the aura of worries too big to be shared. What the hell was he doing taking time to look at their two-bit murder case that didn't concern him at all?

Leo Tobin, filled with the expansive good cheer of the short-timer, said, 'Pull up a chair, Don. Any number can play this game.' He handed over a fistful of paper. 'Here's your first brainteaser: why would anybody keep chits from casino slots in with paperwork from home sales? Which, by the way, I thought I understood flipping houses, but some of these deals—' He was too intent to notice that his sentence had run completely off the rails.

'Here's a house on Valencia Avenue that our man bought in April, for instance. As near as I can tell it was paid for with eighteen thousand in cash, a land swap from over by Benson, two used cars from the indie dealer on Auto Mall Road and a truckload of wine from a vineyard in St David. He sold it in June to a buyer in Tijuana.'

Jason's face lit up with delight. 'An eighteen-wheeler full of wine from the monastery? Really?'

'I'm not sure yet about the size of the truck, Jason. We'll have to pin that down.'

'And here in my box,' Sarah said, 'is this sheaf of orders for machine tools from a manufacturer in China.'

'Ah, China.' Don Belgrave looked pleased. 'Shipped to where?'

'A maquiladora in Sonora.'

'Uh-huh,' he said, nodding. 'There you go.'

74

'There I go doing what?'

'Looks like your victim's been running a funnel account.' He pulled a smart phone out of an inner pocket and began scrolling through numbers. 'There's a young woman in our DC office, links up with my section when we need her. She's been working on these things almost full-time for a couple of years. She'll be able to help you figure this out.' He paused with his finger poised above the speed-dial button. 'You got the bank records all in order?'

'We haven't found any bank records,' Sarah said. 'What's a funnel account?'

'No bank records? Well, but how can you—' He looked around the table. 'You people haven't seen a funnel account before? Where you been?'

'We're homicide,' Ollie said. 'We hardly ever get to play with the money.'

'Except sometimes in home invasions,' Jason said, 'there'll be some bloody cash mixed in with the corpses.' His face had put on its iron-hard, step-out-of-the-vehicle look. He'd had a tough year – killed a man to save an old woman's life, did it the way he was trained to do it and got a commendation but still had nightmares about it. Sarah could almost hear him thinking, *Ain't no slicker-than-snot Fed guy gets to mark us down as a bunch of candy asses just because we don't know about some downtown accounting dodge with stupid funnels.*

'Where we've been,' Sarah said, 'is right here investigating the death of an elderly man named Calvin Springer, who by all accounts lived a quiet life in his small house under Signal Mountain

75

for fifteen or twenty years until this Fourth of July holiday, when somebody walked into his house and killed him. So if the paper in these boxes gives you some idea of what he was doing that might account for that, we'd all like to hear about it.'

Don Belgrave looked around the long table and saw six homicide detectives watching him with the cold blank stares they usually put on for shackled nogoodniks about to hear their Miranda rights.

He stood up. 'Tell you what,' he told Delaney, 'let's go in your office and sort out the jurisdiction on this thing first.'

So they did that and the homicide crew went back to piecing together the oddball deals Calvin Springer had been making, or at least documenting, in his solitary hours on Alameda Avenue. In half an hour Belgrave was gone and Delaney came out of his office looking cheerful.

'OK, I made the deal,' he said.

'Good,' Sarah said. 'What do we get?'

'A woman named Lois Johnson, how's that for plain and simple? Belgrave says she matches her name but don't be fooled by her appearance – she's wicked smart.' He passed the note to Sarah. 'She spends most of her time in New York and DC but she's scheduled for a visit to Phoenix next week. Belgrave's going to try to get her to carve out a day or two to look this stuff over and decide if they should take the case.'

Sarah turned a protesting face toward him but he held up a hand. 'Just the money laundering part, that's all they're interested in. The homicide

76

will still be ours.' He sat down in the chair Belgrave had abandoned. 'You still haven't found any bank records?'

'Because they're not here to find,' Tobin said. 'We've been to the bottom of all these boxes – of course there are notes on the money but no checks or copies of checks, nothing you could take to court. I see the initials FSCU in several places, though. I'm pretty sure that means First Southwest Credit Union. We could go there with a subpoena and bring back whatever they've got. What do you think?'

'Sounds like a good plan but I've got a better one,' Ollie said. He looked at Sarah. 'You still got the keys to the house?'

Handing them over, Sarah said, 'You're thinking about that hot bathroom, aren't you?'

'You bet. And I don't want to listen to any more belly-aching about your back muscles, so how about it, boss, can Jason come with me and help carry what I think I'm going to find?'

Jason, who had been trying for some time to think of an urgent chore that would get him out of looking at any more handwritten records, was ready to go in five minutes flat.

He looked a little less enthusiastic when they came back, two hours later, pushing another cart containing four cardboard boxes. In the boxes, which they heaved on to the counting table together, were eight family-size coffee cans, each one bulging with tightly-packed paper.

'We had to kind of pry this last one out,' Ollie said. 'It was right where the conduit turned. Shee! Wonder he had any air in there at all.'

Leo was already scanning the bank slips that cascaded out of the cans. 'It *was* First Southwest, by God. Hah! Betcha these babies make that Fed lady smile.'

'Smiling or not,' Delaney said, 'she'll be here first thing Monday morning. Don Belgrave just called.' He did a funny thing with his eyebrows. 'He asked me to say what a pleasure it was to meet you folks.'

'Denny,' Sarah said that night as they filled the dishwasher after dinner, 'could we talk for a few minutes when we're done with this?'

'Oh, please, Aunt Sarah.' Denny was growing a new look this summer – Sarah privately called it her Bunkered Chipmunk look. Maybe it was just tough days with the new braces and a couple of zits that heralded the approach of puberty. Sometimes her whole body seemed to flinch and her small face grew a contemptuous sneer that said the world was not even close to good enough for her. Sarah was trying to decide if this was a phase of near-twelve development that just needed patience, or maybe for the first time since they'd lived together her beloved Denny needed to be told to stuff it.

She'd had good reason for the Dubious Denny look she'd worn when Sarah had adopted her. Her last year with her drug-addicted mother had been scary enough to make any kid insecure. But she was basically good-natured and had bounced back quickly, Sarah had thought, as soon as she got regular meals and a reliable support system. She'd kept her grades up with no urging and done more than her share of household chores without complaint. But this summer she had days when she seemed to be turning into Witchy Denny.

In the dry, snappish voice that went with the new look, she said, 'We went over all that female anatomy stuff a month ago in school. If I promise not to get pregnant for years and years could we please skip the cycles of the moon tonight?'

Sarah managed a laugh. 'Poor Denny. Do you feel like you're getting carpet-bombed with information on sensitive topics?'

'For sure. And most of the teachers are even more embarrassed than you are.'

'I'm not – well, yes, I guess I am a little. You're still not quite twelve and this all feels much too soon.'

'To me too. But what can I do?'

'Same thing we all do, I guess – grin and bear it. Actually I wasn't even thinking about sex education when we started this conversation. Something a colleague said at work made me think I ought to ask you if any of your peer group was getting into drugs yet. Is marijuana circulating freely in the halls? Anybody toking in the showers?'

'Oh – a little sampling going on, I guess. Here and there.'

'Ever get tempted to try a sample?'

'Omigod no. Me? Never.'

'How come you're so sure? Because of your mom?'

'Yes. Watching her ruin herself – I can't even stand to think about it. I believe I'm immune for life. Like I got' – she laughed out loud at the irony of what she was about to say – 'I got my shots for that.'

'Well, at least immunity is good, huh? Would you . . . could we have a hug?' With the small, firm body held close against her side, she said, 'I'm sorry you had to get immune the hard way. And I don't mean to be always lecturing you about something. But you know . . . well, you don't know, so I'll tell you. Peer group pressure works on parents the same way it does on kids – maybe even worse when you're an adoptive parent. People say things and I start feeling . . . like I don't know enough to raise you right. Am I being too nosy? Or not paying close enough attention? I guess you'll have to tell me when I'm too far off the mark, won't you?'

'Oh, sure.' Dubious Denny came back, looking amused. 'Tell you you're all wrong and then duck?'

'I'll try not to heave a brick at your head. But parenting is not an easy job, it turns out. I try to remember that when we talk about your mother.'

'She used to remind me quite often.' Witchy Denny came back and added, 'When she could talk at all.'

Surveying Denny's tired face, Sarah said, 'You know, I haven't seen you close up much this summer. We've been doing a lot of passing and waving, haven't we? You're growing a new look, kind of lean and mean. Is that swim team turning out to be a lot more work than you expected?'

'Well . . . sorry if I look mean. Yeah, right now the coach says we need to, um, *bear down*.'

'Oh, that's right, there's a meet this weekend, isn't there?'

'Yes. All-city. If we could get two firsts and a couple of seconds we could go to the regionals in Phoenix next month. I don't really think we're good enough, but we gotta try, I guess.'

'When you made the team in May I thought you were so thrilled. Now you sound like you're kind of sorry you took it on.'

'I love to swim. I'm not so sure I love to compete. It all gets kind of . . . competitive, you know? And stressful.'

'And who needs stress in the summer, huh? It's supposed to be the time you stretch out and get over yourself, isn't it? Listen, if it's making you unhappy I won't object if you quit.'

'Well, you can't quit in the middle of a season. I mean, this coach is really very good and I wouldn't want to let her down.'

'I suppose. Look, I'll finish these pans. Why don't you go have a little read before bedtime? Maybe you just need some cocooning.'

'Oh, you sure? Well, thanks, Aunt Sarah.' Denny made an effort – flashed a little smile before she walked away. Sarah watched her go, not liking the set of her shoulders.

When the pans were stacked on the drying board she went out the kitchen door onto the patio where Will was raking up dead leaves and trash left by the storm. Her mother was curled on a chaise in front of her *casita*, talking to Will and watching the hummingbirds at a nearby feeder.

The small free-standing house at the back of the

81

lot was one of the features that had persuaded the three of them to buy this property together. It had solved the huge problem of Aggie Decker, totally compos mentis but frail after a stroke. Once a ranch wife who could help deliver a calf at midnight and still have breakfast on the table for family and ranch hands by six-thirty the next morning, during her convalescence she had faced the prospect of assisted living with dread.

'I don't mean to sound ungrateful,' she said. 'I'm glad those doctors saved my life. Sort of. But TV and card games all day – *damn*, Sarah, I can't say I'm looking forward to it.'

It was Will Dietz, the new boyfriend with whom Sarah hadn't even had time to make serious commitments let alone talk about marriage, who had pointed out that they could help Aggie and also rescue Denny from her drug-addicted mother if they all moved in together and Aggie agreed to supervise the hours when Will and Sarah were both working. About the debt the three of them took on together, he shrugged and said, 'Everybody's gotta live somewhere. This house is an *asset*.'

Sarah still held her breath sometimes when she thought how many unknowns their unconventional family had confronted. Would Aggie's recovery continue? Will was still in recovery, too, from a near-fatal shooting. His future in the police department wasn't secure. And Denny, after all, had survived in her mother's turbulent household by becoming a skilled thief and manipulator. Would she adjust to normal living and supervision?

So far it seemed to be working. Will had

resigned from the police department and was thriving in his new investigative job in the county attorney's office. Sarah loved having him home at nights and weekends.

And their hand-tooled version of assisted living suited Aggie to perfection – she had given up her car and driver's license without a whimper, knowing she could still play an important role in the new household. Will and Sarah ferried her to appointments and she supervised housecleaners and did most of the cooking, with Denny's help.

That was the big surprise benefit of this family bargain – the seamless way Aggie had contrived to become a substitute mother to Denny. Except for this recent dust-up about computer games they never seemed to annoy each other. Aggie had pulled out all her old cookbooks and obviously enjoyed sharing her culinary skills with a willing pupil.

'Look here, this amazing girl can even make piecrust now,' Aggie had said, beaming, as they served up last Sunday's dessert.

Better luck than I had any right to expect, Sarah had thought several times, watching them pull one delicious dish after another out of the oven. They were even developing a special patois in which they finished each other's sentences, some-times with words but often with action; if one of them said, 'Now where did I put . . .' the other's hand would likely reach out with the needed tool.

But this summer something was making Denny as prickly as a cactus. Sarah tried to remember – did the approach of puberty bother me this much? Maybe Aggie would remember. Sarah walked across the brick patio to stand between Will and her mother and announced, 'We need to talk.'

'Oh, my,' Will said as he leaned his rake against the trash container. 'This sounds serious.' They pulled three chairs together.

Sarah said, 'Have you noticed how irritable Denny's getting?'

'She's tired,' Aggie said. 'I've been waiting for a chance to talk to you about that swim team she joined. I think their instructor's gone a little overboard about winning. She's working them like they're getting ready for the Olympics.'

Will said, 'I noticed when I pick her up after practice that she doesn't chatter on about it like she did at the beginning.'

'What do you think she's so concerned about? Does she think she's not good enough? She's always been so happy in the water. I'm really puzzled.'

'If I had a way to get there,' Aggie said, 'I could go watch a practice session.'

'I can't get away to take you tomorrow,' Sarah said. 'But we could go together on Friday. Oh, but that's your poker club day, isn't it?'

Aggie waved dismissively. 'Never mind that, they won't miss me. They always have plenty of players.'

When they'd agreed on a time, Will said, 'Then why don't you all meet me downtown after work on Friday and I'll buy you dinner?'

'What a nice thought,' Aggie said. 'Is urban renewal all done, then? It's safe to go downtown after dark?'

'Oh, with two cops along I think you'll be OK,' Will said, not quite able to keep himself from smiling.

'We haven't been getting you out enough, have we?' Sarah said. 'Downtown Tucson is a happening place now, Ma. Great idea, Will. We could all use a treat. There's a French brasserie that just opened, or would you like to try the new Italian place?'

'You pick,' Will said. 'And this weekend I'll see if Denny wants to ride down on the south end and do some car-spotting. That'll cheer her up.'

'Will it ever. She loves that cop lore you teach her,' Aggie said. She privately thought this nudge toward street-cop thinking was a little extreme for a girl of Denny's age but was glad the child had got over her earlier suspicion of 'the boyfriend.'

'She likes knowing stuff other kids her age don't know,' Will said.

'That's true,' Aggie said. 'I enjoy teaching Denny too. I guess because she's a fast learner. I rarely have to say anything twice.'

'And when I teach her something new, she says, "Oh, cool,"' Will said. 'You know how seldom cops get to hear that?'

So the impromptu meeting ended on a pleasant note, but in bed later Will said quietly, 'Send me an email at work tomorrow – everything you can find about this swim teacher. I'll do some digging and see what I can learn before Friday.'

Digging was his passion now. After he went to work for the county attorney, Will had told Sarah, 'It's wonderful how much information you can get on the punishment end after the crime's been committed and it's too late to prevent it.'

'Oh, whoa,' she'd said that day. 'Am I hearing the new, more cynical Will Dietz?'

'Better believe it. The legal end of law enforcement is colder than a witch's tit. Better come over here and warm me up.'

Tonight, when he declared himself ready to start investigating the swim coach, she turned toward him in the dark and said, 'Oh, you mean – oh.' She hadn't given any thought to twisted coaches. 'I wasn't thinking . . . I mostly just thought she looked *tired*, Will.'

'Which I agree she does. But Denny's usually a pretty cheerful kid and now that you mention it I think she's been looking worried about something. So let's find out what it is and get it fixed.'

Will Dietz, my own personal Mr Fixit, who knows as well as I do that we can't fix everything. She listened to his breathing in the warm bed, thinking as she drifted toward sleep, but hang on, Denny, we'll make this better if we can.

'Let's not spend any more time on these records,' Delaney said Thursday morning, ''till we get the woman from ICE here to help. In the meantime, I'd like to get back to where we were before we got buried in all this paper.'

'Where was that?' said Leo. He had been in cold cases when they found the boxes and had been hoping to be so helpful with them that Delaney would not send him back.

'Looking at all the rest of the forensic evidence.

Let's not forget that our basic task is to find out who killed Calvin Springer.'

'I never forgot that,' Ollie said. 'But I thought we decided he must have been murdered over this funny business with the money.'

'Sounds reasonable but we haven't proved it yet. I think you should talk to some of the people in that parade that was passing while the murder took place.'

'How would we ever find them now?' Sarah said. 'I could talk to those day-care women again but they never said they knew anybody in the parade, did they, Jason?'

'Nope.'

'Ah, but I talked to Tucson Parks and Recreation,' Delaney said, 'and got them to send me the names of people who signed up for each float. This list,' he handed it to Sarah, 'has even got the order of the march. Start here' – he'd marked an entry with a red Sharpie – 'with the mariachi players, see? Here's the headman of the band, address and three phone numbers. Find him and get him to give you the same info on his players. Ask every one of them what they saw that day. Bring me back everything they say, even if it isn't much.'

'Even if it's nothing?'

'Come on. A murder, yelling, blood on a broken window – somebody must have seen *something*. If you don't get anything from the mariachi players you'll have to go on to the llama day-trippers behind them and the . . . what was it? Cowboys, I think. Yes, here it is, trail riders on paint horses – they were in front of the mariachis.'

87

The detectives held a strategy huddle before they went out. 'Let's each take our own car,' Sarah said. 'That way we can spread out and find them fast when we get the names.' Looking for the leader of the band, they turned on University Avenue and drove in caravan behind Old Main. As usual, they found no place to park, so they turned on their light strips and stopped at the curb outside the CESL building.

'I feel like putting a sack over my head,' Ollie said, getting out of his car. 'We just changed campus traffic from tight to gridlocked.'

'We won't be here long,' Sarah said. 'Come on.'

'Oh my God,' Pepe Montoya said, looking up from the desk in his tiny, crowded office, 'what have I done?' Six detectives stood in his doorway, holding up badges.

'Don't panic,' Leo Tobin said, oozing kindly-old-flatfoot reassurance, 'we just need to ask you a few questions.'

'I don't know anything about Islamic terrorists.'

'We don't either,' Sarah said. 'We're here to talk about the Fourth of July parade in Menlo Park. You were in it, weren't you? You and your mariachi band?'

'It's not my band,' he said. 'I belong to a group and we just . . . play together sometimes. I did sign the form that got us a spot in the Fourth of July parade, but— Is that a crime now, for God's sake?'

'Of course not,' Sarah said. 'We're hoping you can answer a few questions about what happened on Alameda Avenue on Sunday.'

'On the day of the parade? I'd probably be the last to know. When you're in a parade that's all you see – your own little part.' He glanced around his tiny, crowded space where piles of paper occupied the spare chair seat and every other surface. 'Well, we can't sit in here; let's go in the lounge.'

Fortyish, thin, balding, a tense and overworked teacher of English as a second language to freshmen students, he was not the dashing trumpeter with the sexy suit today. He had just conducted a round of pop-up quizzes, he explained as he led them out to the lounge, and this morning his teaching assistant had called in sick.

'So all those piles of paper are going to sit there giving me guilt till I correct them myself. By the time I get that done it'll be time for another test.'

'Whatever happened to that paperless society the softwear designers used to promise us?' Leo said.

'Forget about it. Testing is where the rubber hits the road in my end of the teaching profession,' Montoya said. 'Most of my students are on scholarships and they need to show constant progress to keep the cash flowing.'

Montoya brightened when the conversation turned to his music. 'I *love* to play,' he said. 'Such crazy music – we all get high and silly and laugh all the time. But leading a mariachi band is like herding cats. I really need to get rid of that part of the job. We're all moonlighters, you know. We all have day jobs.'

One or two bands play regularly in bars in

Tucson, he explained, 'But otherwise we mostly get a *quinceanera* or a wedding here and there, and then pop-up chances to show-off, like this parade. So the membership of the bands is quite fluid; whoever can get time off when the gig comes along.

'Let's see, there were five of us marching on the Fourth, as I remember. I played the trumpet, Luis was on guitarron, Miguel on vihuela, and two violins – that'd be Felix and Fred.'

'Wasn't there a singer? Martina said—'

'We all sing. Usually Miguel does the solos – he has the best voice. Are you going to try to find all these people? Hold on, I'll go get my address book.'

Ray Menendez typed addresses and phone numbers into Sarah's tablet while she asked the professor what he could tell her about the murder that took place during the march.

'Murder? My God, I don't know anything about that.'

'Are you saying you never heard that big fight?'

'I certainly did not. I was in the middle of five musicians pouring their hearts out in Mexican folk music. All singing, sometimes. A dozen half-drunk faux cowboys were up ahead of me, yelling insults at each other while they twirled their lariats. And somewhere to the back of us, I remember, was another band with tubas. Parades are a free-for-all to see who can make the most noise.'

'And I suppose the clown created noise too? Kids yelling?'

'What clown?'

90

'The one with the limp marching with your band.'

'We don't have a clown. Mariachis never have clowns. Red noses? They would clash with our outfits.'

'Really? He wasn't with you? But you must have noticed him, didn't you?'

'Sure didn't.' He threw his hands up, palms outward. 'We were *busy*, OK?'

'Well . . . I guess he must have been with the group behind you. Was that llamas?'

'There was a hiking guide with llamas, yes – the animals carry the luggage for the hikers, they told me. Awful animals, angry, spitting . . . I don't know why people think they're so cute. I never saw a clown. We formed up in the parking lot of the El Rio health center and marched west on Congress. Our group was near the front so I saw most of the floats, but then people mill around so much. Are we about done? I have a class in a few minutes.'

'Just about. You've given me home addresses and phone numbers, but you say you all have day jobs. So can you tell us where I'd be likely to find these people now?'

'Oh, God . . . well, let's see . . .' So they started over. 'Felix is a house painter; you'd have to call his store to find out where he's working.' He cudgeled his brain until the store name popped out. They went on down the list: Luis was a kindergarten teacher, Miguel a pastor at a tiny Christian church in a strip mall and Fred a retired fireman who sometimes volunteered at homeless shelters for men. When she had all he could tell her in her tablet, Sarah thanked Montoya and they hurried out to their cars.

The row of flashing lights had already drawn several spectators. The detectives waved away their questions and divided the list. Sarah took the kindergarten teacher, Luis Calvo. She found him right away, because Pepe Montoya had guessed correctly that his kindergarten was the one on Magee Road. Luis was opening cardboard boxes in a chaotic classroom filled with many more cardboard boxes.

'The kids aren't here yet,' he said, 'but school starts in two weeks so we're getting the rooms ready and holding training courses. We have a lot of new teachers and many changes in policy, so we have to re-train.' He rolled his eyes up. 'Some year we're going to stop training and actually teach. Just kidding – I love my job, and all-day kindergarten, whatever else you can say about it, is a godsend for working mothers.'

He was even more modest about his career as a mariachi. 'I just do it because my wife gets turned on when she sees me in those pants. Actually, we kind of have a nerve even claiming to be a band. It's really whoever shows up out of a group of ten or so players. You know mariachi is mostly an oral tradition? Hardly anything written down – it's all passed along from one group to the next. That's why we often look so joyous; we're so glad when we all hit the right chord at the same time.' He laughed out loud after that zinger, his white teeth gleaming beneath his extravagant mustache.

'It's wonderful music,' Sarah said. 'I was

92

hoping you could tell me what you saw in that house and yard where the murder took place. It seems to have happened just as you marched past it.'

'It did? Really? My God. I read about it in the paper the next day but I didn't know. Jeez, it must have been a nice quiet murder – I never heard a thing. And I don't believe I looked at any of the houses – there were people all around us and these days you kind of keep an eye on them, you know. Any crowd is likely to draw a crazy with a gun.' He stared at Sarah, appalled. 'Where did that murder take place, exactly?'

'On Alameda, between Grande and Melwood.'

'Just before we made the turn. We went south on Melwood and marched back to Congress, then east and back into the parking lot in front of the El Rio health center where the parade started and ended. We were all dying of thirst by then; we went across the street to the Mercado San Agostin and got huge icy drinks. Drank them right down and hopped on the streetcar to go back to our cars on campus. We'd no idea we had just strutted right past a murder – *oy vey*. That's not Spanish, by the way – my wife is Jewish and I pick up the Yiddish from her. They have all the best – what?'

'I was just going to remark that except for names your group does not seem very Hispanic; at least, the ones I've met. Your accents – you could be from anywhere.'

'Yeah, we're all second or third generation – the lucky ones who got the degrees and didn't have to do the stoop labor. And then there's Fred

93

– his last name is Jorgenson. His dad worked in Mexico for a couple of years while Fred was in high school and he picked up his music then.' A big shrug. 'He just likes to play. We're all like that really – it's a labor of love. The money is,' he rocked his hand, 'not so much.'

Her phone rang. Ray Menendez said, 'Hey, Sarah, how you doing at that kindergarten?'

'Just finishing up.'

'OK, we found the pastor and the house painter. When Hector and Jason went after the retired fireman they got a long list of homeless shelters and so far they've tried two with no luck. We thought we'd triple-team it, see if we could find them all. You want to join up?'

'Sure. Give me an address and I'll start.'

She was pulling in to an ancient motel on Oracle when Ray called again and said, 'Leo finally got Fred's wife on the phone; she says Fred took a day off and went golfing. And she's sure he doesn't know anything about that murder because now that he's retired, she says, Fred tells her everything. It's the first thing he does when he comes in the house; as soon as he's gone to the bathroom he finds her and tells her everything he's done since she saw him last. Are you glad to know all that about Fred Jorgenson?'

'Enchanted,' Sarah said. 'Where shall we go for coffee?'

'We're mostly in the south end. How about the Dunkin Donuts on Broadway?'

'Deal.'

They persuaded the counterman to make a fresh pot and each drank two cups and ate big frosted apple Danishes before they called Delaney. 'Because you know what he'll do when we bring in this big nada,' Ollie said.

'Of course we know that,' Leo said. 'He'll send us out in search of llama keepers and that noisy pack of dentists that ride the paint ponies.'

'And he can keep on sending us out till hell freezes over and we'll never come back with anything,' Jason said, 'because like we already reminded him ten times, everybody was watching the *parade*, and then the *storm*. Why does he find that so hard to accept? He was there himself; he knows it's true.'

'He's the head of the section,' Sarah said. 'He wants to be sure we can show we did our due diligence.'

'Well, I think we've duly drunk enough of this diligent coffee so we can go in now,' Ray said. 'By the time we've detailed this waste of a morning it'll be time for lunch.'

But Delaney wasn't buying delay. He twitched through three versions of 'my guy didn't see anything.' Then he threw up his hands and said, 'Why are you dragging this out? None of the mariachis noticed anything in that yard, is that it?'

All the detectives' heads bobbed sadly.

'Time for the next pivot, then. Banjo called; he wants to tell us what he's learned about the Smith and Wesson. So why don't you all take an early lunch and get back here by twelve-thirty. Banjo's got a full afternoon but he'll squeeze us in, he said, if we can make it early.'

Still full of sugared pastry and coffee, the crew

hurried out, trying to think of a place to buy thin soup or a no-calorie salad. Unable to think of anything she could eat right now without gagging, Sarah took a paperback to the main library, enjoyed a cool read for half an hour and drank a bottle of water on the way back to her desk.

Six

'Smith and Wesson called this gun the K-22 Masterpiece because they honestly felt they had made the best revolver in existence,' Banjo said, talking fast, glancing at his watch. 'And marksmen ever since have endorsed that opinion. There's a history on their website of its iterations over the years since they introduced it in 1939, with comments from shooters so detailed and respectful that sometimes you think, "In a minute, I'll hear organ music."

'Here's an example. "In 1955, the four-screw side plate was eliminated and replaced by one using only three screws, with the earlier top screw replaced by a tongue on the plate that fit into the frame."' Banjo pushed his wire-rims onto his forehead and pursed his whole face into a pained squint. 'The gospel according to Saint Wesson. I sent you several pages of this stuff, Sarah – you should read it to get a feel for why your otherwise plain-living victim hung onto this weapon.

'So when Smith and Wesson tell me that our

gun was shipped in 1990 to a gun dealer in Grosse Pointe, Michigan, I believe them. They have the serial number, they know its various features, they don't mess around. Grosse Pointe is a classy suburb of Detroit, the gun shop they sold it to is still in business and the owner keeps records almost as extensive as S and W. My man at the store wouldn't give me a phone number till he checked with the buyer. But the buyer, on the other hand, was so eager to talk about this gun that *he* called *me*.

'Norman Wasserman, that's his name. He's still a hobby shooter but he doesn't have a Masterpiece any more – the one you found was stolen from him on New Year's Day, 1995, while he and his family were skiing in Vermont. The thieves took many other items of value but what he remembers with the most regret was the loss of his best guns out of locked cases in his study. He calls it his study but the way he describes it I think it's more like the coolest hobby room ever. Kind of a man cave with two toy train sets and a big pool table. He says he's got a steel door and frame on it now and a deadbolt lock; nobody's ever getting in there again till he lets them in.'

All the men in the room, Sarah could see, were leaning toward Banjo with shining eyes. Any minute now they're all going to drool, she thought.

'Naturally, what Norman wants is his gun back. I told him to be patient. "All investigations end eventually, Norman," I said.'

'Unless they become cold cases,' Leo said.

Jason walked into the group just then, very late

back from lunch. Delaney raised his eyebrows and said, 'Nice of you to join us.'

His sarcasm didn't put a dent in Jason's good humor. 'Hey, I had a string of phone calls, all related to this case. And the last call I took was the best.' He turned his cheery smile toward Sarah and said, above the thunder just then rolling across mid-town, 'Remember when we told that Martina lady she should call us if she thought of anything else she wanted to tell us? Well, she called me just now and she thinks she's got something we ought to see, so' – he turned his optimistic smile on Delaney – 'can we go see her now?'

'Maybe later.' Delaney looked cross. 'We only have Banjo here for a few more minutes. I'd like to concentrate on—'

'We pretty much promised her we'd come if she called,' Jason said. 'She was really spooked about having a dead body next door. Can't blame her with all those kids in the house.'

'OK.' Delaney sighed. 'You can go see what she needs. But you don't need Sarah along for this, do you?' Seeing Sarah making the time-out signal, he turned to her and said, 'What?'

'I don't think Jason should go to that house by himself, boss.' Her face pleaded with him not to make her say why.

Delaney opened his mouth, saw Sarah's expression, paused for two beats and said, 'OK, both of you go, but hurry.' He called after them as they headed for the stairs: 'Let me know right away if you got problems at that house.'

They ran downstairs together, checking phones,

Glocks and recorders. In the car, Jason driving, Sarah said, 'Did she sound scared?'

'No. Excited, though. Said she'd *found* something.' As a few big drops of water hit the windshield, he said, 'You think Mother Nature just passed some new rule that we can only talk to this woman in a rainstorm?'

But the storm fizzled quickly, becoming statistically one of this monsoon's many 'trace amounts.'

From Martina's sunlit front doorway, Sarah saw she had more children in the house today. The floor inside was a hazardous waste dump of toys and small bodies and the air was filled with little piping cries. Sofia sent Jason some blazing eye signals but Martina said quickly, 'It's outside in the trash.'

She turned at the doorway and told Sofia, 'Don't let Timothy get his hands on this doorknob.' She explained as they walked into the yard, 'He just got tall enough to open the door and he's *determined* to do it.'

The city dumpster stood next to the street, on the property line between her lot and the house to her right.

'I heard something that day,' she said, 'while I was dialing nine-one-one. But there was so much going on . . . I never thought of it again till this afternoon when we started carrying out bags for tomorrow's pickup. So many kids, you know – we have a lot of trash. We take it out a few bags at a time so we don't get sore backs. I threw a couple of bags in here and let the lid fall, and I remembered that noise. So I came back out here and took a look. Careful, now, don't let

99

this hit you.' She let the big lid fall back and they all peered into the smelly interior.

'See that red and white dotted thing just peeking out of the brown paper bag? Under the plastic sacks on your side?'

'Yeah,' Jason said, putting on gloves. 'Almost looks like . . .' He reached as far as he could, stood on tiptoe and started to tilt inward. Sarah grabbed his arm and he tilted back. Martina pulled a pair of kitchen tongs out of her apron pocket and said, 'Try these.'

Jason snagged a corner, tugged carefully and teased out a brightly polka-dotted, very dirty garment. It had a stiff frilled collar, speckled with dried blood and bits of garbage, a big red shoe and a grotesque . . . mask? Yes, a grinning face with a big red nose rolled up inside the costume.

His expression as he held the filthy thing aloft would have been appropriate for a precious art object. Turning his dazzling grin on Martina, he said, 'Do you have any idea how much easier our jobs would be if all the homeowners were as smart and helpful as you are?'

'Oh, homeowners, don't I wish,' Martina said. 'I just rent.' But she was blushing, looking young and pretty and pleased.

The rest of that afternoon was a blur of work. Sarah made many phone calls, beginning with the support crew to ask them to impound the trash container and the crime lab to tell them they were about to get the mother of all searching and testing jobs. She insisted Jason should have the pleasure of calling Delaney to tell him they

100

had just found the answer to how their murderer got away without being noticed.

Somewhere in that busy afternoon Sarah remembered to ask Martina, 'Have you seen anybody prowling around your neighbor's house since the day we found the body there?'

'Oh, yeah, people come by all the time and take pictures,' Martina said. 'They think it's fun to tell their friends they know where a murder happened. Like it makes them glamorous to know where the house is that was on TV.'

'Any of them ever try to get in?'

'No. Well, there's one car with the blackened windows that came a couple of times with a key.'

'Oh?' Sarah said. And then casually, 'You notice a license plate on that one?'

'No. But he had a key so I knew it must be one of yours.'

'Sure,' Sarah said, careful to keep her voice matter-of-fact. 'I don't always know what everybody's driving.'

They were getting back in their car to leave when Sarah, standing by the driver's-side door, said, 'Wait.' She stood for twenty seconds with four fingertips pressed to her forehead then sprinted back to Martina's door and stuck her head in. Scanning the confusing roomful of moving bodies, she said, 'Sofia?'

The girl's pretty face appeared at the far side of the dinette table, above the whimpering child she had just picked up. 'What?'

'The day of the parade – did you say the clown was lame?'

'Yes.'

'Lame in what way? Did he walk funny? Was he limping?'

'He didn't exactly limp. He just had a funny, um, gait.' Looking thoughtful, Sofia laid the squirming child across her shoulder and patted its back absent-mindedly. 'And he was leaning on a cane.'

'A cane. Ah.' Sarah smiled at the attractive girl, so like her mother, who seemed destined for a future very much like Martina's. And why do I think that's such a bad thing? she thought. Maybe because she does. 'Did you get a look at it? Can you describe it?'

'What, the cane? It was wood, I think. Looked kind of, like, carved? Had a big knot on the top for a handle.'

'Thank you very much, Sofia,' Sarah said. 'You and your mother would both make very good detectives.'

As she turned to go she got her first friendly look from Sofia.

Back at the car, she asked Jason to drive and started a phoning fit of her own – to the crime lab, first, to tell them that besides another red clown shoe, size thirty or so, they should be on the lookout for a bloody wooden cane. 'I think it's uneven and has a big knot for a handle. Like a, what's that Irish word? Shillelagh. You know, a carved wooden thing with knots. Fine.'

When she got off the phone, she told Jason, 'I'm making a note but help me remember to tell Delaney about the car with tinted windows, will you?'

'Yeah. Sounds like a cartel guy has a key that'll get him through a crime-scene lock.'

'Sure does.'

'You think he got anything?'

'Not where I was looking. That one must be a better shooter than searcher. He didn't get the stuff in the vent pipes or above the soffit.'

'That one? You think there's more than one lurker?'

'Well, she said a lot of people were hanging around taking pictures. Could be one or two of those were bad guys acting like tourists. But – hell, I don't know. One more puzzle.'

She called Will to make sure he could pick up Denny after swim practice, then rang her house to tell Aggie they had made an important find and she would no doubt be late getting home. 'So tell everybody to go ahead and eat; don't wait for me.'

When she pulled in her driveway a little after nine she found all her family members reading in a favorite chair in an otherwise dark and silent house. They gathered at the round table to watch her eat warmed-over stew and listen to her story of the find.

'Looks like he just stripped off his bloody clown costume and mask, stuffed them in a grocery bag, dropped the bag and the cane in the trash and boogied on out of there,' she said. 'Probably on that streetcar that leaves the Mercado every ten minutes now. One of the merchants told me he saw the mariachis piling onto that train after the parade, and I bet the shooter blended in with that group, or one like it, and rode back to

103

campus, waving a little US flag like the rest of the patriots.'

'Makes quite a picture, doesn't it?' Aggie said. 'There's a little more stew; would you like to have it?'

'Uh . . . sure. With another piece of bread? This all tastes good beyond belief, you know.'

'Better have another glass of wine to go with it,' Will said. 'It's been a long day and you're off tomorrow.'

'Great idea. Spoil me some more,' she said, stretching.

'You should sleep in a little in the morning, too,' Aggie said. 'I told Denny that you and I would like to come and watch her practice tomorrow and she said the best time would be early afternoon. They do most of their lap timing early in the class.'

After a pause, Aggie added, 'She got kind of anxious, though, about why we wanted to watch.'

'I know I look pretty dragged out after practice,' Denny said. 'But really, Aunt Sarah, nobody's beating on me with ropes or anything. It *is* hard work but it's all voluntary.'

'I would never think of interfering,' Sarah said. 'Is that what you're worried about?'

'Well . . .'

'We just want to enjoy watching your progress,' Sarah said. 'You know how parents are. Always looking for something to brag about.'

'Don't get me wrong, it's very nice of you to take some of your precious time off just to watch us flounder in the pool. But—'

'What?'

104

'Well, Jill's mom came to watch a lot and now Jill quit the team.'

'Oh, and she was kind of your buddy, wasn't she?'

'Yeah. Her and Mickey, they're the ones I like.'

'Did she say why she was quitting?'

'No.'

'Why do you think?'

'Just got sick of working so hard, maybe,' Denny said.

'But you suspect her mother saw something she didn't like and talked to the coach about it?'

'Yeah. Or Mickey says maybe she didn't talk to the coach, maybe she just told Jill it was OK to quit.'

'And Jill was ready to quit?'

'Mickey says so.'

'Why?'

Denny shrugged.

'Too much work?'

'I guess.' Denny was looking at the ceiling light as anxiously as if she thought it might explode. Aggie was shaking her head at Sarah. Damn, she thought, I'm blowing this, getting too nosy.

She leaned toward her niece and said, 'Trust me, Denny, I will not say anything to your coach but hello, and you can pretend we're not there, OK? I just . . . I thought it would be fun for Ma to get out of the kitchen for a change. And it would be a great rest for my brain to spend a couple of hours not thinking about this crazy case I'm working on. But if it will bother you too much we'll stay away.'

'It won't bother me a bit unless you make me quit the team.'

'Of course I won't do that. It's your summer and you can do whatever you like with it. Well, as long as it's legal.'

Denny giggled. 'What could I do in a pool that wasn't?'

Aggie said, 'She's got a point. I can't think of any stories you've ever told me about crimes in a swimming pool. But then I'm getting old; maybe I've forgotten some.'

'Well, I did have one a few years ago,' Sarah said, 'but it was so sordid I think I spared you the details.'

Denny said, 'Ooh, sordid. Am I old enough to hear about it now?'

'Probably, but I'm never going to talk about that one again if I can help it.'

'Well,' Will said, 'I can certainly see why your brain would need a rest from that murder in Menlo Park. That story's way too neat to be true, isn't it?' He had finished pouring her wine and stood by her chair, listening to them while he replaced the cork.

'I guess it is. When we came back with the dumpster story today, Leo Tobin said, "Tell the truth, Sarah – you guys are just making stuff up now to entertain the old boy in his last month on the job, right?"'

'I feel the same way,' Will said. 'Like you must be testing my gullibility.'

'Why, because the parade came just in time?'

'Yeah. Such a masterpiece of timing – the parade that covered the noise of the fight and distracted everybody so the attacker could leave. But how could a would-be murderer possibly have known there'd be a parade there when he needed it?'

'I don't know,' Sarah said. 'But who else would put a bloody clown costume in that dumpster? Somebody knew about the parade or he wouldn't have been dressed that way. Somehow he got word and joined the march.'

'It just sounds way too convenient.'

'I know. But I've heard you say it yourself, Will; sometimes it seems like murderers have all the luck.'

'When did I say that?' He looked thoughtful, putting the bottle back on the sideboard. 'Must have been back in the olden days when I was still working in Homicide.'

'I guess it was, yes.'

'Well, I've changed since then. Now I think murderers are mostly just losers with poor impulse control.' He sat back down at the table and looked around at three generations of the same features, rearranged slightly on each face and marked differently by age. 'The amazing fact I've discovered in recent years is that even old beat-up detectives with marks and scars can have plenty of luck.'

Around the table, the three similar faces lit up with differing degrees of pleasure. Aggie shook her head and smiled ironically. Denny rolled her eyes up to the light again but then did a little humorous bounce. Sarah got up and fetched a fresh fork from the sideboard, touching the back of his neck as she passed him.

* * *

'Denny said you'd probably be coming to watch this afternoon,' the young coach said and touched her whistle. She did that frequently, Sarah had noticed – the whistle seemed to be her amulet. 'I'm Joan.' She had team lists on a clipboard, sharpies clipped to the lists. Her T-shirt carried the team logo – a barracuda with many sharp teeth – and said, 'Go Cudas!' They shook hands.

'My mother, Aggie Decker.'

'Oh, a grandmother, how lovely.' Joan had a beautiful smile for grandmothers. 'We're so pleased when families take an interest.'

'Denny's been telling us how hard you're working,' Sarah said. 'We thought we'd come and see the progress.'

'You want to sit here on the end? You'll get a good view of the take-off and the turn.'

Eight girls were lined up on the far end of the pool. Denny was near the middle, wearing vest number ten. Was the lineup random or according to ability? Sarah watched, wondering if she'd be able to tell. She knew, from things Denny had told her about the team, that the girl next to her in the number sixteen vest was Mickey. Denny was the second smallest girl on the team. Mickey was half an inch shorter; all the other girls were bigger.

'We're going to do some warm-up laps and then we'll time some of the different strokes,' Joan said. She blew her whistle. All the girls jumped into the pool and swam two lengths each of freestyle, backstroke, breaststroke and butterfly. Denny just about held her own on the freestyle but picked up a small advantage on the turns.

Mickey pulled even with her on the backstroke and the two of them were by then half a length ahead of the rest of the pack. She and Mickey matched each other almost stroke for stroke in the breaststroke section, then Denny pulled decisively ahead of Mickey in the butterfly but was almost caught by number three, the biggest girl in the class, who staged a brilliant streak of speed in that stroke. The other five trailed by one to two lengths.

Joan blew her whistle when the series ended and called, 'All over here.' The whole team swam to her side of the pool and listened as she told them, 'Most of you could improve your times by several seconds if you'd sharpen your turns. Mickey and Denny are doing it right, so, Denny, I want you to swim four widths from right here. The rest of you watch now . . .' She described what was right about Denny's slick little flip. 'Now, Mickey, you.' Then she praised the superior speed that Jean, number three, was getting with her butterfly and asked her to swim a length. 'You see how much power she's getting with her kick?' She had Jean swim a length holding a board so they could all watch her feet. 'I want you all to get in the pool now and do two lengths of butterfly, trying to match Jean's kick.'

Joan was scrupulously fair and praised every sign of progress, Sarah thought, including some so subtle that she herself, watching carefully, didn't see. But it was clear that Denny was the best swimmer on the team, overall, and Sarah thought she'd improved her kick in the butterfly a little after watching Jean.

The other thing Sarah noticed was that the poorest swimmer, a thin girl named Brady, was at the bottom of some kind of pecking order being established by the four-girl pack that ranged in skill below Jean but above Brady. As the practice went on the group of four found ways to mock her performance with little eye-rolls and snickers. They clustered during breaks and did a lot of giggling and whispering behind their hands. Brady stood by herself during breaks and Sarah saw a member of the brat pack stick out a foot and try to trip her. Brady noticed the hazard and dodged it without looking at the trickster behind the foot.

Joan managed to appear oblivious of their sniping, which was probably the best way to be in a summer class with short-term goals. But Sarah longed to send Patty, the snarky leader of the mean-girl pack, to the locker room for a time-out.

Sarah and Aggie watched for another half hour while the team did timed laps in each stroke. When Aggie said she was getting tired on the hard bench, Sarah took her home. On the way, Aggie said, 'You kids have fun at your dinner out. I'm going to get in my jammies and open a can of soup.'

Sarah drove back for Denny, who curled into a ball on her seat and muttered, 'Some days I wish I'd never joined this stupid thing.'

'They bother you, too, huh? The mean little girls with the jokes about Brady.'

'You saw that?' Denny sat up with her eyes blazing. 'Isn't it just a damn shame? That's what they did to Amy and she quit; now that she's gone they've decided to pick on Brady. The kid is trying her best! Just because she hasn't had all the lessons they have.'

'What have they got against her, do you think?'

'Oh, I think she's kind of poor – her clothes are pretty dismal. I remember so well how that felt, that last year with Mom, when I didn't have clean clothes half the time. Brady's so shy and quiet but look how hard she's working! Why don't their parents make them stop? Or somebody from school?' Abruptly, she changed tacks. 'You didn't say anything, did you? To the coach?'

'Of course not. I promised, remember?'

'It doesn't feel right to me, pretending I can't see them being so awful to her. But if you get known as a snitch or a suck-up it's just *death* for the rest of your life.'

'Denny, do you think I was never in school myself? All I meant to say is I know you're between a rock and a hard place and I'm sorry.'

'Yeah.' She leaned back with her eyes closed again, then opened them and said, 'Hey, there's a fun thought.'

'What?'

'Be good to catch Patty's gang on a hard place and hit 'em with a rock.'

'Oh, well, now . . .'

Denny giggled. 'You can't go to jail for what you're thinking, right? I heard that in a song the other day and I like it.'

'Such an old song – where'd you hear it?'

'Grandma was playing golden oldies on the radio.' Then she pulled another of her lightning changes. 'It's so nice of Will to want to take us to dinner but do you think I could be excused? I'm really beat. I'd like to heat up some soup and go to bed.'

'Good, you can keep your grandma company,' Sarah said and called Aggie to make the deal. Denny rode home the rest of the way curled up in her seat with her eyes closed. In the driveway she opened them and saw her grandmother standing in the doorway.

'Look at Grandma – isn't she cute in her fuzzy pink slippers?' she said. 'Why is she so anxious about me? Have I got some zits I haven't noticed?'

'She's afraid the swim team is wearing you out,' Sarah said. 'Try being cheerful, will you? Make her feel better.'

'Now I've got to cheer up Grandma? Life gets more and more complicated.'

'I'm almost certain you can handle it,' Sarah said and called Will to tell him the party had shrunk. 'Mom and Denny are both too tired to go out so this just turned into a dinner date for two.'

'Hey, a treat. Let's shoot for the moon,' he said. So she changed into the best dress she owned and took time over her hair and make-up.

'Damn, woman,' Will said when she met him at the restaurant, 'you look good enough to distract me from eating.'

'Good. But hold that thought for later, will you, please? Because every molecule of my body is demanding food right now.'

They had picked the Italian place. As they passed through elaborately etched doors into a gleaming space filled with miles of white linen,

Will said, 'What do you think, babe? Is this place good enough for us?'

'I believe it is. And I hope they mean to feed us well,' Sarah said as the waiter seated them with a flourish, 'so we'll be strong enough to hold up these menus.'

'They are a little large,' Will said, 'but I see that one of the items they offer is *osso buco*, so my contentment level is already inching up toward the max.'

'And if I offer to split a cannoli for dessert?'

'Better be careful,' Will said. 'I might cry.'

Denny's swim team acquitted themselves very well in the all-city meet the next afternoon. Denny, Mickey and Jean all won firsts in their best events and the team was placed second overall.

Will didn't go to watch the meet. 'I'd get too nervous,' he told Sarah. 'This parent stuff isn't easy, is it?'

But when they came home with the great results he told Denny she'd made him proud. He asked her, 'So do you get to go to Phoenix?'

'Yup. First weekend in August.' Her expression wavered between proud and grim. 'Now we really get to bear down.'

Seven

'Well, it does look like he might have been running a funnel account,' Lois Johnson said on Monday morning.

Don Belgrave had been right about her appearance. Sarah's first thought when she saw her was, Grant Wood: American Gothic. But a few seconds later she decided, well, not exactly. Lois was plain-faced like the picture but her body was taut as a drum – if Lois Johnson had been in that picture, Sarah thought, she'd probably have been the one holding the pitchfork. At a minimum she probably did three miles on an indoor track and had a quick swim before breakfast.

When she began to talk, though, Sarah heard the flat Midwestern vowels of the women in Aggie's family scrapbooks, the female relatives they had once visited on a farm in Iowa. Take away the cottage apron and add fake nails and an assured touch on a mini iPad and you'd have Lois Johnson.

'It'll take a crack team of accountants to prove it, of course,' she said. 'Luckily, I have one of those.' When she nodded, which she did often to endorse her own statements, her light brown Dutch bob swayed easily – a subtle cut that fit her head like a cap. She used very little make-up and wore a plain blouse and skirt but had a certain shiny perfection that made you want to keep watching her. Her clothes were all cut from some wrinkle-resistant fabric and fit her slender body closely without being at all provocative. 'Are these all the bank records?' She blinked at the coffee cans.

'All we've found so far,' Delaney said. 'We just got this case on Sunday.'

'Ah, yes, your Fourth of July celebration. I heard about that.' She favored them with a caustic smile that enlisted them into her tough-as-nails team. Her eyes were pale blue and evidently near-sighted, enlarged by trifocals in beige plastic frames.

'It's a homicide case with some funny kinks in it,' Sarah said. 'The victim has lived in the neighborhood for a long time but seems strangely detached from it. We can't find anyone who knew him. I'm sure you understand that we're anxious to continue that investigation.'

'Of course.' She smiled around the table, looking for a moment as if she might be going to hand around a plate of brownies. Then the Iron Lady from ICE came back. 'My office is only interested in the money laundering part of the case, but I'm sure *you* understand we have to have total control of any portion we agree to accept.'

'Well,' Delaney said, 'Special Agent Belgrave indicated we could expect full cooperation if your people turn up anything on the homicide that we can use.'

'I suppose.' Lois rocked her hands. 'You and Don signed a memorandum of agreement, as I understand it?' She fixed Delaney in a blue-laser stare through her thick lenses. All the detectives in the room watched Lois Johnson closely, trying to get their heads around her curious blend of country girl and big-city powerhouse.

'That's right,' Delaney said, still pleasant but getting cooler fast. 'Don and I reached an understanding without much difficulty. I have a copy in my office and you're welcome to read it any time.'

'I'll certainly do that,' Lois said. 'I do hope

115

Don didn't give away the farm.' She looked back at them thoughtfully. 'I would have supposed that anybody in law enforcement this close to the border would be running into these cases all the time and we wouldn't need all this . . . *dickering*. But I guess . . . We all drive the same highway but in different lanes, don't we? I actually don't have much idea how you do your jobs, either. Well!' She sat up straighter, if that was possible. 'Let's get the preliminaries out of the way, shall we?'

She leaned her gym-toned body back in her chair and tented her fingers. 'Funnel accounts are usually opened by a person or company in a bank near the border. It has to be a bank with branches in at least several, sometimes hundreds of other cities. The account is set up with the proviso that it will receive deposits in certain other locations which are specified in advance but subject to change upon notice. Typically, deposits get made to the account in several of the distant branches and withdrawn from the original branch, usually within a day or two, sometimes within hours.'

Sarah's initial impression of a thirties heartland hausfrau disappeared as Lois gave them a crisp summary of funnel accounts. She offered to deliver examples, variations and anecdotes if she thought they needed to hear them. She obviously knew her subject cold and was patiently trying to help them catch up.

'That's part of the picture we look for – lots of churn. Fast, hard to follow. The money, which is deposited in dollars, is often used to make purchases in foreign countries. The merchandise it buys is sent to a business address in Mexico, where it will be sold for pesos. So the money is converted without going through a currency exchange in this country.'

'I get that,' Leo said. 'That's part of what's going on in my box, I guess.' He told her again about the house.

'Yes, that's a good example. A trifle more complex than usual but not the most convoluted I've ever seen.'

'This takes a lot of coordination, though, doesn't it? You'd think we'd be looking at a lot of computers and cell phones, a whole network of smooth operators. What we seem to have here is one old guy with a Ford pickup and an adding machine.'

'An adding machine? Are you serious?'

Beaming, Leo showed her the tapes – his favorite part of the puzzle.

'Well, there has to be more to it than this. If Mr Springer was doing what I think, he works for a highly sophisticated syndicate and has many partners. Not necessarily known to him by sight, however. One feature of this level of money laundering is that many of the players are unknown to each other and play their parts without knowing the whole game. These people adhere strictly to the concept of need-to-know. It's quite possible your victim is dead because he got some information he wasn't entitled to.'

'They'd kill him even if he learned it by accident?'

'Absolutely. He may not even have known he had it. Drug cartels don't take chances.'

'What about the casino chits, though?' Ollie said. 'Almost every box has a batch of them. Was he skimming and gambling with the money, you think, or—'

'No, that's part of the job, to feed cash into the gambling machines. They don't care if they win or lose because when they take the money out they have a chit that shows a legitimate source for it. That money can then be sent directly to an account below the border – it has been given a credible source other than drugs, you see? And as you have already noticed, that's been happening here. Springer occasionally sent a deposit made up entirely of gambling returns to his Mazatlan bagman, Felipe García.'

'So the neighbor who thought he saw him at the Indian Casino,' Oscar said, 'wasn't mistaken.'

'Probably not. I'd guess that Springer was gambling to launder the money. Then he brought the chits back to his bank and used them instead of checks as the basis of the deposit. When he sends it across the border he just has to keep the dollar amounts below the currency reporting threshold of ten thousand dollars. You know about that rule, right, that banks have to report—'

'Yes,' Sarah said, 'we know about that rule.'

'Good.' Lois sent a high-beam smile to Sarah over the tops of her glasses. 'Let's not get testy with each other; I'm here to help.'

'And we know we need help, and we're very grateful to you.' Well, I am grateful, Sarah thought. Doing my best to be, anyway. OK, maybe not succeeding a hundred percent. She shared the street cop's view that the Feds always managed to flit along the flowery top layer of cases and leave the locals slogging through the grit and gravel below.

'Your man,' Lois Johnson said, 'appears to have been running a hybrid of several forms of funnel accounts. Usually they're more specialized – just do one or two types of laundering. But he was buying and selling, *and* gambling . . .'

'Plus he seems to have Shylocked the money for a couple of people-smuggling runs,' Oscar said. 'At least, I believe that's what I have here.'

'I'll look at that next.' Lois got up and moved her chair beside Oscar's. Sarah thought, Oh, I just bet you will, Lois.

'I don't usually get to follow anybody quite so resourceful and versatile,' Lois said. 'The way he combines the funnel accounts with old-fashioned TBML.'

'Now wait,' Jason said. 'What's TBML?'

'Trade-based money laundering.'

Jason laid his face down sideways on the cool table surface and muttered, 'Had to ask.'

After several more lessons in criminal pursuits, they broke for lunch. Sarah, trying to be hospitable, asked Lois to join them and began naming off the varieties of Mexican cuisine available nearby.

Lois gave her a restraining wave and said, 'I'm on the road fifty weeks a year. I always stay in a hotel that furnishes me with continental breakfast and will make me a brown-bag lunch. That way I control the calories, the time and the money.'

She pulled a paperback whodunit out of the same

bag that held her lunch and retreated behind it, indicating she knew how to fend off random chats, too. Oscar offered to make her tea but she pulled a thermos out of the same handy satchel.

Good, we won't worry about Lois, then. Sarah went out with the rest of the crew. Feeling gleefully hedonistic away from that relentless nasal narrative, she broke training entirely, went to a Greek restaurant and ate a gyro with plenty of sour cream and a fluffy heap of herbed rice.

When they got back they found Lois already back in her chair at the table, speed-dialing her smart phone, issuing rapid-fire orders to the underlings who seemed to wait somewhere, tablets poised to receive her orders. When she finished the call she was on she clicked off without saying goodbye and resumed the morning's conversation with Delaney's crew before they realized she was talking to them.

'This strategy your victim had,' Lois said, 'of somehow doing his jobs with lo-tech and antiquated equipment – have you any idea why he was doing that? Any notes anywhere on how it fits with the rest of the operation?'

'Haven't found any,' Sarah said.

'My guess is,' Leo said, 'he's been doing this for a long time and he got himself grandfathered in to do it his way.'

Lois looked at Sarah. 'Did you tell me that – that he'd been doing this for a long time?'

'I said living in the house a long time,' Sarah said. 'We don't know yet when he got into cross-border crime.'

'Well, it's one of the things we'll find out

when we find the rest of the bank records. This must be just the tip of the iceberg you've got here.'

'You keep saying that like you know something we don't. Why are you so sure?'

'Because this operation isn't moving enough money. A few million a year . . . big-time crime syndicates deal in billions – they've got a lot of thugs and ammo to pay for. We have to find a bigger honey pot.'

'Where do you think we ought to be looking?'

Lois tipped her head on one side and screwed her mouth into an ironic smirk. 'Maybe in another bank? Under the mattress doesn't seem to work anymore.'

'OK. We can go back and crawl through the house again, when we have time. Right now we're concentrating on the homicide and there's a lot to do.'

'I agree. I've got all your paper records now anyway; my people will be working on it. I'll let you know what I've found when I get back.'

'Back from where?' Delaney said. 'I thought we were going to wind this up today.'

'Can't. I've got to be in Boca Raton tonight and Chicago by lunchtime tomorrow. Then back to DC for a couple of days, and I have to stop in Dallas on the way back here. Look for me on Friday. I'll let you know what time.'

Sarah opened her mouth to say that her section of homicide worked four tens, Monday through Thursday, and would not be in the building on Friday. But she met Delaney's eyes, saw his quick little headshake and realized that rather than tell a 24/7 powerhouse like Lois Johnson that they did not work Fridays he would personally see to it that some of them were in this office whenever she chose to return.

'We swabbed the truck and the bike last week,' Gloria said on the phone. 'And got the latents at the same time. Jody and Sandy went up together to that hellhole of an impound lot. When are we gonna get one that doesn't have dog shit and spiders all over it?'

'Don't know,' Sarah said. 'What I called to ask . . . Are you all done with those items, then? You don't put it up on a hoist and sample the truck from underneath, do you?'

'What? No. We're not a bunch of damn auto mechanics, Sarah. You can't lift latents off the underside of an old pickup, for God's sake. What are you looking for?'

'I just wanted to make sure you were done with the bike and car, that's all. So if we go up and take another look at them we won't be messing up your work.'

'Well, that's very nice and polite and one of these days I'll certainly try to return the favor,' Gloria said, 'but right now I'm too busy to talk. Goodbye.'

'It's too bad she doesn't have one of those old phones you slam into a cradle,' Sarah said as she hit OFF. 'Then she could break my eardrum while she's at it.'

'Oh dear, Sarah's talking to herself again,' Leo said from her doorway. 'Come on, didn't you hear Delaney say to meet in his office?'

'No. I was on the phone taking abuse from another source.'

'Poor, poor Sarah. You never got the memo warning that a detective's life is not an easy one?'

'Sure. But I thought they were talking about simple stuff like knife fights and gunfire.'

'Ah. So you were unprepared for something really terrifying like bullying by phone. Who's on your case?'

'Gloria Jackson.'

'Oh, that. Be patient with Gloria; she's fighting with her boyfriend.'

'Is that what it is? Leo, you mustn't retire. You're the only one who knows the really useful stuff.'

They all crammed into Delaney's office, dragging chairs.

'OK, the Fed lady's not very impressed by our boxes. It doesn't sound like she's going to be much help. So what's next?'

'I think somebody in a car with tinted windows has searched Calvin Springer's house at least once since we put the crime-scene lock on it,' Sarah said.

'What? Why do you say that?'

'I suspected it the day Ollie and I went back and found the records. A couple of drawers were out of the dresser that I was pretty sure we put back the day of the murder. So I asked Martina if anybody else had been at the house since we were there. She said she saw a "car with blackened windows." She took it for granted it was one of ours because the driver had a key.'

'Shit.' Delaney brooded a minute. 'But you and Ollie found all the good stuff, right?'

'We hope we got it all. Who can say?'

'Yeah. Damn. It kind of stands to reason they might be afraid he left some evidence around, though, doesn't it?'

'Yes. And I suppose they're still looking for more money. I think we should wait a while to turn that house over to the cleaners.'

'Agreed. Anybody else got any thoughts?'

'We haven't talked to anybody in the new part of Menlo Park,' Ollie said. 'The parade formed up in the parking lot in front of the El Rio health center, across the street from the Mercado and all that posh housing in the part they call the Convento district. Somebody in that section must have seen the clown, maybe with his mask off.'

'OK, canvass the new housing under Signal Mountain. Good idea.'

'That little credit union branch where the funnel account is,' Leo said. 'We haven't dug all the way to the bottom of that yet, have we?'

'No, and it's certainly time we did.' Delaney was making a list with handwritten bullet points.

'Lois kept saying this is just the tip of the iceberg – there has to be more,' Sarah said. 'But we haven't found any more, and I've been thinking . . . Wouldn't the underside of a Ford pickup be a good place to hide something secret that you wanted to keep handy?'

'Like a key or a number or . . . yeah.' Delaney was writing fast.

'And don't we have a homicide detective sitting right here who can find something hidden in a six-year-old Ford chassis about as fast as anybody in Tucson?' Sarah said and watched the light come up in Oscar Cifuentes' eyes.

'They don't have a hoist in that impound yard,' Jason said. His eyes were shining too. 'Remember, buddy? You'll need the creeper.'

Jason and Oscar were not normally buddies but he had helped Oscar dismantle a vintage Jaguar in that yard a couple of years ago and had entertained his buds for weeks with the pictures they took as the auto was reduced to heaps of parts. He did not intend to let anybody else get to be the designated helper on this job.

'Yes,' Oscar said. 'And I'll need my coveralls and my good wrench set and the best flashlight we own, with plenty of batteries. Will you ask the proprietor to have the vehicle moved out onto the cement slab by tomorrow morning, please, boss?'

'Well now, wait a minute,' Delaney said. 'Let's use our brains here a minute and save some brawn. If Springer kept a hidden key it would be to something he'd want to be able to access quickly, right? So he'd keep it where he could get at it easy.'

'I guess,' Oscar said. He had been looking forward to reducing a Ford pickup to its constituent parts and the dream died hard. But he had begun to enjoy some signs of favorable regard from Delaney and he would not risk that. 'You're right, come to think of it,' he said. 'He's not going to dismantle his Ford whenever he wants his stash, is he?'

'No. So just get under that pickup with a good

125

light and bring back whatever you can find in a reasonable search. If that's nothing, it's nothing.'

They split into teams, Jason with Oscar to search the Ford and Ray and Ollie on the canvass in the Rio Nuevo-developed section of Menlo Park. Delaney called the president of the First Southwest Credit Union and made sure Sarah and Leo were cleared to talk to everybody who'd ever handled the Springer account.

They drove together to the credit union Tuesday morning at nine. The staff were pleasant and wanted to be helpful. But they were so shocked by the news of Springer's murder that they found it hard to move on from their indignation. The women, particularly, complained bitterly and repeatedly, as if they thought they might get Springer's death canceled if they lodged a loud enough protest.

'One of my favorite customers,' Mattie Entwhistle said. 'A nice, polite man, never a bit of trouble, always asked about my grandchildren. I feel so *outraged*.'

Maria Lopez was actually crying. 'He sent Christmas cards to all the tellers,' she said, 'every year, with a nice little bonus check. What kind of beast would kill such a man?'

Frank Entwhistle, Mattie's husband, was the vice president who had handled most of Calvin's wire transfers. He was less emotional and a lot more defensive, determined to head off any notions the detectives might be getting about causing trouble for the bank.

'You seem to think we should have been asking more questions,' he said, 'but hell, doing business

126

this close to the border, we handle a lot of money transfers, all across Mexico, all the time.'

'We're not here looking to hang anything on First Southwest, Mr Entwhistle,' Sarah said. 'But we've got a homicide to figure out so we have to ask questions of everyone who knew him. That's our *job,* you see?'

'Of course I see that – I'm not stupid,' he said. 'I just want to be sure *you* see what *I'm* pointing out: whatever else Calvin Springer was doing he wasn't doing anything illegal in this credit union. The politicians these days all want to make Mexico into the boogie man but the growth of cross-border traffic in goods and services is rapidly becoming the lifeblood of this area, as anybody in business can tell you. We were very glad to have his account, and pleased about how it was growing.'

They took a deposition from Lyle White, the bank president, a much cheerier fellow. He got his secretary to run off a history of the account since its beginnings twelve years earlier. Lyle was proud of how smoothly the account had been managed. 'We were all a little nervous about it at first. Seemed pretty complicated, all those deposits coming from different places, but once we got the hang of it, it was never any trouble.'

Leo interviewed Archie Simplot, another vice president who had helped Calvin get the exchange rate figured out for the China orders. 'Kind of a learning experience,' Archie said. 'But the information's all there if you dig for it. I don't know how he found the manufacturers he was working with but that was Calvin for you – a quiet older guy, didn't look like anybody much but very enterprising. Always looking for new ways to make a buck.'

They spent two days listening to stories like that.

'Once again,' Sarah said as they headed back under the highway on Wednesday afternoon, 'we come back with Big Nada. Calvin Springer was just a prince of a guy who somehow got himself killed by some ruffian – probably all a mistake.'

'Maybe our comrades did better,' Leo said. Every day now brought him closer to his last day at work, so he was mellow and easy to please.

But Ray and Ollie, after two days of talking to the well-off tenants of the new homes around the Mercado, declared they had never found a less observant group.

'Going around with their heads up their ass, jeez,' Ollie said. 'All they care about is their foot-thick walls and their stupid balconies with the pots of trailing ivy – who lives in a dream world like that?'

'Attorneys and insurance brokers. Affluent realtors with no small children,' Sarah said. 'So you didn't get anything either?'

'One: parades are a noisy nuisance. Two: why don't we put the money into something useful like another golf course?' Ray ticked off responses on his fingers. 'Three: I try not to waste my time on anything worth less than a million dollars. Four: was there a parade? I was at an Open House in Oro Valley.'

Ollie said, 'Well, come on, guys, who's got the

next bright idea we can fling at Delaney in the morning?'

'Not me,' Sarah said. 'I'm tapped out.'

Their mood was not improved when Oscar and Jason stepped out of the elevator covered in greasy dust, showing evidence of spider bites and, on Jason's left arm, a long, painful welt from a wire gate that swung shut on him.

When he saw he had everybody's attention, Oscar took his hands out of the pockets of his coveralls and held them up, empty.

He said, 'Tell me again. Why are we so sure there's another stash?'

'Lois says there has to be,' Sarah said. 'Lois works for ICE and she knows things like that.'

'Well then,' Oscar said, 'looks like Lois will have to find it. Because there is nothing in the Ford pickup except the standard equipment.'

'I was half right,' Lois said. Constant travel seemed to agree with her; she looked energetic and focused in a fresh blouse and skirt, taupe over charcoal, with a single string of silver beads. Delaney had offered her coffee and water but she waved it all away; she had, as usual, a plane to catch. 'There *is* more to the Calvin Springer iceberg but it turned out to be less than I expected.'

'You've found more bank records?' Sarah said. They were meeting, as Lois had predicted, on Friday morning. Delaney was still concerned about the budget, though, so it was just the three of them in his office.

'Yes. The slips from your coffee cans were all for First Southwest Credit Union. That's the funnel account; it gets deposits from a dozen branches more or less in a row across New Mexico and Texas. Looks like the yield from one mid-size distributor, making deliveries on a regular schedule. His dealers are moving the product and making the deposits. It appears to have been a stable little organization for some time – years, in fact. They sent the money to Calvin and he got it back to Mexico in all the ways you described to me, based on what you saw in those boxes.

'We've requisitioned a history on all these accounts, of course, and my people tell me the traffic has followed the classic money trails. There's less gambling involved now than formerly because they have more manufacturers in China to order from and more assembly plants in Mexico where merchandise can be sent. The house-flipping fad went the same way for drug dealers that it did for everybody else – very popular in the early part of the century and a market bust starting in early two thousand and eight.

'Here's one thing you ought to know: Calvin Springer's social is bogus. Lifted off a grocer in Douglas who died in nineteen fifty-three. Did you find any Medicare records for him?'

'No. We really dug through his house, because at his age—'

'I know. But we can't find any either. Whatever he did to stay so healthy he must have done it on his own dime. He's a slippery one – we haven't been able to establish a bio for him before he appeared in Tucson eighteen years ago. He bought the house you found him in, paid cash for it and established a checking account at the credit union which he still had at his death. He evidently conducted his money laundering in cash and postal money orders for the first few years he lived here. Twelve years ago he set up the funnel account called Argos Inc. that was still going strong when he was killed. He must have had help with that – it doesn't fit with the plain and old-fashioned way he did everything else – but whoever it was stayed out of sight. Calvin fronted the operation from first to last.'

Sarah said, 'We haven't been able to match his prints on any crime database and I couldn't find any service records. Have you looked for him in Canada?'

'Not yet. I'll let you know when we find him. All the other depositors, in New Mexico and Texas, check out. All American citizens with social security numbers and driver's licenses. We're moving to establish the sources of the money they've deposited. We've not established any indictable offenses as yet, and we probably won't now, since all traffic has ceased and the accounts are closed. We've tried to interview some of these people and we will in the end, but so far they all seem to be out of town and a couple have already closed out and moved away.'

'Is it always this difficult?'

'Yes. These people have years of experience and good lawyers. But there's one thing that happened to the account in Benson that's unique, and maybe since you're here you can follow up on this. The name of the original depositor was Clifford Mays. He kept the account going for

131

eight years before he died. We found funeral and burial records, and an obit praising him as a vet and local merchant and so on – nothing fishy about his death.'

'Or about his life? I mean, if he was laundering drug money, isn't it likely he was into other kinds of corruption?'

'Not necessarily. This part of the industry is often performed by small merchants, bar owners and dry cleaners and so on, people who deal in a lot of cash and can easily hide some more from the IRS. They get paid a percentage and can usually skim a little more without getting caught by the cartel, so they cheat a little all around and they see it as a convenient boost that helps out in the hard years. Small-town merchants see all years as hard years.'

'Maybe because they are,' Delaney said. His father had managed the feed store and grain elevator in a small town in Kansas. Delaney still sometimes heard the rant about taxes and regulations in his dreams.

'Maybe so. Anyway, Clifford Mays was replaced on this account by a man named William F. McGinty. And what we noticed is that while almost all the other deposits to this funnel account grew quite substantially in the next couple of years, McGinty's stayed just about steady.'

'So you think McGinty was skimming a little extra?'

'Looks that way. There's something else interesting about him. He's kind of like the flip side of Calvin Springer.'

'You mean he also appears somewhat fictional?'

132

'No, he's real enough – or at least he used to be.'

'What?'

'William F. McGinty is the name of a real person who lived in LA and then Phoenix until eighteen years ago. That William McGinty had the same date of birth as this one. Sold real estate, had a couple of fender benders and a DUI, had an address, driver's license – and the same social security number this one uses. He surfaces briefly as the buyer of a forty-two foot catamaran in San Diego harbor shortly after he sold his house in Phoenix, jointly with his wife, Pauline. After that he disappears from the records nationwide. Doesn't have an obit or a burial record, didn't go to prison. Didn't buy a house or a car. But now he, or somebody using his stats, is making deposits to this account in Benson.'

'So he went to some other country to live and now he's back,' Delaney said. 'Why is that so mysterious?'

'Because he's not back all the way. I've had my people looking for what else William F. McGinty does in Benson and so far they can't find a thing.'

Sarah said, 'No address? Phone? TV service?' Lois kept shaking her head. 'How does he live?'

'Probably the same as all the rest of us but he does it someplace else.' She watched them both for a few seconds. 'You haven't run across this name before?'

'No,' Sarah said, and looked at Delaney, who shook his head.

'Well, we're still looking. To me it seems

133

reasonable to suppose that he's a member of the cartel, probably a watchdog planted by them. If that's the case he probably lives across the border and he may be the one who fingered Calvin and got him killed.'

'But wait a minute, what about the funnel account? If he's a member of the cartel he wouldn't be skimming it, would he?'

'Sure, they all steal from each other all the time. So here's what I want you to know: this account had not been closed by McGinty and in the end we decided not to close it either. William F. McGinty is a little past due on his next deposit, but just in case, if he comes back, the bank will call the police at once and then call you, Captain Delaney. If he's been out of the country he might not have heard the news, and then you'll get him there.'

'Wouldn't that be sweet?' Delaney said.

Sarah said, 'Can we back up a little? You're pretty sure Calvin had his fingers in the till too?'

'Yes. My team set up a spreadsheet to tally the total deposits in the funnel account against the totals getting sent to the cartel. It's never going to come out exactly right since it passes through all this buying and selling, but over a year or so it should be close.

'And Calvin's deposits were pretty close, for years after he got set up here. I did tell you, didn't I, that in the early days he actually sent postal money orders? And about once a year cartons of guns from Brazil and Colombia.'

'You told me about the money orders. Not about cartons of guns.'

'OK, forgive my rambling . . . it just sticks in my mind, how recently things were a lot simpler – grab and go, shoot and run. Now they've got all this incredibly sophisticated . . . Ah, well. It is what it is. Since they set up the funnel account and the deals got bigger and more complicated, Calvin stuck with mostly shipments of merchandise and wire transfers through the bank. And my team showed plainly that, in the course of a year, if you added up the money and the merchandise he was coming up short – anywhere from fifty to a hundred thousand dollars a year.

'That's not a big percentage if you think about a total of four to five million a year he was sending to the cartel. But for cautious old Cal it was beginning to amount to quite a tidy nest egg. What we don't know is where he was keeping it.'

'You don't think he had an account in the Caymans, something like that?'

'Can't find one. Probably would have been too complicated for him. Calvin's probably got a stash pretty close by. When you crawl that house again, look for secret numbers. Could be written on the bottom of a drawer or inside a lampshade . . . anywhere.'

'We've already done all that a couple of times but we'll look again. How much longer are you going to need to keep our records?'

'It's all being scanned into our system now and the originals will be boxed and on their way back to you via UPS in a week or two.'

'You mean you're not going to pursue—'

'Oh, we're not giving up. We'll be following

the money trail and we'll let you know what we find. We're convinced your victim was working with the Sinaloa operation but frankly this is too small a part of that system to be very relevant. Four or five million a year – I'm surprised they let him continue as long as they did. But I suppose . . . he was established and reliable and he wasn't causing any trouble. Till now.'

'You're quite convinced his own organization killed him?'

'Oh, yes, I assume so. But it's not exactly on my job sheet to prove it; we've got plenty on this cartel if we can ever seize some of the top people. That'll probably be a cold day in hell, though. In the meantime, the homicide investigation is back in your hands. We expect to be informed of anything you find, of course.'

'And you'll file a report on what you've found so far?'

'Yes, of course. Including the money we've agreed to split, which is in the joint account Don and you agreed on, Captain Delaney. And I'll notify the home office of all the ways we're continuing to cooperate. If you want more help at any point you can contact Don.' She looked at Delaney. 'Anything else?'

'Don knows all about this? He's satisfied with this arrangement?'

'Of course.' She smiled. 'He's a very busy man but I'm sure he'll be in touch. Meantime, he asked me to convey his congratulations on the way this joint effort has worked out.'

She leaned toward them then, looking anxious to make a point. 'TBML crime isn't just for the drug lords any more, you know. It's an ocean of unrecorded currency circulating in an increasingly globalized black market. Unregulated and untaxed – governments hate that. We're getting into bitcoins now. Your worst nightmare – no records on those at all. Upsetting legitimate markets, funding God knows how many escalating wars and revolutions – Isis is learning to play this game. And there's this nasty sideline, smuggling people – the clergy of all denominations are pushing their legislators to fund an all-out *war* against what it's doing to women and children. What you've stumbled into here looks small by itself—'

'It doesn't look small to us,' Delaney said.

'Maybe not but believe me, it's just a few drops on the edge of a vast Sargasso Sea of undercover money that's becoming the enemy of well-ordered societies everywhere. Make what you can of Calvin's quaint maneuvers with adding machine tapes. I'd love it if you'd nail a bad guy or two.'

Sarah said, 'But something tells me you don't think that's going to make much difference.'

'Listen, they put El Chapo in jail every time they grab him but you notice the flow of drugs goes on without a hitch. There'll always be three or four candidates standing in line to take the place of every one you finally put behind bars. Most of the ones we really want will never see a courtroom.'

Delaney said, 'Our job is still to find out who killed Calvin Springer.'

'Oh, that.' Lois shrugged. 'You may have quite a bit of trouble nailing that down. Cartels use

137

teams, usually, and the men on the teams often have several identities.'

'Some things about the crime scene suggest one man and a lot of rage.'

'Oh? Interesting.' Lois was already putting a few notes back in her briefcase. 'I suppose it's possible that Springer offended somebody in the cartel who bore a personal grudge – they're not robots, after all.' She shrugged a quick *whatever*. 'But it still looks like an organization hit to me.'

She hung her neat case over her shoulder and shook hands with them both, saying, with one of her little nods, 'My message to both of you and the rest of your crew is be careful. Watch your own backs for a while. Big-time drug dealers are very dangerous.' She walked to the elevator, looking at her watch, which Sarah felt certain would always be accurate to the last second.

'I made a fresh pot of coffee to offer her,' Delaney said when Lois was gone, 'and we never got to drink any. Let's have a cup now and decide what's next. You got time?'

'Sure,' Sarah said. On the way to the break room she decided to get one of those crullers she had seen there earlier . . . wasn't sugar a proven antidote to frustration? But the pastry was all gone by the time she got to the console so she put double cream and sugar in her coffee.

Delaney had already swallowed several swigs of hot black brew, she saw when she got back to his desk, and was looking even pinker and itchier than he usually did in hot weather.

'Well, she's a little hard to take,' he said, putting

138

his cup down carefully, 'but she did leave us with something, didn't she?'

'Did she? What Lois always leaves me with is the feeling that in her eyes I'm kind of a small-time dweeb.'

He made the amusement noise she didn't get to hear very often, something between a snort and a chuckle. 'I think Lois read that book about how to win friends and – what was it?'

'Influence people.'

'Yeah, that. And she decided it would be more interesting to try some other way.'

Sarah drank some of the incredibly delicious rich coffee, enjoying the mellow side of Delaney that Lois Johnson's hard edge had uncovered. 'So what do you think she left us?'

'That name we've never heard before, William F. McGinty. I feel like I've been buried up to my eyeballs in information ever since we found Calvin Springer, don't you? So much evidence but it doesn't seem to fit together very well. In fact, I only believe about half of it. I mean, a clown suit in the trash container – what the hell? I don't feel right even talking about it.'

'But if that's what we've got—'

'I know. But now I'm thinking about a simple story, something people can understand, that we can release to the media along with this new name. Person of interest, we'll call him. Say we want to question him in connection with the death of blah blah blah. You know the drill.'

'OK. Let's see, it's early yet, I can get that onto the six o'clock news. That'll repeat at ten and then there's that Friday night *Week in Review.*'

'Fine. That might get it mentioned by some of the weekend talk shows and maybe by Monday, who knows? Somebody will come up with . . . something.'

'Worth a shot,' Sarah said and went to work on it. She privately thought it was about the lamest move she'd made all week but it pleased her boss and wiped out the sour feeling she'd had when Lois Johnson zipped up her soft leather briefcase and strode out the door to her next, much more important meeting.

'Tucson homicide detectives are anxious to question this man in connection with the violent death of Calvin Springer in the Menlo Park neighborhood on the Fourth of July.' Sarah finished the story, hit the print key and called the information officer.

Driving home, she thought some more about Calvin's stash. If he was skimming as much as Lois says he was, and he kept it in cash, there has to be quite a pile. He sure didn't spend it on anything in that house and yard.

He liked to keep things simple.

And she's probably right – a hidden account in the Caymans would seem too risky to him. So what then?

A suitcase in a storage unit near his house. Maybe more than one suitcase.

Storage units all have locks. Padlocks or those combination things with dials.

He hated complexity. I'm betting on a key.

Damn, do we have to go back to his yard and turn over all those river stones?

Eight

At ten o'clock on Monday morning, a woman on the phone, not young by the sound of her voice, said, 'My name is Mabel Conway.'

'How can I help you, Mabel?'

'Are you a detective?'

'Yes, ma'am.'

'I believe I have something to tell you.'

'All right.' Sarah put all the helpful vibes she had into her voice. Her caller had already talked to the switchboard and the information officer before being forwarded to Ollie who, forewarned at the morning briefing, had passed her on to Sarah. By now she was probably beginning to be sorry she'd called. 'I'm listening, Mabel.'

'Something to tell and then something to ask, I guess.'

'Fine. Let's start with what you have to tell me.'

'That name I read about in the paper . . . and then I heard it on TV. William F. McGinty?'

'Yes. You know him?'

'The one I knew was called Bill, but I suppose it could be the same person.'

'Well, sure. Most Williams *are* called Bill, I guess.'

There was a short silence filled with breathing. Mabel was a little anxious. 'Why do you need to find him? You think he's done something?'

141

'He's a person of interest,' Sarah said. 'That just means we want to talk to him. It doesn't necessarily mean he's in any trouble. Tell him he shouldn't be afraid to come in.'

'Oh, well, I don't know where he *is*. I mean, the last time I saw Bill McGinty was, my gosh, it must be almost twenty years ago. And that was in Mexico.'

'I see,' Sarah said. *Mexico.* This might actually be something. 'Do you remember where in Mexico you saw him last?'

'Sure. La Paz, on the Baja peninsula, when I was down there sailing with my late husband, Fred, who sadly departed this earth just over six months ago. We had – I still have – a long-time friend here in Marana who was down there with us. He keeps saying it can't be the same person but it just seems so odd . . . that familiar name coming up in the Tucson paper, in connection with somebody who died.'

Sarah said, 'Why is that so odd?'

'Well, I mean, after all these years? Jack said forget about it, it's got nothing to do with us, but I couldn't get it out of my mind so I finally said well, heck, I'm just going to call and find out what's going on.'

'Good for you! What's going on is a homicide investigation, Mrs Conway. What's your address in Marana – can I get that first?'

'Wait a minute, I don't want to get involved or anything. I was just asking—'

'You're not involved – I'm just making sure I know who I'm talking to. Would you rather give me your email address – do you prefer to be

142

contacted that way?' She was Googling Mabel Conway, getting nothing so far, and making signs to Ollie. He came over and looked at her search, made a circle 'OK' sign and went back to his desk. But Mabel was getting ready to bolt.

'I mean, I don't really know anything at all,' she said. 'And I've got all I can handle right here at home. Fred's only been gone six months and, believe me, after forty-three years of marriage it isn't easy. I just called to get one simple piece of information—'

'Which was what?' Sarah waited through the short, crackly silence that followed her question and finally said, 'Mabel? What is it you want to know?'

'Well . . . if you find this William McGinty . . . you want to talk to him about a dead person, is that it? The man who got killed there in Tucson on the Fourth?'

'That's right.'

'It just seems so darn *spooky*,' she said in a wondering voice.

'Mr Springer's death seems spooky? In what way?'

'The fact that you want to find Bill McGinty to talk about it.'

'Why is that spooky?'

'Because all those years ago in Mexico, that's the last thing we said about him: "We've got to find Bill McGinty and talk about this." But we never did. The police came and took Poppy's body away, and after that they didn't want to talk to us anymore. And Bill never came back and it was Mexico, you know? Everybody had been so

143

friendly and kind to us but all of a sudden they were suspicious and hostile. They didn't appreciate our questions one bit.'

'Was Poppy a friend of yours?'

'Well, yes, she was Bill's wife.'

'Oh. And you never found out where McGinty went?'

'No. And we finally realized if they didn't want to talk to us there was nothing we could do about it. Fred said, what are you going to do, start a revolt in a harbor in Mexico? Three Anglo sailors . . . They see a hundred new ones every day, why should they care what we want?' The quiet woman had conquered her initial shyness and was letting it all spill out.

When she paused for breath, Sarah said, 'That does sound like a tough situation.'

'Tough is right. We certainly didn't want to stick around La Paz and *play* anymore. So we got our boats ready and went home. Twelve days up the Baja in the teeth of a filthy wind, every other wave slapping us in the face – I've never been so cold. I wore foul-weather gear over my oldest clothes, the same set for eight days; I never changed anything. I couldn't stand to smell myself. But you have to get undressed to change clothes so I didn't even consider it till we got to Turtle Bay.'

'You're not making me envy your trip.'

'Well, there were things to love about that adventure but not the trip home. Besides that, I felt so *guilty* the whole time, sneaking off to the north that way, even though I had nothing to do with Poppy's death. I kept thinking no, no, we've got to go back and straighten this out. But we hadn't been able to straighten anything out while we were right there in front of a dozen policemen, so what was the use?'

'Sounds pretty discouraging, all right.'

'For sure. I felt bad every time I thought about it, all these years. And then last week I read in the paper about this other murder and the next thing the story says is that the Tucson Police want to find William McGinty and talk about it.' She breathed into the phone a few times and added, just above a whisper, 'Spoo-*key*.'

'Yes,' Sarah said, 'I agree, Mrs Conway, that seems like a very strange coincidence. So unusual that I think we ought to get together and talk about it, don't you? You live in Marana, right? What's your street address?'

'Jack is going to be so disgusted with me,' Mabel said. 'I promised him I'd leave it alone.'

'Mrs Conway, you're not in any trouble. I just need to talk to you. Shall I come and see you or send a police car to bring you in here?'

A silence followed, filled with little mouth sounds, a gasp and a swallow, maybe. Sarah said, 'Mabel?'

'Oh, well, just let me think a minute,' she said miserably. At that moment Ollie thrust his notebook in front of Sarah's face with Mabel Conway's name and address displayed. Sarah read it off aloud and said, 'Is that your correct address, Mabel?'

'Yes.' Once it was out and she couldn't call it back she grew calmer, even sounded a little relieved. She gave good directions to her house in a subdivision.

145

'Fine. We'll be there in about twenty minutes. Nothing to worry about, Mabel, we just want to talk!' She hung up the phone and said, 'Ollie, you got time to go with me to talk to Mabel?'

'Absolutely, I wouldn't miss it. How'd this happen?' he said as they started toward the elevator. 'This woman just read the paper and remembered something?'

'Yeah, but we chummed her – just a minute.' Passing Delaney's office, she saw him on the phone and made an urgent time-out sign. He said something to the phone and punched his HOLD button. 'What?'

'The news release worked. Woman in Marana wants to talk about William McGinty. Ollie's free to go so we're heading out now.'

Delaney beamed, put two thumbs up and said, 'Stay in touch.'

In the elevator, Sarah asked Ollie, 'Will you drive so I can look some stuff up?'

'Sure. My car's over there in the shade.' As he pulled onto South Stone, he said, 'Chummed how?' The morning brief had included a report on the Friday meeting with Lois, so Ollie knew most of the McGinty story they'd received from Lois Johnson.

Sarah told him about Delaney's inspiration to get the name out to the media. 'I thought it was a waste of effort but I did it to please him and here we are, first thing Monday morning, getting a response. Shows you what I know. You need I-10, we're going to Marana.'

Remembering what Mabel had said about being a new widow, she tried Googling Fred Conway

146

and hit the mother lode. As they rolled westward she developed a profile on him, reading it off to Ollie as she found it: Marana resident since the late nineties, prominent in trail building and hiking activities, Vets' Club, golf tournaments. 'But Fred succumbed to Alzheimer's six months ago.' Now finally some facts about the widow: newest member of the Marana Technology Club, volunteer with a literacy program. 'Mabel doesn't have a lightweight's bio. She sounded a little scattered on the phone at first but that must have been because of her uncertainty about telling me her story. She seems to have a friend who thinks she has enough on her mind right now and she shouldn't get involved in anything new.'

'Probably true. But you don't think we're heading for a total Nimrod?'

'Her bio says not. But Bill McGinty's name seems to trigger some unpleasant memories. And she's just lost her husband so . . . we better take it slow so she doesn't start crying before we find out why the memories make her jumpy.'

'OK. You seem to have a feel for her so you ask the questions. I'll stand around looking brave and strong the way I do and keep an eye peeled for concealed weapons.'

'I really don't expect any sneak attacks. But she is on edge about something. However, this woman went to Mexico with Fred on a sailboat and stayed there for a couple of years, so we're not looking for any weenie.'

'I'm looking forward to meeting Mabel. You're sold on her except when you're not.'

'Which just means I don't have a read on her

yet. But we baited a hook with Bill McGinty and Mabel nibbled, so—'

'Now – is this the Bill McGinty the ICE lady told you about?'

'That's what we want to know. Lois's McGinty has a strange bio and possibly works for the Sinaloa drug cartel. But Mabel says she knew her McGinty in Mexico years ago when they were down there on a boat. So at this moment she's a *major* person of interest.'

'Good, this is interesting, huh? And look, what a beautiful day we have for going to Marana. Aren't the Tortolitas pretty from here? This beats pulling coffee cans out of vent pipes by a mile.'

'Can't say we don't get variety in our work, can we? This is it, I think – she said she's the one with the red bougainvillea by the door.' Sarah checked the number. 'Yup, this is it.'

'Wow, it wouldn't do to come home drunk around here, would it?' Ollie said. 'All these cul-de-sacs look the same.'

They were in one of the clusters of cookie-cutter houses by which Marana was growing, in lurches of development that burgeoned and paused in response to the state of the economy. This neighborhood had beige stucco walls, red tile roofs and two-car garages, all with terracotta or dark green trim. They walked up to Mabel's door and rang the bell.

The woman who let them in wore no makeup but appeared younger than Sarah had expected from the voice on the phone. Solid and fit, she looked as if she enjoyed three meals a day and plenty of mountain hiking. She swung the door open wide with no hesitation and said, 'Come in. You made good time.'

'Your directions were excellent. This is Detective Oliver Greenaway.' They shook hands.

She had a fresh pot of wonderful-smelling coffee. Ollie helped her carry the mugs in from the kitchen. Mabel brought along a plate of cookies, home-made, smelling like dates and nuts.

'It's a little too hot to sit outside,' she said and offered paper napkins from a box on the dining-room table.

All her surroundings were like her: worn, solid, serviceable. Many family photos, no art. A few books on a shelf and a quilting frame holding a work in progress.

Sipping the fragrant coffee in the comfortable room, Sarah began to see Mabel Conway as a reasonable person who knew how to manage a good life. Definitely not a dingbat. If William McGinty gave her the jitters, he must be an odd one.

'How long ago was it,' she asked Mabel, 'this trip to Mexico?'

'Been trying to think,' Mabel said. 'I believe it must have been eighteen years ago. We met Jack and Molly just as we moved in here and that was twenty-two years ago in October. We were from Minnesota, they were from Wisconsin and we hit it off right from the start. But we'd only been settled a couple of years when Molly – oh, it was terrible, she got that fast-growing cancer and was gone in just a few months.

'Jack kept her at home, nursed her like a mother, never gave up hope. Kept talking about the

149

wonderful trips they would take when she was better. But it was obvious before long that she was terminal. When she died he was just beside himself. His grief was terrible to see. Fred and I tried to help him but there isn't much you can do for a man in despair. We got through that dismal winter with him and in the spring Jack said he felt like he needed to get out of here for a while. He told Fred he knew of a marina in San Diego where he could rent a sailboat, a thing called a bareboat charter where they furnish everything but the crew, and he talked us into going sailing with him. "It's just wonderful out on the water," he said. "You and Mabel will have fun and maybe I can start to heal up."

'We didn't really want to go – we were still getting settled in the neighborhood and there was plenty to do here. Fred said, "Jack, I'm not much of a sailor." But Jack said he had plenty of experience and he'd help us with everything. And after all, the farm was sold and the kids were running the hardware store. We were free of responsibility after years of hard work. We looked at each other and said, "Well, we said we were out for adventure." So we went.

'The three of us rented one sailboat together. A sloop, not that I knew what that was. The guys did all the sailing, mostly day trips out of San Diego harbor, and I had to learn how to keep house for all of us in small spaces. Actually that was kind of fun, almost like playing house. We were always in a harbor at night, so if I was too tired to cook we went to a restaurant.

'About the most exciting thing that happened

was that Fred fell overboard on the way to Catalina, which in a way was kind of lucky.'

'Falling overboard was lucky?' Ollie had obviously liked Mabel all along and now she'd really pleased him.

'Yes, because he'd been getting feistier all the time; going to sea made him feel like a kid again. Jack was a very careful sailor and he kept warning us both to keep our life jackets on and to hook onto the lifeline whenever we were out of the harbor. But Fred hated the jacket and just despised being tied down to the boat, so he began taking the gear off whenever Jack wasn't watching him.

'The day we sailed to Catalina was very fair, smooth sailing, and when our course was set Jack went down for a nap while Fred stood watch. I stayed up on deck with him, enjoying the sights. Fred saw a line flapping loose up forward and just hopped up on deck in his shirtsleeves to tie it down.

'Just then a much bigger boat passed us, going fast. It created a big bow wave that almost capsized us. Fred wasn't holding onto anything and when we heeled over he flew off into the water like a flipped pebble, just a little splash and there he was, out in that big ocean.

'I had no idea what to do. I just stuck my head down below and screamed for Jack. He flew up the ladder and got the sail down, started the motor and turned the boat around. Oh, and he threw the wand thing over, the one with the light that they'd practiced with in the harbor. Fred was a strong swimmer so he was able to reach it, and luckily the wind was calm so we were not making much speed when he fell off. He looked a long way away, though, by the time I spotted him, hanging onto that marker and yelling his head off.

'It was the one time I ever saw Jack get mad at him. He rarely gets annoyed at anybody, actually, he's a quiet, patient man. But that day – it was very scary. I hope I never get that anxious again.

'We got Fred back on the boat, eventually. It took both of us heaving with all our might because Fred was getting too cold to help much. We piled blankets on him and I fed him broth by the spoonful – I was a long time warming him up. Jack had the sail furled by then and was running on the motor, back toward San Diego.

'When Fred felt better Jack told him we were all done sailing. Said he would not stay on a boat with a man who was too stubborn to listen and insisted on taking stupid chances. "You didn't just put yourself at risk," Jack said. "Mabel and I could have been hurt or killed trying to save your stupid neck."

'Fred had to just beg him not to cancel the lease on the boat. My husband wasn't usually much given to admitting mistakes but he loved being on the water, so he humbled himself. And from then on he was the most careful sailor you could ever hope to see. Anytime he wasn't on the lifeline it was one hand for the task, one hand for the boat.'

'That's a terrific story, Mabel,' Sarah said. 'But now, about Bill McGinty? When did you meet him?'

'Oh, well, yes, I guess you'd like me to get to

the point. We went home a couple of months later but Fred and Jack just couldn't settle for card games and hiking any more. They spent that whole summer planning the next boat trip. They went back to California twice to shop for the boats they wanted. I wasn't as crazy about the idea as they were but I went along because Jack was recovering from his terrible grief and Fred was just over the moon with joy. Every last turnbuckle and cleat, he loved it all. He told me once, "It feels like the reward I worked for all my life."

'Long story short, we went back to San Diego in October. That time we moved right onto the boats and began getting them ready – there's a lot to do to prepare for live-aboard sailing. We named our boat *Agnes Anne* after our two daughters and finally left San Diego in late February.

'That time, we went right down along the coast to Cabo San Lucas. Went south with the grey whales – they migrate down from the Bering Straits to Magdalena Bay every spring, mate and give birth there. Oh, it was exciting to see their spouts rising from the water all around.

'We stopped for one night in Mag Bay. I was sitting on deck after supper when a grey whale rose right alongside the boat, a couple of feet under my hand. She had her baby kind of tucked alongside and was covered all over with barnacles and seaweed. She was as big as the boat. I held my breath but she didn't seem to mind us at all. Fred brought a blanket and wrapped us in it and we sat on deck till dark, watching mamas and babies out for their evening exercise.'

'Wow, Mabel,' Ollie said, 'I'd love to see that.'

153

She gave him a happy little nod and said, 'Well, you can. And it's worth all the effort it takes. I've never felt the same about the world I live in since that night. I know how lucky I am to have my tiny slot in the animal kingdom.'

She glanced at Sarah, who was beginning to twitch. 'Hang on, Detective, I'm getting to the main event. We anchored in the big bay at Cabo San Lucas and began to learn the ropes. It was a much simpler place then. I've seen pictures taken lately and it seems to be all built up with resorts. When we got there it still had vestiges of the fishing village it had been, though it was getting very touristy. We did the things you do, took clothes to the laundromat and swapped books with other boats. Went to town for what we called a "celebration dinner" and got roaring drunk.

'That's when we met the McGintys. Bill and his wife Poppy. They had a forty-two-foot catamaran named *Pretty Baby*, named after Poppy, Bill said. People had already pointed it out to us as the party boat in the harbor. The owners were at a long, noisy table with a dozen other people, drinking, eating dinner and telling hilarious stories about mistakes on boats. Bill was loud and funny, Poppy was pretty and sexy. She seemed to be close friends with everybody there. There was lots of hugging.

'Jack kept looking over at the table and I could see that he wanted to join it. He saw a couple of boaters he'd met in San Diego while we were outfitting and pretty soon he went over to talk to them. Then he was back at our table, saying, "Come over and join up, these folks are fun."

'We told each other we'd go over for one drink and leave, but of course we didn't. Tell you the truth, I don't remember how we got back to the boat that night. By the grace of God is probably the right way to say it.

'Fred and I were basically Minnesota farmers, definitely not swingers. Cabo has a lot of experience with drunken sailors and I guess they took care of us. We did more partying in the next couple of years than ever before in our lives, but we took care, after that first night, not to get carried away. Jack just went for it, all the way. He was coming out of that terrible depression he went into after Molly died – laughs felt very good to him and he wanted all he could get.

'I knew, of course, that most of the party people were enjoying weed along with their drinks, and maybe some stronger stuff. But in that setting it didn't seem like a very big deal. Or it wasn't as long as we stayed in Cabo – six months, more or less. Then the McGintys said they were moving around into the sea of Cortez and going to hang out in La Paz for a while. Little by little most of the sailors who made up their merry band began to drift around the corner to join them and before long the three of us followed. La Paz is a very old city on a big sheltering bay. It's been catering to adventurers of every description for eons.

'Dozens of boats were anchored there ahead of us. We had to be careful about picking our spot because there's a lot of swing every time the tide changes. Besides the anchorage there were boats in a couple of marinas and up in dry dock in a repair yard. Busy place. Even so, *Pretty Baby*

155

was easy to find, especially in late afternoon when they turned up the music. Then the sailboards and dinghies began to raft up around it and the party animals climbed aboard clutching their jugs of margarita mix.

'I didn't go to the parties much in La Paz but I loved the place for other reasons. I learned to ride a sailboard there and took Spanish lessons. Made a couple of friends I've kept ever since. Fred changed too; he got serious about sailboat maintenance, bought many books and *crates* of tools. We spent so much time in the air freight office we made a friend there, took him to dinner in Pichilingue – that's a whole other story. Fred was always Mr Fixit on our farm and at the store – he just reverted to type. The longer we lived on that boat the more he seemed to love tinkering with it as much as riding around in it.

'By the second summer we began to notice Bill left his boat for days at a time and was very tired when he got back. Poppy used to say he was off playing macho games with a bunch of Mexicans and that he thought it was so cool to go native.'

She carried on bravely with the parties – of course by then she had a host of friends who were glad to help. But gradually it became taken for granted that her most reliable helper on party nights was Jack Ames. In fact, more and more, party nights got to be mostly on the nights when Bill wasn't there. When he came back from one of his trips it would take him a couple of days to get his game face on. And even then he wasn't the anything-for-fun guy he had been when we first knew him. Poppy never talked about where he was going or what he was doing. She didn't seem to want to and we didn't really want to know.

'Jack was always on *Pretty Baby* on party nights, and then I began to see Poppy on Jack's boat on quiet afternoons. I told Fred I was afraid Jack was getting pretty cozy with Poppy. Fred just snickered and said, "Yeah, I think he's recovered from the blues, don't you?"

'I said, "I just hope he doesn't end up in a big fight with Bill – that Poppy's kind of a wild one."

'Fred was down in the sole, bent over some coupling – I was having this conversation with his bare back, as usual those days. He stood up so his head came out of the hole in the deck and said, "He's a grown-up, Mabel. Keep out of it." He wiped sweat off his face with an oily rag and spread brown stains down his cheeks. That made me laugh and we dropped the subject.

'But the subject didn't go away, of course. The more Bill McGinty stayed away from his boat, the more time Jack Ames spent there. I forgot about all three of them for a while though because Fred and I got snorkeling gear, learned how to use it and left La Paz to run up further into the sea. We hooked up with a group exploring bays and islands, snorkeling every day and learning the names of fish and birds. Then a hurricane came into the bay and we ran further north to get out of the way. We went as far as Loreto and a little beyond, found a quiet bay where several big spotted rays were living and floated around watching them for a few days – it was kind of an enchanted time for us.

'Jack spotted the *Agnes Anne* as we came back into La Paz harbor, and as soon as we got the anchor down he pulled alongside in his dinghy. He came aboard for lunch and we had a big happy reunion and told him about our adventures. Before he left, he told us where to go on the beach that night for a picnic.

'"Couple of guys are going to roast a goat – bring whatever you want to eat and drink with that," he said. We were happy to see him again, all smiley and tanned. And late that afternoon we followed the noise to the picnic. The usual rowdy crowd around a big fire with a goat roasting on a spit and everything you could imagine to eat and drink on a long table nearby. Bill and Poppy were there, cool and jolly at first, Poppy looking adorable in a coral outfit that showed off her wonderful body. There was lots of laughing and story-telling, but after the drinks had been flowing a while Bill and Poppy began sniping at each other. Gradually it turned into a serious argument that none of us wanted to hear. But they wouldn't stop; I think Poppy had been waiting to have this fight when there were plenty of her friends around to referee. Bill said they were leaving day after tomorrow, period – nothing to make waves about.

'"Headed back to San Diego," he said. "I got things to do, people to see." Poppy said he always thought he should decide everything and it wasn't fair. He just shrugged and said, "It's too bad, baby, but business is business and I gotta go."

'Poppy said she wasn't ready to go so he should just go do his business and come back for her. The goat was dripping grease into the fire by then, flames shooting up; we all wanted to carve it up and eat. But there they were by the fire, yelling at each other, waving their arms, and then Poppy threw her drink in Bill's face. The guys running the goat roast got seriously annoyed at that point and told them to take their fight someplace else.

'Bill was always kind of a mouth, even sober. That night he tossed off some insults about goat herders that don't know their place. One of the roasters picked up a rock and threatened to bash his head in with it, and then you know how these things go – Poppy flew to Bill's defense.'

'That happens to cops a lot,' Ollie said.

'I bet. Jack was standing nearby in great distress, wanting to help Poppy but not seeing a way to do it without making things worse. Fred put his arm around Jack's shoulders and said, "Steady, Sport, you don't want to get in the middle of this."

'He handed three plates to me with some pieces of goat on each. I piled about nine kinds of beans and potato salad alongside and found us a nice quiet rock to sit on. Jack was somber but he ate. Bill and Poppy had disappeared somewhere and the rest of the party went on, a little fragmented now.

'When we finished we paid our share to the goat roasters and went back to our boats. The next morning we were quietly nursing our hangovers when some Mexican harbor patrolmen knocked on the side of the boat. They were looking for anybody who might be able to identify the body they'd found on the beach. We didn't want to go with them but Jack was in their boat; they'd come to him first. We didn't want him going alone with the *policia* so we got in their launch.

'It was Poppy's body on the beach. She had bruises all over her body, the pretty coral outfit was ripped and stained and her face was all bloody but she wasn't bleeding any more – anyone could see she was dead. The police were looking for Bill. He wasn't on their boat or at any of the usual hangouts. Most of the party people were staying out of sight, trying not to get involved. The harbor patrol opened up *Pretty Baby*'s big storage compartments and found almost a ton of pot, a couple of tight-wrapped bundles of cocaine powder and a suitcase of money. That gave them carte blanche to seize the boat and you could tell by their attitudes that they didn't care if they never found Bill McGinty.

'We kept saying, in our crippled Spanish, "You have to find him. His wife is dead." They nodded wisely and said, "We're looking for him. We have made enquiries." As we grew more insistent they got less polite. Jack was determined that they must perform an autopsy on Poppy.

'"She had blood running down her cheek," he said. "You should find out where that came from and determine what happened to her."

'"We have no authorization for that," they said. One of Poppy's party friends, a woman she's been particularly close to, looked around and found Poppy's address book, then remembered she had a sister in a suburb of Minneapolis – Edina, actually. The Harbor Patrol called her. She sent money for an immediate cremation and the shipment of the cremains to her. The authorities found an undertaker to comply with her wishes and away went what was left of Poppy to her childhood home.

'Even before Poppy was gone, the *Pretty Baby* had been impounded and towed out of there. Bill never showed up. By the following week there was nobody left around who would even talk to us about the case. It was kind of like, what case? So, it felt as wrong as anything I ever did in my life, but I helped Fred get the boat ready to sail. Jack's boat seemed to be always ready – he was a neat sailor. Our two boats pulled out of Cabo San Lucas harbor together on a warm, clear morning, turned the headland into the teeth of a stiff breeze and started to fight our way up that long peninsula, tacking into prevailing winds. Oh, well, I told you before about that trip. Twelve days later we pulled into San Diego Harbor – very salty indeed. I wanted to yell where are the water cannons, where's the marching band? Don't you people know how to greet heroes? I mean, for the first time in my life I felt like a bona-fide sailor. Adventurer, even. But instead of a cordial greeting all we got was, "Pull around the corner there; two more boats are coming in behind you."

'We were home, though. I don't think I knew till that morning how American I was. We got a room and took, God, showers with streams of hot water. I went to the grocery store and Fred found me there a few minutes later with tears in my eyes. He said, "What's wrong?"

'"Oh, God, Fred," I said. "Look at the lettuce."

Ten different varieties, surrounded by more fruit and vegetables than I could name. I understand the Baja's all built up now – they probably have stores filled with Brie and arugula and better champagne than we have here. But that day, after that journey up that dead brown coast and one wormy head of cabbage for sale in the store in Turtle Bay, I stood in the supermarket and cried with joy. I know prosperity isn't everything. But combine it with a good distribution system and a government that isn't overtly hostile and it bends toward happiness, doesn't it? We're very lucky to live in this safe, comfortable country – I never forget that now. We should quit bitching about taxes and try to make it work a little better for everybody.

'There, now, I've spoken my Shameless Liberal spiel. Call the thought police and turn me in.'

'Mabel,' Sarah said, 'did you keep any pictures from those times? You think you might have one of Bill McGinty?'

'You know, I brought home boxes of slides from that trip. I'm sure Bill was in some of them. But when the technology changed Fred got rid of the projector and I threw all the slides away. Since digital cameras and Facebook nobody wants to take the time to set up a screen just to look at your old slides. Now,' Mabel Conway said, 'are you going to tell me what it is you want to ask Bill McGinty about?'

'Oh . . . yes, since you've been so forthcoming with us, I guess you feel we owe you that, don't you?' Sarah sorted through her thoughts for a few seconds and said, 'Your friend Jack Ames is

162

right – it's really got nothing to do with you. We're investigating the death of a person named Calvin Springer, just as the paper said. Did the McGintys ever mention him?'

Mabel shook her head. 'I don't believe so.'

'Have you ever heard that name elsewhere?'

'Not till now, that I remember.'

'McGinty's name is on one of the bank accounts with which Calvin Springer was, we believe, transmitting drug money from the US to a cartel in Mexico. In view of what you've told us about those last days in La Paz, that doesn't sound too far-fetched, does it?'

'No. I don't know anything about it but I wouldn't doubt it. Fred and I just happened to be on the fringes of a crowd of Americans cutting loose in Mexican ports. Nothing new at the time and it's still going on today. There were always rumors – this one or that one was doing drugs or dealing drugs. It wasn't what I wanted to do; I didn't really want to hear about it so I didn't pay much attention. I haven't thought about those days for a long time. When I do, I remember the natural beauty of the place, the thrill of the life we found under the water. I kind of rubbed out the sybaritic stuff but it was there all right. Do you know for sure this William McGinty is the same one we knew?'

'No. We want to find our William McGinty and I'll let you know if we do. Now, we've taken up a lot of your time and I appreciate your patience. If you can give me a phone number for Jack Ames we'll get out of your hair.'

'Oh dear, he's going to be cross with me about

163

this. He keeps saying this can't be the Bill McGinty we knew. He says the reckless way that Bill was living he's surely been dead for years. But you can call him and ask what he remembers. I told him: talking never killed anybody. Why can't I ever find a pen when I need one?' She rummaged in a drawer, ignoring the two pens Sarah and Ollie held out to her. 'I owe Jack more than I can ever repay – he spent countless hours here while Fred was . . . You know my husband died of Alzheimer's?'

'Did he?' Sarah said. She didn't want to talk about the bio she'd dredged up on the way out here. 'How very hard for you.'

'Hardest thing I've ever had to do in my life, seeing him through to the end of it. You lose the husband you had but you're left with this . . . body to take care of. Hospice is wonderful but I don't know how I'd have managed that last year if Jack hadn't stood by us. As long as Fred was able to walk, Jack took him for a walk every day. But it was after Fred couldn't walk any more that Jack was a real hero – he read to him and played some stupid child's card game by the hour.'

Ollie said, 'Sounds like Jack Ames is a very kind man.'

'Yes, he is. He has this . . . quiet way of knowing what you need and being there with it. Dogs and children trust him right away. Fred needed constant monitoring the last couple of years – he couldn't be trusted out of sight. He'd just . . . wander off. Most people would soon tire of taking care of a patient so untrustworthy but Jack had infinite patience with it. It kind of suited

164

him to be in charge of somebody whose judgment had gone – Jack's always liked being in charge. Fred did too when he was his old self – they were both used to being the boss at work. That's why they clashed sometimes, like over the life-lines. But usually they just saw eye to eye about everything. Jack seemed to actually enjoy caring for Fred after he had to be watched every minute, like a child. Or so he made it seem, maybe so I wouldn't feel too indebted. Anyway, he kept up his good deeds right to the end, gave me free hours, stayed with Fred while I went for groceries or had a coffee with friends.

'I think Fred's death was just as hard for Jack as it was for me. You know, final caretakers . . . for months you don't have a minute to yourself and then boom, they're gone and for a while it feels like there's more free time than you're ever going to fill up. Here it is!' She stood up in triumph, waving a pen and a pad of paper.

'Here's Jack's number. And his address; it's only two blocks from here. He's in and out of here most days but he's gone off with his fishing buddies down to Arivaca Lake today. Fred used to be part of that group – he loved it. Jack has this disgraceful-looking fishing car he somehow keeps running. He's got a perfectly good Toyota but he and his buds are happiest rattling around in that old wreck of a Dodge with the mismatched doors. What is it with men and old cars?'

'I have one,' Ollie said. 'They're fun because they're so worthless you don't have to worry about what happens to them.'

'I guess. And the ugly old hats are part of the

fun. They call themselves the Marana Hunt Club, which is really a joke. Mostly what they do is fish. Between you and me they're not even very good at that – they don't come home with much. Once in a while they take out some old rifles they've had forever, go out in the desert and plink at tin cans and bottles.'

Sarah said, 'You're still close, then?'

'We're like brother and sister. No less and never any more. We need to ease away from being so close now because it's not going anywhere. We each need to find other people and the next big thing to do.'

'I see you've started a quilt,' Ollie said.

'Just last week and I already know the next big thing isn't going to be quilting. Call me if you have any more questions.'

'Well, once again we come back with something very close to zero,' Sarah said as they rolled past the gravel pit and headed back to their desks. 'What time is it? God, the whole morning's gone.'

'Hey, ease up. Did you expect to solve this whole crazy puzzle by yourself in one morning? Why are you so wound up?'

'Well, I thought, a fresh lead, and she mentioned Mexico – maybe we're finally getting somewhere. But as usual we just opened up more questions.'

'Did we? Like what?'

'Like we'll probably never know if the Bill McGinty Mabel knew in Mexico killed his wife on the beach or just left her there drunk for somebody else to kill. And so far we're not even sure if we're talking about the same William McGinty.'

'Well, we can't be sure until we get some concrete evidence about the one who's been making the deposits.'

'Which we already knew we wanted to do before we came over here.'

'But we can get that evidence fast enough, can't we? Surely the bank in Benson will have his picture?'

'Yes. I called them to make sure. We have to take along a subpoena but then we can get a nice clear picture, they said. They're proud of their camera equipment.'

'Come to think of it, though,' Ollie stretched like a cat in the sunshine, 'why do we even care if it's the same Bill McGinty she knew? If that ICE lady is right and he's a plant from the cartel, he's probably the murderer, isn't he?'

'Or he knows who did it. He's almost certainly back in Mexico by now. And if he works for the cartel we won't be able to get our hands on him. You see what I mean?' Sarah twitched restlessly. 'This case is like smoke – every time I get close it drifts away.'

'Look at it another way, though. We got out of that dungeon we work in for a whole bright morning and we met a terrific woman. That's never a waste of time.'

'I could see you were favorably impressed. I liked her too. What was it for you?'

'She's so enterprising. She went to Mexico on a sailboat to accommodate the two men in her life but then she found ways to get a memorable experience out of it for herself.'

'Yeah, she did, didn't she? And now she's being refreshingly unsentimental about her need to move on from her husband's death. I never got the feeling she was lying or holding anything back, did you?'

'No, it all came rolling out like she was just unspooling the tape. She's a great storyteller, isn't she?'

'She is. We should all be more like Mabel, who by the way also makes a great cup of coffee.'

'And the best date-nut cookies I ever tasted, and— Oh my God, look at that baby coyote, he must be lost.'

They watched in breathless silence while a small russet creature darted through roaring Interstate traffic, looking desperately right and left. He escaped death by a couple of inches and disappeared into a culvert in a terrified streak.

Exhaling, Ollie said, 'I love these parts of the desert where it's still a little wild, don't you? Mabel's right, we're lucky to live here.'

'Yes. I'm not quite ready to stop bitching about taxes but I agree, this is a great place to live.'

Nine

'Ease up, I never expected her to have all the answers to everything,' Delaney said after Sarah had shared her frustration with him. 'But think about it, Sarah, it's not just nothing. They did know a man named Bill McGinty and he sounds like a possible match for the one we're trying to find.'

'And the way to find out,' Sarah said, 'is to get over there to that bank in Benson with a subpoena. They can print out a history of the Argos account. That'll give us the date and time of his last deposit and we can run that segment of the tape. They say they don't discard or print over them – they've got miles of film stored.'

'Good. I'll put in a request for a subpoena right away. And in case the pictures aren't perfectly clear I'm going to send a tech team along with the detectives. We might be able to lift some prints or DNA off anything McGinty handled there. Another thing: maybe if you talked to this Jack Ames just right – without accusing him of anything, just asking. Sounds like he got pretty close to that swinging wife. Maybe he hung onto a keepsake or two from her boat. If he did he might not tell Mabel about it.'

'You're probably right about that.'

'And anything the wife had the husband might have handled. It's a long shot but these days they only need fragments of DNA. You need to talk to him anyway, don't you?'

'Yes. OK, I'll call Jack Ames tomorrow. And in the meantime I've been thinking some more about Calvin's skimming.'

'Oh? What about it?'

'I mean, I've been thinking about what Lois said about it. She claims her team proved he was definitely skimming. And we've examined his house enough to know he didn't spend much of it on anything we can see there. So there must be a pile of money somewhere and we know he liked to keep his business simple.'

'For sure. So?'

'So aren't the chances pretty good that it's in cash and that he kept it close by?'

'Yes. But none of those boxes held an extra key, did they?'

'No. Nor a slip of paper with numbers for a combination lock. I've checked with four local storage businesses and they all said their customers furnish their own locks, either a padlock or a combination lock. But we haven't cleaned up the crime scene yet, have we?'

'No. I've been thinking we should give it to the cleanup crew pretty soon. It's part of the forfeit we've agreed to share with ICE.'

'So let's all go over there today and crawl around that house and yard one more time.'

'In the afternoon? It's predicted to get to a hundred and five.'

'Oh, well . . . all right, how about tomorrow morning?'

Delaney stared at her for a few seconds, put his pen down with a click and said, 'Oh, what the hell, it'll be hot in the morning too. Who's around? Could we get a team on the road without debating for an hour?'

Leo Tobin was back in cold cases and in the interest of his blood pressure they left him there. Ray Menendez was across town interviewing a witness on another case that Delaney felt might be going to court soon. All the other detectives were at their desks. They took a crime-scene van and all rode under the highway together. Delaney stayed behind to do a couple of chores. He said he needed his own car anyway in case he got called to some new calamity, so he'd catch up in a bit. His detectives left him behind with his phone at his ear.

The house smelled worse than ever when they first opened it. Even the seasoned noses of Tucson's experienced crime crew quivered with distaste. But nobody said anything – they just slogged on through the usual moves: open all the doors, turn the fans on, resist – just in case – the urge to wipe up. They got ready to take notes as soon as the A/C started putting out because Delaney was already parking behind the van, looking pumped. Delaney had found no new calamities and was suddenly overtaken by a feeling, like a break was close by waiting for him to catch it.

He began firing orders as soon as his foot hit the threshold: Ollie must go to work on the vent spaces inside and out since he knew them so well. Jason should survey the backyard and Oscar the front, looking for fragments of evidence out there, paper, footprints, wheel marks – anything they might have missed in the storm.

'Even under the rocks?' Jason asked him, cocking an ironic eyebrow.

'Especially under the rocks,' Delaney said and turned away from Jason's startled expression.

Sarah was to look again at the rest of the interior – windows, doors, furniture, shelves. 'Every last freaking inch,' Delaney said.

He was going to be watching the whole operation, thinking about corners they might have missed, and of course talking on the phone.

They went to work. As the A/C groaned on, Sarah and Delaney grew more comfortable and thoughtful. Ollie alternated inside and out, working his way around the overhang again and coming in panting from time to time to rip up the vent pipes some more. The two men scanning gravel in the yard drank water constantly and gradually reduced their clothing to sweaty rags but made no comment. They were Tucson police detectives, it was July; what else was new?

By four o'clock Ollie had ripped out the bathroom vent all the way into the crawl space. After he muttered briefly about meeting himself coming around the other way, he retreated to the kitchen and went to work on the larger vent pipe there.

Sarah had finished a second look at the bottoms of all the furniture and begun opening and closing the old-fashioned wooden windows, shining a flashlight along all the sills and the grouted tunnels that carried the sash supports. Closing the last one in the back wall, she paused for a moment, watching Jason pick up river stones out of the ditch. He turned each one over in his hands, stuck a green marking circle on the bottom and set it aside. A row of green-dotted stones stretched behind him to the fence that bordered the alley. A longer row of unmarked stones lay ahead, stretching toward Oscar, who was working in from the street, turning over stones along the same ditch, marking his with blue dots. Sarah shook her head, thinking, *In case there's an argument later about who looked at which stone?*

She noticed that Jason's last bottle of water lay empty nearby him on the gravel and thought that in a minute she'd take out a fresh bottle and remind him to keep drinking.

A movement caught her eye – a spotted cactus wren, hopping from post to bush to power line, flicking his tail. She thought idly, how do they always seem to know which lines are safe to sit on? The line ran down from the big pole in the alley to the post at the back corner of the yard that held the power feed for this house. The wren hopped off the line on to a smaller green post, deeply buried in the weeds, that she would never have noticed if he hadn't sat on it. It must be the metal cover that kept rainwater out of a junction box – probably the TV feed, since Calvin had no computer.

Sarah stepped away from the window and out the back door. As she walked past Jason's bent back, she said, 'Did you look at that junction box in the alley?'

Jason stood up with sweat dripping off his face and said, 'What?'

'You look a little dizzy,' she said. 'You'd better go inside for a while and get some more water.' But she kept on walking, to the little metal gate that led into the alley, through it and around, kicking her way through tall weeds. She had to search again to find the green metal tower, barely as tall as the weeds. When she bent over it and lifted, the cover came off easily – it wasn't bolted on.

And when she turned it over and looked inside, she saw a clear plastic baggie, small, snack-sized, duct-taped to the side, high up near the top.

Heat radiated against her back suddenly as if a fire had sprung up. She turned quickly and saw Jason standing behind her left shoulder, looking at what she'd found. She thought again he should get inside, at the same time reaching for the baggie. But the long tube tilted away.

'Hold this, will you?' She handed the closed end of the cover to Jason and he held it, shaking a little. *He really needs to get inside.* The duct tape peeled off neatly, bringing the baggie along. She pulled the baggie off the tape, unzipped the plastic track and turned it over.

The key that fell into her hand was three inches long and heavy for its size, a chunky brass key with the tumbler pattern serrated along one side. Oscar was with them now, radiating heat along her other side. All three of them said at once, 'Padlock key.'

Then Jason exploded. 'Oh, for shit's sake!' he yelled and threw the green cover across the yard. 'I'm out here all these hours turning over these fucking rocks' – he turned and began kicking the rocks he'd piled so neatly along his section of ditch – 'and she walks out the door and finds that key without even breaking a sweat? What kind of fucking justice is that?' He kicked his rock pile again, as hard as he could. The rocks barely moved but on his second kick he hurt his foot. He yelled even louder then, hopping around holding his toe.

Ollie came around the corner of the house round-eyed and stood watching. A couple of neighbors came out of their houses and gaped, and then Delaney, hearing the noise, came out of the house frowning, saying, 'Jason, for God's sake, what—?'

But Oscar had been through the torment of the rocks too. He saw what was happening to Jason and he'd been a street cop long enough to know the beginning of hysteria when he saw it. In two long strides he had caught the smaller detective, had his arm around his shaking shoulders and was saying, as softly as a loving uncle, 'Jason, Jason, come on now, it's very good luck. It means we don't have to lift any more stones, don't you see? Come on, now, we need to get inside and cool off.'

As one unit, radiating heat, Oscar and Jason entered through the back door and sat down at Calvin's round, bloody table. They stayed there for some time, talking softly, gulping bottle after bottle of cold water.

In the yard, meanwhile, Delaney looked at Sarah standing awestruck in the blazing sun. 'You found something?'

She held up the baggie and the offending key. 'Where was it?'

'Inside the—' Ollie had gone across the yard after the thrown cover and was coming back with it. 'That,' she said when he reached her. 'It goes on that junction box out there in the weeds.'

'We all think it looks like a padlock key,' Ollie offered and ventured a smile.

'It does, doesn't it?' Delaney said. 'Hey, cheer

up, Sarah, I think you just earned yourself a big attagirl.'

Sarah said, 'You think he's going to be all right?'

'Who? Jason? Sure, he's just a little over-heated, isn't he? Talk to me about this key.' He turned it over in his hand, admiring it. 'It probably opens a padlock on a rented storage space, what do you bet?'

'Yes,' Sarah said. 'And there can't be more than a few thousand of those in Tucson, do you think?'

'Oh, come on,' Ollie said. 'Don't let a little yelling make you go all negative. You keep saying Calvin liked to keep things simple. I bet his stash is close by.'

'I think so too,' Delaney said. 'But let's go inside before we start making the list. This yard really is just a slice of hell, isn't it? I should have thought about it earlier. I wonder if I should send Jason to one of those urgent care places and get him rehydrated.'

Jason had recovered by Tuesday morning, but even so Delaney didn't want to send him or Oscar on any more outdoor assignments for a while. So Ray and Ollie, the two most cheerful detectives on the homicide crew, drew the tedious job of searching for the padlock that would open with the mystery key. They found an association that listed storage vendors by zip code and made a long list of phone numbers and addresses that spiraled around Calvin's house in an extended oval. Then they loaded a crime-scene van with energy bars and fruit, and a whole case of bottled water in a tub of ice. Sarah ran out at the last minute, carrying a fresh tube of sunscreen.

'Use plenty,' she said. 'I'm afraid most of these places are outside.'

'We'll call for backup if we feel ourselves growing faint,' Ollie said. He turned the A/C on high and added, 'Actually, this beats vent creeping by a mile.'

'When we find that big pile of cash,' Ray said, beaming down at her, 'we promise not to steal more than a few thousand apiece.'

Sarah went on the hunt for Jack Ames. She had his address and phone number so she took an hour to make a list of questions before she placed the call. When he didn't answer his phone she called Mabel to ask where he might be at nine-thirty on a Tuesday morning.

'Playing bridge, I expect, at the rec center,' Mabel said. 'I'll put out the word that you're looking for him. We'll round him up.'

He didn't answer his messages on Tuesday. Sarah wasn't ungrateful for the free time. By five o'clock she had a clean desk and was current on case reports.

Ray and Ollie were a little less perky when they parked the van at four o'clock. 'You were wrong,' Ollie told Sarah. 'There might be more than a few thousand of those freaking spaces and they all look a lot alike.'

They went out again the next morning without any jolly farewells.

By noon on Wednesday, when Jack Ames

hadn't answered any of the messages Sarah had scattered in his path, she told Delaney she was feeling snubbed.

He said, 'I bet I can fix that.'

He had a friend in the Marana Police Department, he said, with whom he'd shared a training course. They'd kept in touch and traded a few favors over the years. Delaney reached out to him now and his old buddy said, 'I bet I can fix that.'

When Sarah got back from lunch at one o'clock there was a message from Jack Ames waiting for her. Before she had time to place the call her phone rang and a man's voice said, 'Detective Burke? This is Jack Ames.'

'Well, hello there. For a guy who lives in such a small town you can be very hard to find, Jack Ames.'

'I sure didn't mean to be, Detective. I apologize if I've caused you any anxiety. I just happened to have a whole list of people I'd promised to do things for and I was working my way down a list. Is this an emergency? Mabel said you just wanted to chat.'

'It's a police enquiry, Mr Ames. That's a little more serious than a chat.'

'Well, please accept my apology and tell me what I can do to make amends.'

He sounded so nice she was tempted to cut him some slack but reminded herself it had been a long wait. 'You can meet me at Marana Police Station. Do you need directions to find it?'

'No.'

'Good. Can you make it by one forty-five?'

'Yes.'

'Good. See you then.' She hung up on his monosyllables, called the Marana dispatcher to reserve an interview space and walked around the corner to find Jason typing fast in his workspace.

She said, 'You got time for a trip to Marana?'

Without taking his eyes off the monitor, he said, 'To do what?'

'Interrogate an innocent man in a cool, quiet room full of clean tables and chairs.'

'You must have me confused with someone else. I'm a homicide detective, accustomed to work with hoodlums in sordid bloody spaces full of heat and bad smells.'

'But couldn't you make an exception just this once to please a colleague who admires your work?'

He took his nose out of his keyboard then and sat back laughing. 'Hell, yeah,' he said. 'I bet you admired the way I put the fear of God into that pile of rocks, didn't you?'

'Yes. So can we go right now? Because I've kind of got this guy on the defensive and I'll lose my advantage if I'm late.'

'Well, hell, we can't have Sarah losing her edge. Let's go.' He limped out of his cubicle then and she saw he was wearing an orthopedic frame instead of a shoe on his bandaged right foot.

'Oh, Jason,' she said.

'Broke the big toe. Serves me right. Now will you drive and can we please never talk about it again?'

'My fondest wish.'

'Now,' he said when they were strapped in

their seats, 'tell me more about this innocent man, will you? I don't believe I've ever met one of those.'

'Point taken – he's probably not innocent of everything. But he does sound like an exceptionally nice guy.' On the trip west she summarized some of Mabel's great sailing stories and her glowing description of how much her friend Jack Ames had helped her during the sadder times just past.

'He does sound like a wonderful friend,' Jason said. 'So why do you think you need me along?'

'I just like to have a second set of eyes on interviews,' Sarah said. 'Especially when I have to question somebody who sounds a little too good to be true. I usually pretend I'm considering buying his used car. Will you do that for me today? Ask yourself if you believe everything he's saying about the tires and transmission.'

'You're putting up a high wall for him to jump over, Sarah. I never believe what guys say about their cars.'

But when they saw him standing in the shade of a mesquite tree with a small dog sitting primly by his side, he did look very likeable – a slender, white-haired man with bright blue eyes talking softly to his well-groomed Sheltie. Mabel was right about one thing, Sarah saw at once – Jack's dog trusted him absolutely and was ready to follow him anywhere.

After they introduced themselves all round, Jack Ames said, 'I hope you don't mind waiting just a minute while I set Meggie up in her favorite waiting spot.' He walked her across the parking

180

area to a row of leafy acacias in a divider. He put down the small plastic dish he was carrying, filled it with water from a bottle, unclipped her leash and hung it from a low branch. He leaned and said something, patted her head and left her there in deep shade.

'Will she stay there?' Sarah said.

'Yes. I volunteer with Search and Rescue and we train in this area once a week. I've taught Meggie to wait in this planting strip while we practice. It's got nice shade and a little grass so she's happy here. Everybody who works up here knows her – she'll be safe.'

They checked in with the duty sergeant and were directed to a room down a short hallway. Two patrolmen greeted Jack warmly as they signed in.

'It's not locked,' the officer said. 'Go right in. There's water on the table. Anything else you need?'

'Not a thing, thanks,' Sarah said. To Jack Ames, she said, 'Looks like you're well known around here.'

'Well, I drive for Meals on Wheels too, and I groom trails with the hiking club. Just about everything we do in Marana revolves around this city center.'

'So you're doing what Mabel said, moving on after seeing Fred Conway through his final illness.'

'I was doing that before she began talking about it. Mabel was too deep in grief to notice anything else for a while. It's hard to get over losing a mate you've had for forty-some years.'

'I guess you know about that from experience, don't you?'

'Yes. Not quite thirty years, for me, when my wife died. And I have to admit, Mabel's doing better at it than I did. I was kind of a wreck for a while.'

'But Mabel said the boat trips helped you recover. Is that how you remember it?'

'Well, yes.' A little ironic chuckle. 'Either of you ever spend any time on a live-aboard sailboat?'

Sarah shook her head. Jason said, 'Always wanted to try it but never had a chance so far.'

'Well, when you do you'll find out there's not much time to think about anything but survival. It's great fun but it's also a lot of work. So yes, I'd call it a sure cure for the blues. One human brain can only hold so many thoughts at once.'

'And you met some interesting people down there?'

'We sure did. Some wonderful people and a few I hope I never see again.' The chuckle again – he seemed to enjoy his sailboat memories.

'Which was Bill McGinty?'

'Oh, Bill was a fun guy when he was more or less sober. Some of his party-hearty friends I could live without.'

'Did you take a lot of pictures? Any chance you might have a picture of McGinty?'

'No. Fred and Mabel took a lot of pictures, I remember. Did you ask her if she kept them?'

'Slides, she said, that they threw away when the technology changed.'

'That's life in our times, isn't it? I got rid of a lot of eight-track tapes back in the day.'

'But you never took any snapshots?'

'I was single-handing so . . . I suppose I must have had a camera on the boat but I don't think I ever took any pictures. I remember it all very well, though – better than some of those people who had their eyes stuck in a viewfinder all the time.'

'Could you describe him?'

'Who, McGinty? Sure. Big, handsome guy, black curly hair, solid build, very strong – he was a great swimmer and a tremendously capable sailor. Also a free-spender – loved to party.'

'And his wife? Pauline, was that her name?'

'That may have been the name on her birth certificate but I never heard her called that. Bill and all their friends called her Poppy. Or Baby, Bill called her that a lot – he had that way of talking, you know, kind of like Humphrey Bogart? Imitation gangster style.'

'Did she enjoy living on the boat?'

'Oh, yes. The free and easy life down there – that was their style.'

'So they got along well?'

'Most of the time. He loved to give her orders – fetch me another drink, Baby. Wear the blue outfit, Baby, that's the one I like. Their boat was called *Pretty Baby* and he said it was named after her. "You might have noticed," he said to me once, "my wife is quite a dish." Like she was part of the equipment.'

'Did you like her better than him?'

'Yes. Everybody did. Poppy was sweet to everybody. Bill was . . . He could be kind of crude sometimes.'

'And yet Mabel said they always had crowds of friends around.'

'Sure, because he had a big, well-appointed boat that was always loaded with good things to eat and drink. And great music playing. They had a killer sound system on board and piles of tapes.'

'You seem to be describing plenty of money.'

'Oh, yes. Their dinghy ran into shore every day and came back loaded with goodies. In between times they took deliveries from the harbor vendors. If you wanted big shrimp and lobster with your margaritas the *Pretty Baby* was the boat to be on.'

'Was Poppy working all the time, then, serving up all this hospitality?'

'Oh, no, Poppy was no galley slave. She was a real party animal – she liked to dance and have fun. When they started one of their mock arguments, Bill always said, "Come on, now, Baby, don't I take good care of you?" And in his way he did. They never carried a crew along but every port they went into Bill recruited some locals to do the cooking and cleanup.'

'But Mabel said he was gone a lot.'

'Yes. After they moved around to LaPaz.' Jack Ames sat silently tapping his fingertips on the table for a couple of beats while his expression changed from serious to sad. 'I guess the three of us, Fred, Mabel and I, should have seen that trouble was coming. I've always felt we should have done . . . something. Although to this day I don't know what.'

'You mean trouble between the McGintys or—'

'No. I mean I think Bill came down to the Baja

as a small-time dealer, making extra travel money selling pot to sailors off his boat, but after they'd been there a while he upgraded, if that's the right word, to the big time.'

'Cocaine, Mabel said.'

'And from the looks of some of the people who came to his boat around that time, a little of whatever else they wanted him to do.'

'Like what, for instance?'

'Some deliveries to contested territories, I think. I never knew any of the details – but I could see how bruised and sore he was some-times when he came back. I think he was making his bones, as they say, and it made him jumpy and short-tempered. He got more aggressive and he couldn't seem to sit still. But Poppy went right on behaving like she had no idea what could be troubling him.'

'You think she knew more than she was ready to admit?'

'Or even think about.' Jack Ames did some more silent finger-tapping. 'She began saying things like, "As soon as Bill gets over this *funk* he's in . . ." trying to pretend it was just a bad mood. But we could see – Fred agreed with me – that Bill was in up to his eyeballs in some serious shit, getting scared and trying to bluff his way out and go on his carefree way. I suppose Mabel told you about the fight, didn't she? That night at the goat roast?'

'Yes. It must have been pretty embarrassing.'

'It was worse than that. It brought something to a head that they'd both been trying to avoid, I think. Poppy wasn't usually a nagging wife.

She always said she'd rather dance than fight. But that night, when she had too much to drink, she did want to fight. And she blew the lid off some things she'd been trying not to talk about.'

Sarah had often observed that talking to the police turned people into toe-tapping, ear-pulling fidgets. Especially if they were trying to put a little lipstick on the pig, they couldn't do it sitting still.

Now she sat quietly watching Jack Ames, who had begun to tap his fingers and move his feet around. 'I've been trying to think of some tactful way to ask this,' she said, 'and I can't. But I need to know – were you and Poppy lovers?'

He re-crossed his legs and raised his eyebrows. 'I'm not sure you do need to know that.' He was silent for a few beats and did some more tapping. 'But no, we weren't. I hadn't been a widower very long – I was still missing my wife. And Poppy – it was sort of legendary about her. A beautiful woman alone on her boat so much of the time, she could have had half the men in the harbor. Guys asked each other, what would it take to soften her up? Especially after Bill began to leave her alone so much and to bully her when he was aboard. But he seemed to be the only one she wanted in bed.'

'Pretty frustrating, huh?'

He pulled on his right ear. 'Well, I thought about it sometimes – I'm not made of wood. But we were such great friends and every time I was tempted to try something I thought no, why rock this wonderful boat? Pardon the pun.' The little laugh again; he was a great chuckler.

'Do you by any chance have any keepsakes

from that time? Something she might have given you as a memento of all your good times together?'

'Keepsakes? Like what, a Saint Christopher's medal or something? No, I certainly don't. What would you do with it if I had?'

'DNA. Fingerprints. Anything she had that Bill might have handled.'

'Humph.' He looked as if he found that idea disgusting. 'You're still thinking the William McGinty you're after now might be the one we knew?' He shook his head. 'I'm pretty sure you're wasting your time with that idea.'

'Mabel said you think the one you knew would be dead by now.'

'I think he was at the bottom of the Sea of Cortez before the year was out. He had made friends with some very bad guys and you could see it in his face. He knew he was just low-hanging fruit to them.'

'So you think this person making deposits is just somebody from the cartel using his credentials?'

'Sure. He was working for them; they would have kept all his cards. Nothing they like better than American ID.'

'True.' Sarah folded up her tablet and tucked it in the side pocket of her daypack. 'Mr Ames, you've been very helpful and I appreciate it.' She put out a hand and they shook.

'You're quite welcome.' Jack Ames squinted humorously at Jason Peete. 'You've been strangely quiet during this conversation. Are you just here to pass judgment on the cut of my jib?'

Jason smiled. 'That's a very astute question,'

187

he said. 'We could sure use an analyst like you down at headquarters, couldn't we, Sarah?'

'We used to say so,' Sarah said, ''till you came to work there.' They all had another warm chuckle over that witticism while Jason shook Jack Ames's hand. Then Ames went out and got the most perfectly behaved small dog Sarah had ever seen out of the shade in the parking divider. She sat down beside Jack Ames with her lovely tail furled around her feet and looked up at him as if he were God.

'Well, so, any thoughts about Jack Ames?' Sarah asked, rolling southeast on I-10 past the new Marana mall.

Jason rubbed his face, looking tired. He was not entirely recovered from yesterday's overexposure to sun. He stared along the bright ribbon of highway for a minute before he said, 'He's just the way Mabel described him, isn't he? An amazingly nice guy. Did she mention how much his dog loves him?'

'Yes. She said kids always trust him, too.'

'I can see why they would. Jack Ames reminds me of DeShawn Williams.'

'Who's he?'

'My last stepfather. I told you, didn't I, that my brothers and I all have different fathers? My mother never had any trouble attracting men but every one of them left her in the end. DeShawn was Leland's father, the last of all the boyfriends who moved in and out of our house. The best one, too, and he lasted the longest. He didn't leave till Leland was eight.'

'And you missed him when he was gone?'

'Still do, some days. He was so good to us – while DeShawn was with us we always had food on the table and decent clothes to wear to school. We knew he traveled for a living; he was usually gone during the week. But he explained he sold roofing and siding on the road so we just felt glad that he was almost always with us for weekends and holidays. He did fun stuff with us, took us camping and fishing. One year during the monsoon we played a lot of silly card games in a tent in the backyard. He made that seem like the greatest adventure, being out in that tent in the rain.

'DeShawn said he loved us and we believed him because we loved him back. To this day I believe he told the truth about the love part. But there were times he would go quiet and thoughtful, and in the fall of the year when Leland was starting third grade, we found out why.

'Turned out there were a few things DeShawn neglected to mention. The most important thing he left out was the fact that he had another family over in Willcox. I guess he'd probably forgotten to tell them about us, too – I never found out where they thought he went on weekends.

'What wrecked the arrangement was the other wife got cancer. She began raising a ruckus, I suppose, about needing more money and a full-time husband. I never knew exactly what DeShawn and Mom said to each other. The worst part for us kids was DeShawn couldn't face us to say goodbye. He just quit showing up. When we started asking, "When's DeShawn coming

189

home?" Mom had to do all the explaining. In retrospect, I think the most amazing thing she said was, "Let's try to be charitable. DeShawn was good to us while he was with us, and being angry just makes everything worse."

'She was right, of course. But I was thirteen that year, a difficult year at best. Nelson was eleven and it damn near killed him. He had a bad overbite and a stammer – DeShawn was the only man in the world he ever felt close to. His own father hadn't come around since he was a baby. Pretty soon he was in trouble in school, and—' There was silence in the car for a minute before Jason said, 'I guess I still can't talk about Nelson.' After another silence, he said, 'Funny thing was the one with the most skin in the game suffered least. Leland was the youngest so he had the fewest memories. He got over it fast and he's always been the happiest one in the family.'

Sarah drove for a couple of miles before she could ask, 'Why does Jack Ames remind you of DeShawn?'

'Well, see, what DeShawn left me with is a very keen sense of when something is being left out.'

'Ah.' She drove a while longer. 'The tapping fingers, is that his tell?'

'Yes. And the twitchy toes. Followed by a tendency to tell you a little more than necessary about some things.'

'Like the bit about how he was still grieving for his wife and Poppy was in love with her husband?'

'Exactly. He could have just said "No, we didn't have that kind of chemistry." Nobody ever questions that.'

'So you think he's troubled about something that he doesn't want to tell me.'

'Yes. And I think a detective who can look out a window and spot a small key, hidden inside a metal box that's buried out of sight in the weeds, can surely find a way to get that troubled man to tell her what's bothering him.'

Sarah drove in silence for a couple of miles before she said, 'You think I should go back to him and ask some really rude, intrusive questions about what she was doing on his boat all those afternoons if they weren't making love?'

'That might work. Ask him if they weren't getting it on, was she teaching him how to sell weed during loud parties on a boat? That's another possibility, isn't it?'

'You think nice Jack Ames might have bought into the drug biz? I suppose that's possible.'

'Sure. Put the blame on me since he already took a dislike to me. Say that your colleague doesn't think the sexy wife of Bill McGinty would have been keeping him around so close just to help carry the snack trays.'

'Uh-huh. That would be rude all right.'

By then they were close to the Miracle Mile sign. They rode the rest of the way to South Stone watching the spiky mass of the Catalinas turn lavender in the late afternoon sunlight.

Back in the station, Sarah's phone rang as she walked into her cubicle.

Delaney said, 'Lois Johnson called from

somewhere on the road. She says there appears to be a small drug war going on in Agua Prieta, just across the border from Douglas. She thinks it might be a fight over who gets to keep Calvin Springer's funnel account. A running gun battle has lasted for three days, there are two dead cartel members and one of her ICE agents is hospitalized with serious wounds. She asked me to notify you and the rest of the crew because she thought you were all taking the threat a little too lightly. She said to watch your backs, travel in pairs with backup nearby for a while and . . . Oh, well, you know, the usual. I agree; it's the sensible thing to do. I'm putting out a directive now.'

'So . . . you want us all to know that Lois thinks we're too dense to look after ourselves down here.'

'Well, I'm sorry it strikes you that way. But do it anyway. How'd it go with Jack Ames?'

'Kind of interesting.'

'How so?'

'Well, he didn't exactly contradict Mabel's story but he puts kind of a different spin on it.'

'Really? I think maybe I'll call a short meeting in the morning, get everybody on the same page about Bill McGinty.'

'That sounds good.'

She tidied her desk, getting ready to leave, when her phone rang again and Delaney said, 'Ray Menendez just called. I told him about the morning meeting and he said, "OK, then I won't take the van home." They were hatching some plan to speed up the start in the morning because they're down to the last third of that list they started out with and they figure tomorrow's going to be the day they find the stash.'

'Ray and Ollie make the perfect pair, don't they? Two days of that stupid drudgery with the key and they're still optimistic.'

'There's some logic to what they said, though. They seem to be more convinced than ever that our search area is the right one. Some of the people they've talked to say they've noticed a truck like Calvin's around the neighborhood.'

'And there can't be more than a few hundred of those in the south end of Tucson.'

'Well, now, Sarah,' Delaney said, dredging up a well-worn department mantra, 'even Tucson cops are sometimes right.'

'True. See you in the morning.' She was turning to go when the phone rang again.

It was Mabel Conway, talking fast as soon as she said hello. 'I know it's probably quitting time but I just remembered something I forgot to tell you before. And I told Jack I'm going to tell you right now before I forget again.'

Damn. I should have let this go to voicemail. 'What is it, Mabel?'

'The last time Jack and I took Fred for an outing,' Mabel said, 'we went down to Convento Street, parked in that vacant lot in front of the Mercado and went into the farmer's market. Fred couldn't talk much by then but he enjoyed the music and watching people get on and off the streetcar. It was a busy day, crowded inside. I stopped at a booth to buy some bread and, just that fast, while my back was turned, Fred

193

wandered off. When I turned and couldn't see him I called to Jack, who was watching the musicians, "Where's Fred? I can't see him."

'Jack looked over a lot of heads and said, "I think I see him. He's over there talking to a guy. Don't worry, I'll get him." He disappeared into the crowd. When he came back he was practically dragging Fred, who kept saying, "Why didn't you stay and talk to old Bill?"

'I asked Jack, "What old Bill is he talking about?" but Jack just shook his head. And when I asked him privately later, he said, "Oh, he had some stranger by the arm and was sure we were old friends. You know how he is now – sometimes he remembers dreams and thinks they were real."

'Fred said to me as we got in the car, "Would have been fun to talk to old Bill." But when we got home and I asked him if Bill remembered him too, he said, "Who?" So maybe Jack's right and it was nothing, just another hallucination. Fred slid in and out of reality a lot in the last couple of years. But sometimes he'd surprise me with something he understood very well. So when I remembered that day I thought you should know about it.'

'You're right, we should. Thanks, Mabel,' Sarah said, 'I'll keep that with the rest of your story.'

194

Ten

'Ray and I better hit the road,' Ollie said Thursday morning. 'One meeting more or less, who's ever going to remember? But I can feel in my bones – this is our day to bring home the stash.'

'Me and Oscar need to hustle the flab too,' Jason said, 'if you want us to catch that ride to Benson. Those women in the crime-scene van don't wait for *nobody*.' He wanted to go in the van, he had told Sarah, so he could get better acquainted with Jody. He thought it was interesting, that day at Calvin Springer's house, how she stayed so unflappable during the storm.

'Don't worry, it takes them forever to get all the right stuff in the van,' Delaney said. 'You can take ten minutes now so we're all on the same page about the Jack Ames interview. Go ahead, Sarah.'

Jason had asked Sarah earlier not to share his DeShawn Williams story with the team, so that morning she just said they both felt Jack Ames was less forthcoming than Mabel. 'But then Mabel is unusually open and frank.'

'But Ames isn't? You think he's hiding something?'

'Maybe. Or he just has a stronger desire for privacy. Also, he insists that this William McGinty who's making deposits can't be the one they met in Mexico all those years ago. Says it was obvious the Mexican police were in league with the cartel. They didn't care who'd killed Poppy, and when they saw how much value there was in the boat and cargo they didn't even *want* to find McGinty. He says anyone could see Bill was beginning to be afraid of his new Mexican pals.'

'So Ames thinks the cartel probably killed that Bill McGinty?'

'Yes. He figures they would have kept Bill's social and other numbers, and now one of their guys is using those records to make deposits to the funnel account.'

'We've got to prove that, one way or the other,' Delaney said. 'Oscar and Jason, do your best to get some decent pictures from that bank in Benson.'

'We'll do the best we can with what they've got,' Oscar said, 'but it's a small bank and they might not have great equipment.'

'True. The next time I talk to Lois Johnson I'll ask if she's given me copies of everything she got there. She called me again yesterday, by the way. Wanted to be sure I told you all about the killings in Agua Prieta.'

'Who'd have thought,' Jason said, 'that Lois had a muffin side?'

'Not me,' Ollie said. 'I thought she was titanium all the way through.'

'Does she really think,' Oscar asked, 'that we have worked all these years eighty miles from the border without learning how to watch our backs?'

'Well, just keep it in mind and take the safety precautions I'm asking for in the directive,'

196

Delaney said. 'There are two dead Mexicans and one badly injured American, Lois said.'

All heads went up then. Ray said, 'An American? Anybody we know?'

Delaney shook his head. 'An ICE agent named Gilmartin. If it's true it means the gloves are off. They've been pretty much leaving Americans alone lately.'

'OK, we'll be careful,' Ollie said. 'Now can we all haul ass?'

'Both teams go. Leo, back to cold cases. Sarah, sit still, I have a few more questions.'

'Good. So do I.'

When the four men were gone, Sarah said, 'Mabel called me yesterday because she remembered something.' She told him about the hurried phone call that had ended her day.

'Interesting,' Delaney said. 'Have you asked Jack Ames if he remembers that incident?'

'Not yet. I'll call him today. Now what's your question?'

'Mine also concerns Jack Ames. He called my office yesterday afternoon to lodge a protest. Got the information officer first and said he needed to talk to "whoever's in charge of detectives." So we talked and he said he wanted to file a protest. Said he felt the two detectives who'd just left him were kind of arrogant. Especially the black one, he said, who was "uppity." He didn't actually say "uppity nigger," but it was clear that's what he meant. I managed to get off the phone without calling him a bigot, but I have to ask, what went on during that interview?'

'Actually it was all very cordial till the end.'

197

Sarah told him about the final exchange, when Ames questioned what Jason was doing there. 'Jason hadn't said one word until then. When Ames questioned his reason to be there he gave – we both gave – kind of humorous answers, I guess. But I don't think we were out of line. It's not up to us to explain what we're doing to everybody we question, is it?'

'Certainly not.'

'Good. That brings me to my question.' She told him about Jason's feeling that Jack was leaving something out of his story. She left out Jason's family details but included his later suggestion. 'He thought I ought to try jerking his chain a little, see if he'd get angry enough to blurt out something more about Poppy.'

'So, now you've talked to him, what do you think? Good idea to try a little rough stuff?'

'Sure. This is a homicide case – anything's fair that works. And if he's that touchy . . . Jack Ames has never been on my suspect list for the murder of Calvin Springer, but after that conversation yesterday I'd be glad to put him there.'

She called Ames as soon as she got back to her cubicle, got no answer and left a message.

He must not have liked getting reprimanded by Delaney's friend in Marana PD. He called back in four minutes. From some noisy place, he said, 'I bet you want to talk about that phone call from Mabel yesterday, don't you? But I just realized it's so noisy in here I can't hear you. Can you hold on a second while I step outside?'

There were other voices and a door slammed.

198

'There,' he said. 'Nice and quiet out here but very hot.'

'I'll be quick. Mabel called about an incident at the farmer's market on Convento when her husband disappeared into the crowd and you found him and brought him back. You remember it?'

'Vaguely. It was just one of many times during his last two years when I rescued Fred from disaster. He went through a kind of unruly two-year-old stage where he kept wandering off.' He sighed. 'That seemed very troubling at the time, but now I remember those as the good times. Later on, he couldn't walk at all. At the end, he couldn't eat.'

'It must have been very hard.' She waited a beat before she said, 'Mabel remembers that he kept saying he'd seen "Old Bill." She seemed to think he might have seen Bill McGinty. But you were the one who found him that day and you never mentioned that.'

'No, because it never happened. It was like a hundred other times when he imagined he saw something. Or heard from somebody he used to know. Sometimes his body wandered; other times he stood still and his mind left the room. He would see a neighbor he saw every day and call him a name from childhood. Alzheimer's is a very unpredictable disease.'

'I understand that. But when you retrieved him out of the crowd that day, was he talking to a man named Bill?'

'Oh, let's see, I think by the time I got there he was talking to the wall. People around him were kind of edging away.' He sighed again.

'So you didn't see anybody that day that reminded you of the Bill McGinty you knew in Mexico?'

'No. And I didn't expect to. Mabel's prone to remembering Fred's last two years a little better than they were. It's hard for her to accept that she put all that effort into caring for a man who didn't know, by the end, who she was.'

Sarah was trying to think of a way to transition to Poppy McGinty after that but he went right on. 'By the way, did you see the stories in the paper and on TV? About those drug dealers killing each other down in Agua Prieta? Looks like they shot an American agent, too.'

'We heard about it.'

'I hope you and your crew are looking out for each other?'

'Don't worry, Mr Ames, we always do that.' Then outrage put a red halo around the desktop screen she was looking at. What hypocrisy pretending to care about their well-being after he had just done his best to get Jason in trouble. In the bright light of her anger she saw, as if she were looking down from a height, the two of them talking to each other politely without communicating at all. Maybe Jason's right, she thought. Let's try rude. 'It's really good of you, though, to be concerned about our safety.' He made a sort of purring noise. 'But listen, while I've got you on the phone, I'd like to go over your story about Poppy McGinty again.'

'Oh. What part of that—'

'The relationship part. Because frankly I find it incredible that a red-blooded sailor like you would hang around a beautiful, neglected woman for so long just for the fun of helping with the snack trays. Some of those nice long afternoons on your boat, now, come on—'

'No,' Jack Ames said. 'You are not going to talk any filthy talk like that about her, not to me, ever. In fact, we are not going to talk about the McGintys any more.' His anger grew as he spoke. 'You are a very rude woman and if you ever call me again I'm going to lodge a complaint with the Tucson Police Department. You got that? Never. Call me. Again.'

After the line went dead Sarah put her phone in the cradle and stared at it for some time, thinking, well, that went well. Didn't it? She was roused from her concentration by a commotion coming off the elevator. There was a lot of thumping and the smell of dust and engine oil, then Ollie's voice, loud and triumphant, 'Didn't we tell you this was the day?'

She poked her head out and saw him, very dusty but gloved up and grinning beside a pile of dirty hard-sided suitcases. Ray Menendez, equally grubby and gloved, had his foot in the elevator doorway, holding it open while they dragged out the suitcases and one transparent plastic box.

Ollie held up a #10 business envelope with a strip of tape along one end. 'This was taped to the bottom of the light switch,' he said. 'I think these are all the keys to these cases.'

'Excellent,' Delaney said, pulling on gloves. 'Let's get Leo out here to help. He deserves a treat.'

'Tell me quick,' Sarah said as she gloved up. 'Where was it?'

'Two blocks from where we started, goddamn it,' Ollie said. 'In a storage unit at the back of the gas station where he probably went every week. We'd passed it on the first day and speculated about it, but the doors all face the back of the lot so the address was wrong for what we took to be the entrance. We thought we were looking at a gravel yard.'

'Well, it is a gravel yard,' Ray insisted. 'They sell some gravel and some of that decorative paving stone, and some slate—'

'Yeah, yeah, yeah,' Ollie said. 'It was dumb we didn't drive in and take a closer look that first day.' He handed the keys to Delaney and said, 'We still got that long table around here somewhere?'

When it was set up they put all the cases on it. 'The keys all have tags with a number but I can't see any numbers on the cases, can you?'

They turned one case, looking and looking. Ray lost patience and began trying keys on another case until he found one that fit. When the lid came open the detectives all made the same sound, a gasp like, 'Whoa!' Ollie stopped grumbling over his case and turned to look. It was full of large bills. So much money in such a small space, it seemed to raise the temperature in the room.

They shared the task of counting that first cache. The grubby little case contained half a million dollars.

'Jesus, and there are, what, eight of them?' Leo said. 'Do you suppose they all—?'

Delaney had two lawyers and a couple of security guards in the room by then. The lawyers got pretty jazzed by the money – the tall one's childhood stammer came back and the short, stocky one sweat so much he kept fogging his glasses – but they both worked at keeping their voices matter-of-fact. The guards were a special detail out of the chief's office, doing what guards get paid to do: look brain-dead while they notice everything, especially hands.

'You just never see this, do you?' one of them said. 'It's kind of like a thousand-year storm.'

When they had all the money uncovered and were halfway through counting it, Delaney turned to Ray Menendez and said, 'Now let's see what you've got in that plastic box.'

'Just records, I guess.' Ray pulled the cover off. 'We could see it wasn't money so we just loaded it up. Shall I?' He put on gloves and got a knife out.

'Go ahead,' Delaney said.

Ray cut the tape on the box. There were two big manila envelopes inside. He opened one and dropped the contents on the table: a driver's license, SCUBA certification, social security and Medicare cards and a set of fingerprints in a glassine folder. The second contained several passport books in the name of William F. McGinty.

The oldest passport picture showed a handsome, smiling man in early middle age, with plenty of well-tended flesh on his bones and a full head of curly black hair just turning silver at the edges. In subsequent passports he looked older and more serious, and he was completely bald.

'For God's sake,' Sarah said. 'That's Calvin Springer.'

'Wait, now,' Ollie said. 'I think I'm going into brain freeze. Didn't we just decide Bill McGinty was the cartel bozo who got Calvin killed by the cartel?'

'That was a guess,' Delaney said. 'This is evidence. Shall we all sit down a minute?'

They sat around the long table, listening to each other breathe.

Delaney said, 'I have to hear you say it out loud. Why would Calvin Springer's picture be on Bill McGinty's passport?'

Sarah opened her mouth and closed it a couple of times, and finally said, 'Because he is Bill McGinty.'

'But he's been Calvin Springer ever since he lived in that house under Signal Mountain. How could such a plain, ordinary man pull off a trick like that?'

'I expect he had a lot of help from the guys who were setting him up to launder money for them. Don't you think?'

'Yes. With the part of my brain that isn't too overloaded to think, that's what I think.'

Sarah said, 'May I have that curly-haired one and one of the bald ones to show Martina?'

'Yes. And take this one to Gloria,' Delaney said, handing them over. 'Tell her to test it for prints and DNA. Oh, and here's a full set of prints she can try for a match on. Why did he have this full set of prints, by the way?'

'Because,' Ray said, reading off the termination record that was attached to the prints, 'are you ready for this? Because he was working for the First Federal Bank of LA, how's that for the fox getting into the henhouse?' He passed the record to Ollie.

'Actually,' Ollie said, waving another sheet of stationery, 'it looks to me like the bank owned this real estate office and McGinty worked for the realty. Selling houses? The drug honcho must have gone through a tame phase.'

'Oh, LA,' Ray said. 'I got a cousin who lives there. He told me by the nineties even the guys on the garbage trucks were moving cocaine on the side.'

'Tell Jody,' Delaney said, impatient as always with urban legends, 'we need a match on those prints as fast as possible.'

'I will,' Sarah said. 'Please tell me they're going to prove that Calvin Springer was really Bill McGinty.'

'If they don't, I'm going to go work someplace else.'

'Oh, please don't leave now. Whoever he was, we still have to find his killer.'

'Aw, hell,' Ollie said. 'I suppose now we're back to Lois Johnson's theory of cartel hitmen.'

'For today, anyway,' Sarah said. 'So are we still traveling in pairs? Who's available to go to Martina's house with me?'

'I am,' Leo said. 'I been inside long enough; I'm starting to grow mold.'

He stood up and began putting on his jacket, energized by the prospect of outside air. But just then Jason Peete and Oscar Cifuentes strode off the elevator, wearing expressions of extreme self-satisfaction.

'Here you are, all together,' Jason said. 'How convenient. We brought home some beautiful pictures to show you. Let's put them out here, compadre.' He was so full of himself he didn't notice that the table he was indicating with his triumphant ta-da! gesture was already littered with dirty old hard-sided suitcases and a great deal of dirty old paper.

As he turned back from Oscar, though, his eyes focused and he saw the money – piles and piles of cash money being counted by strangers in suits. He saw Ollie and Ray at full beam across the table, their faces saying plainly, *We found the stash*.

The air went out of Jason's balloon slowly as he realized his great find was being upstaged by an even greater find. His cheeks took on the iron-hard consistency Sarah remembered from the day he felt the ICE lady's condescension. Watching his anger grow, she thought, he's going to kick another rock.

'Jason,' she said, 'you can't possibly know how much we need to see those pictures right now.' She pushed a suitcase out of the way and cleared a spot on the table. 'Put them right here, Oscar.'

Oscar laid them out the way he did everything – meticulously – in a neat, perfect set of two straight rows. They were all good, clear shots of Calvin Springer depositing cash into his bank account, filling out a deposit slip made out to William F. McGinty.

'There you go, boss,' she said. 'How's that for good ID?'

'Jesus,' Leo said. 'That's some camera, isn't it? It even got the hairs in his ears.'

Sarah felt a deep need to sit with her crewmates in some clean, quiet space where they could talk all day about this day's work. She wanted to ask, over and over, 'Can you believe this?' Hear them say how unlikely it was that on the same day they would find the money stash and the Medicare records they'd been looking for from the beginning and then get clear pictures from the bank in Benson that would really pull this case together.

She wanted them to take turns telling the story over again from the beginning. When she was sure she had every detail straight in her mind she would write her part into the case file.

But the money was there, the lawyers and the guards were still there and as usual there was barely time to do the necessary. They settled for high-fives all round and got back to work.

'What do you say, gents,' Delaney said, turning back to the attorneys. 'Let's get this money counted and put away before we all yield to our natural desire to grab some of it and go to Brazil.'

Leo drove Sarah to the crime lab and said he'd wait in the car while she ran upstairs.

'Take your time,' he said, tuning the radio till he found some golden oldies. 'I'm about to retire, remember? I'm in no hurry.'

Gloria looked up from her cluttered lab table and said, 'Girl, you look like you just struck gold. Whassup?'

'Remember that crime scene we worked on the Fourth of July, down there under Signal Mountain?'

'Who could forget that one? You got something?'

'Quite a bit. Did you get any good pictures of the victim's head that day? Can you bring them up?'

'Right now? I'm in the middle of . . . Never mind. It's a big deal, your stuff, huh?' She moved to another computer and did some rapid-fire clicking. Ghastly crime-scene photos appeared. 'Here we go. Whatcha want?'

Sarah held up a bald passport photo. 'Anything close to this?'

'These are all so beat up.' She squinted. 'This one, maybe. That's not the right name, though, is it?'

'He was Calvin Springer when you photographed him that day of the storm. But we think now he was also William F. McGinty. Look, I've got a set of fingerprints we found in a box of bank records – you don't need to hear all of this right now. I'm going to give this set of prints to Jody and get her to compare them to the ones she took off Calvin Springer. If they match . . . This case keeps lurching along, getting more amazing as it grows.'

'Uh-huh. I can't stop to admire you much right this minute, though. I got a rush order for a child abuse case—'

'Hey, I'll leave you in peace now and go show this photo to another witness. First chance you get, will you crank this passport photo into your

208

NCIC file and see if it matches anything you've got?'

She ran downstairs and hopped in beside Leo, who was nodding off over highway accident reports. He shook his head and said, 'Ready to go?'

'I am. Are you? You want me to drive?'

'Nah. I'm just not firing on all my cylinders lately. That's why I wanted to get outside. I don't know if it's because I feel retirement getting closer but these days when I sit still for a while I fall asleep.'

'Well, drive me to Martina's house, will you? Here's the address.'

'This is the woman who called in the fight on the Fourth?'

'Yes. The mama with the mostest. Wait till you see this example of people making do with what they've got. It's kind of balanced on a knife-edge between inspiring and tragic.'

'Sarah, how long you been a cop? That describes half the south end of Tucson.'

They found Martina very busy, running the day-care center by herself. She had two babies drinking from propped bottles and a one-year-old holding his bottle without support and kicking his heels up happily, admiring his own toes.

'Here you are with yet another man,' Martina said. 'No wonder you like police work.'

'She was just born lucky,' Leo said and introduced himself. 'You run this whole place by yourself?'

'I usually have a helper. My daughter took her

209

baby in for a six months' check-up,' Martina said. 'What you got there, more trouble?'

'Maybe some answers for a change,' Sarah said. She held out a passport photo. 'Does this look like the man next door?'

'Yes. That's him. Better without the blood, eh? Poor man – he won't need a passport no more, will he?'

'Guess not. You ever see him when he looked like this?' She held out one of the old passport pictures of the smiling, black-haired man.

'No.' Martina shook her head, looking down. 'Hoo, he was good looking when he was young, huh? He must have always shaved his head since he lived here.' She thought for a few seconds. 'Lotta times he wore a sort of doo-rag wound around his head. Or he had a big old straw cowboy hat with a wide brim. I never saw him with any hair showing.' She added thoughtfully, 'I never saw him smile like that, either. But the passport says it's the same man, huh?'

'Years ago. Before a lot of stuff happened.'

'Ah. Life.' They turned toward her round table where Leo Tobin sat with a small child on each knee, a third between his knees talking earnestly. Martina's face softened. 'This one is good with kids, is he?'

'Seems to be,' Sarah said. 'First I knew about it.'

In the car she opened her tablet, getting ready to make some notes, and asked Leo, 'Well, what did you think of that little baby factory?'

'It's amazing how well she manages all those kids in such a small space, isn't it?' Squinting into the bright sun bouncing off car bodies, he said, 'You know, I feel a little disoriented.'

'Do your arms feel funny? You want me to stop at Urgent Care?'

'No, not that way. My health is fine now. I think it was the stress of watching Tommy worry his way through training that brought on the heart business. No, I mean . . . I thought we were chasing a badass named Bill McGinty who was skimming off Calvin Springer and probably spied on him for the cartel and maybe also killed him. But now we're saying no, Bill McGinty *was* Calvin Springer and somebody else killed both guys? Is it just because I've been stuck off there in cold cases? I feel like we're coming up one body short.'

'Wait till the rest of the evidence is in. As soon as Jody finds a match for those prints we found in McGinty's box it will start to make sense to you.'

'Well, I'm looking forward to that.' After another humming mile, he said, 'So now we're back to Lois Johnson's theory, hmm? A team hit by anonymous killers we'll probably never identify?'

'I don't like that idea much.'

'Me neither. Let's keep digging till we find one we like better.'

'Deal.' They did a fist bump to seal it.

At the station, Sarah poked her head into Delaney's office. He looked up with a phone at his ear and waved her to a seat. She waited through three minutes of quiet monosyllables till he punched OFF and said, 'Well, where are we?'

'Martina confirms the passport photo is her neighbor. I didn't bother her with the news that the passport belonged to a man named William McGinty. Gloria had work in front of ours but will try to match the photos as soon as she can. Ditto Jody with the prints. I was going to tell you Jason Peete needs a three-day weekend as much as anybody I ever saw, but he got all fired up again this morning when he heard he was going to Benson. Now he seems good to go another couple of laps. Too bad it's Thursday; I feel like everything's starting to pop.'

'Tell me about it. Those boxes of money our team found are generating a ton of paperwork. I like this schedule but almost every Thursday afternoon I wish I had my Fridays back.'

'Good luck with that. I'll let you know if Gloria left me any phone messages.'

Gloria had, and when she answered Sarah's call she was bristling with questions. 'Why the devil didn't it occur to any of us to ask where this man had been all his life? I mean, until somebody offed him, Calvin Springer didn't *have* any records.'

'Oh, we were asking. But we got led down a garden path full of funnel accounts . . . never mind. Fact is Calvin Springer invented himself eighteen years ago and he's been a model citizen ever since.'

'But a model citizen with no medical records? No Medicare card? Doesn't that ring every bell we have?'

'Sure. We were looking for the answers and we followed the money. Now we have some answers. Calvin Springer is really William F.

McGinty who ran a money-laundering operation for the Sinaloa cartel.'

'So that's who killed him?'

'Maybe. Far as I can see he's been doing the same thing for eighteen years or so, getting a little bigger and more successful every year. Why kill him now? Plenty of good questions left, Gloria. Job security for all next week, at least.'

'Oh, you're in a jolly mood, aren't you? There's a big hot rumor going around the halls here about a couple of department lawyers looking for overnight storage for a whole shitload of money. Is that the money you followed to your answers?'

'Could be. I try to keep as much space as possible between me and loose money. Have you found any prison records for Bill McGinty?'

'Haven't had time to search. You think I'll find a lot?'

'I'm betting you don't find any. Have a nice weekend.' Turning away from the phone, she remembered it was her turn to fetch Denny from swim practice. She quickly loaded her daypack, scribbled a note for Monday morning and found her keys.

She ran downstairs, jumped in her overheated car without waiting to blow any air out and drove fast to pick up Denny, who as usual after practice looked wasted. Driving home in rush-hour traffic, she felt suddenly exhausted.

She turned to ask Denny if she wanted to watch *The Price is Right* after supper and saw she had curled up in the seat with her head against the window and was nodding off.

Damn, I'm sick of this boiling hot summer and I'm starting to hate this swim team, Sarah thought. She drove a little slower, careful on the turns, feeling her muscles twitch with fatigue.

As she turned into her driveway she heard a loud *crack!* like a rifle shot. Denny sat up straight, looking out the window, and said, 'What was that?'

'Get down!' Sarah said and pushed her onto the seat. She crouched as low as she could, squinting along the hood to see her way into the carport. Once inside the shelter of the vine-covered lattice, she turned to look at her shattered back window. 'Damn, damn, damn.'

'Aunt Sarah, I saw a man—'

'I know. Look at the window. Somebody shot at us.'

Sarah took Denny, crouching, out of the car on the driver's side, away from the yard. They crept inside through the kitchen and hustled along the hall to the spare bedroom. 'Lie down on the floor. Here's a couple of pillows. Don't go near the windows,' she said, speed-dialing 911 while she pulled the drapes closed. 'I'll get us some help here and then go get Grandma.' Dispatch answered promptly. A few words were enough to get sirens screaming toward her. A few seconds later she crept out the back door with her Glock in her hand.

Aggie was in her casita out back, napping. She hadn't heard anything, she said, but, 'You've got your cop face on. Is it serious?'

'Yes,' Sarah said. 'These shoes OK?' Aggie stepped into her canvas slides and they scuttled hand in hand across the flagstone patio to the kitchen door. Officers in tactical gear were piling out of cruisers in the driveway. Sarah sent Aggie to join Denny on the floor of the guest room and ran to meet them.

The SWAT team was deployed around her house while she showed the hole in her car window to Norman Krantz, the team commander. Norman asked Sarah to stay indoors and away from windows until they cleared the area. She went back down the hall to sit on the floor between Denny and Aggie, listening as more vehicles arrived. Being inactive at a crime scene felt so wrong, her nerves began to jerk.

Her phone chirped. Will Dietz, in the field, sent her a text. 'Call when u can.'

'The cop's grapevine – works every time,' Sarah said. 'Dietz knows already.' She texted him back: 'SWAT team here. All well. 1 shot back wndo my car.'

Aggie said, 'How would it be if I called Howard and asked him to come get me and Denny? We could bunk at the ranch tonight. Two less bodies for you to think about.'

'It sounds like heaven and I'd like to go with you,' Sarah said, 'but I know what Norman would say. They can't protect you at a spread-out property like the ranch – it would take fifty men.'

'Let's not get ridiculous,' Aggie said. 'Whoever's doing that shooting is not after me.'

Sarah agreed but said they couldn't prove it to a SWAT team's satisfaction. Then she remembered that someone should tell Howard what was going on. She started to dial but decided the call

215

shouldn't come from here in case she was being monitored. She sidled to the kitchen, avoiding windows, gave the patrolman stationed at her back door her brother's number and told him what to say.

'Be sure to tell him not to call me here. That's very important. Tell him I'll be in touch as soon as I can.'

When the chief understood that one of his own detectives had been attacked in the course of an active case, he authorized as many extra hours as necessary. After that the yard filled up fast.

Banjo assembled a full night lab crew, which arrived in a van equipped to face anything from blood sacrifice to a flesh-eating plague. They stared in disappointment at her tidy yard and clean house before they set up a bank of super-bright LED lights in the carport and began doing a full work-up on her car.

The bullet had made a small, clean entry hole in her rear left-side window, with cracks radiating out. There was no exit hole in the opposite window so they played lights around till they found a jagged tear in the seat, just where it tucked into the sidewall behind the passenger seat. In a couple of minutes they dug a misshapen bullet out of the right rear corner of the backseat upholstery.

Krantz had the street blocked off in both directions and guards posted all around the yard. He told Sarah it was safe now to move freely within the house but asked her not to come outside until he authorized it.

She spent most of the next hour in the kitchen,

making one pot of coffee after another and pouring cups of it for members of her own detective squad as they arrived. They came in saying things like, 'What the hell, Sarah?' They had all been in touch with their own homes. None had been attacked.

The incident was ridiculously simple to describe, so she had the same short conversation over and over. They knew what she was working on and shared most of her cases. At the end of each conversation another detective thumped her shoulder and said something like, 'We'll get this bastard, don't worry.'

Then they moved outside and walked around shaking their heads during muted conversations with each other. She could see they were puzzled by the behavior of this oddly inept shooter.

Denny and Aggie, glad to be released from the bedroom floor, came down to the kitchen and began filling platters with snacks and offering them to every cop who came through the house. Denny seemed to have forgotten all about being tired. She watched everything with wide-open eyes and occasionally nudged up to Sarah to ask a quiet question. Since there was no way to keep her from being involved, Sarah thought she would be least anxious if she felt fully informed, so she did her best to help her understand the procedure.

The procedure was all she understood herself. The attack didn't seem to her to make sense. But the officers in her yard weren't waiting to ask questions before they got ready to face a massacre. Every day they saw TV reports of terrorist attacks and hate killings. They all wore Kevlar vests and helmets, and carried assault weapons with extra clips.

The bullet was on its way to the lab now and the mobile lab crew was taking photos of the shattered window and the scar in the upholstery. But that's all there is, Sarah kept thinking. Damn hard to make a case out of one mashed bullet.

Then Leo Tobin came into the kitchen and told Sarah, 'They think they found the shooter's hiding spot. You want to come out and take a look? I cleared it with Norman.'

An impressively armored SWAT team member guarded the spot. Between the oleander hedge that grew along the side of the yard and the metal corner post that anchored the front wall she saw a small hollow of flattened gravel under the low-growing leafy branches.

'Nice find,' Sarah said. 'This hedge has gotten so thick – how'd you ever spot it?'

'I had a couple of guys doing assholes-and-elbows all around the yard, searching for that casing. Lopez noticed this funny hollow in the gravel and called me. Looks like the perfect place for the shot to come from. The range is about twenty-five yards. An easy shot.'

'Yeah. Makes you wonder why he missed,' Sarah said.

'Better not think too long about that,' Norman said. 'We're still looking for the casing, by the way.'

Sandy the lab tech stood by, waiting to search for something to swab for DNA in this sunbaked patch of gravel.

'He had good shelter from the street,' Sarah said, looking around. The wall was six feet tall here, the bushes a couple of feet taller. 'But inside—' She turned again to look at the house. 'Four windows on the front of the house and he couldn't have known there was no one in there.'

'He must be slim enough to get all of himself inside the hedge,' Leo said.

'This oleander's big enough to hide in, for sure – fat and bushy all the way up.' Sarah leaned her head between the bush and the post, pulled it out quickly and said, 'But wow, it's prickly in there.' Each slender gray-green leaf was like a serrated double-edged knife. She wiped her face on her sleeve. 'Hot too. If he stood in there very long he must have been sweating like a hog. Sandy, let's give this corner post a good swab, huh? Doesn't this look like a smear right here?'

'Could be,' Sandy said. 'I'll test the whole thing. If he waited very long he might have leaned on it.'

'This is definitely where he went in and out, see?' Leo said. 'There's a little gravel kicked out on the sidewalk there.'

'I see it.' Sarah pointed. 'And hey, isn't that a button hanging in there?'

'By God, you're right,' Krantz said. 'Hanging by a thread from that leaf. Oleanders really are good grabbers, aren't they? Is the photographer still here? Let's get a picture of that before we collect it.'

'He must have parked nearby,' Sarah said as she watched Gloria's flash light up the bush. 'He wouldn't want to walk far in daylight carrying a rifle.' She tried to call back a mental image of the side street as she passed it – was there a car sitting along the curb? She couldn't remember one, but why would she notice?

Will Dietz was suddenly at her side. Reluctant to drive into the security cordon the police had established around his yard and perhaps get his car sequestered, he parked a block away, showed his ID to the guard holding the posse box in his driveway and walked in looking for Sarah. He hugged her hard and said, 'You got time to tell me about it?'

'Yes. Come in the kitchen.' They sat close together on two stools while she told him the short story of the attack and the longer account of everything that had happened since.

Dietz said, 'Is Krantz running the SWAT team today?'

'Yes?'

'I'm going to go talk to him, get his OK to walk around the yard.'

'OK. Watch the team's faces when you do, will you?'

'Because?'

'Something about this whole thing is hinky, Will. And the guys out there – they don't want to say so but watch the way they look at each other, the way they raise their eyebrows. See if you can figure out what's bothering them.'

''K.' Not a big talker on his liveliest days, under pressure Will Dietz could wear silence like a favorite shirt. She saw him drifting around the yard for the next hour, watching and listening, so unobtrusive he was almost not there.

Then Banjo Bailey called from the lab and she got an answer to what was eating them all.

'I can say for sure that the bullet is a .22 Long Rifle,' he said, 'and that it was fired by a Winchester. I've test-fired several similar models and I'm pretty sure your attacker used a Winchester pump action, probably model sixty-one.'

'A squirrel gun? What the hell?'

'Yes. The toolmarks are pretty clear,' Banjo said.

'I'm not questioning your work,' Sarah said, 'only my situation.'

'Which is what?'

'For weeks,' she said, 'we've been on the trail of a drug cartel that we're pretty sure murdered one of their money-launderers. That call we had on the Fourth of July? Yeah, the day of the storm. Lately we all felt like we were getting close, so when somebody shot out my window—'

'You figured it was Pablo's thugs coming after you.'

'Right. But since when does the Sinaloa drug cartel go after its enemies with a pea shooter?'

'Since never before that I know of. But hey, I just work here,' Banjo said. 'I don't get to choose the weapons.'

'So true,' Sarah said. Feeling her sense of humor going south, she thanked Banjo and his crew for working so late. As soon as she got off the phone she went looking for Will Dietz. She needed to vent, and for that you need a mate.

'This whole thing is total bullshit, Will,' she said. 'The bullet is too small, the gun he's saying it came from is too low caliber. Everything Banjo

221

said is wrong – it has to be wrong – but we all know Banjo's never wrong!'

'No need to yell at me, Sarah, I'm right here.'

'OK, sorry. But I'm telling you, this is not how a team of professionals goes hunting, damn it.'

'So it's not a team of professionals. It's one local yahoo on a shooting spree.'

'One shot is not a spree. And why would one local yahoo choose to shoot at my car just when I'm closing in on a pack of international bandits?'

'Coincidence.'

'Will—'

'It does happen, Sarah. You're not immune to the law of averages.'

The phone rang. It was Delaney, making one last call after a storm of phoning that changed a week's schedules around this sudden surge of work in Sarah's yard.

She put the kitchen phone on speaker so Will could hear. 'Boss, you got Banjo's report?'

'Yes.'

'Well, I know Banjo's never wrong, but . . . what do you think?'

'I think we need to find the man who shot your car,' Delaney said. 'Beyond that I don't have an opinion yet. We need more evidence. Meanwhile, the chief says we need to move you and your family to a safe house for the weekend.'

'A safe house?' Three days of sitting aimlessly in some dismal repo in a suburb? 'Come on, boss, two experienced cops in one house in a quiet neighborhood? Give us one man walking the perimeter and we can be plenty safe right here.'

But Delaney was the department's man this

afternoon, not available for a friendly chat. He didn't even acknowledge her objections except to say, 'If the chief says you go, you go.'

She listened in wretched silence as he laid down the orders. 'We're looking for a two-bedroom suite with a sitting room, in a downtown hotel, at least five stories up. We can guarantee safety there with one man in the suite and two in the lobby. There are not many rooms like that to choose from in Tucson and we're not going to select it over the phone, of course. Can you have everybody ready to go in an hour?'

'Of course. But—'

'Good. I can't order Will to go – he doesn't work for my department now. But the county attorney's on board with this plan – her department will pay his share of this operation. Will you tell him we would appreciate his cooperation? Thank you.'

For several seconds after Delaney rang off, Sarah stood with the humming phone in her hand, watching Will's stiff back. He was at the sink, staring out the window. Too angry to speak. She knew, as much as she dreaded inactivity in a hotel room, that he would hate it twice as much.

'I'm sorry, Will,' she said finally. 'But will you help me now? There's a lot to do.'

When he turned, she saw that he had his thoughts collected and was ready, not just to do his part but to think of a hundred details she might forget.

They prioritized quickly. Then she ran and found Aggie and got her started packing a duffle.

Denny was in her room and, unlike the three adults in her household, she glowed with pleasure at the news.

'A free weekend in a big hotel?' she said. 'What's not to like? Can I take my bathing suit?'

'Uh, sure, they might have an indoor pool.'

'Oh, that's right, we have to stay inside, don't we? So what clothes?'

'What you wear here – shorts and tees. One set of sweats or jeans in case the A/C is set too low.'

'OK if I take my tablet? It's got all my good games.'

'Games, books, puzzles. It's going to be a long, quiet weekend. Your job's to keep everybody cheerful. But hurry. You have fifty minutes.'

'Easy-peasy.' In Denny's eyes, Sarah's three days of wretched boredom was a romp.

Sarah ran downstairs and packed the most comfortable clothes in her closet. She found two books on her nightstand she'd been trying to get to for a month and downloaded a third onto her Kindle. Denny's got the right attitude, she thought. We should try to get some fun out of this.

The mood turned a little more somber whenever she crossed Will's path. He was not grim, exactly, but thinking hard, getting tips from the SWAT team members still in the yard. 'They're asking us to leave the house unlocked,' he said. 'They'll secure it if they get cleared to leave.' So they took all their cash, which wasn't much, and locked up their computers and Will's toolshed. The hardest part was leaving their handguns behind, locked in their bedroom cubby. Sarah sighed as she dropped the key into the zippered pocket of her daypack.

'There'll be plenty of guns around,' Will said.

'I know. It just feels wrong.' Sarah ran to Aggie and said, 'Take all your money and your jewelry box. Got your pearls in there?' Her mother had one good strand of pearls and an emerald ring from a couple of years on the ranch when the steers were all fat while the market was up.

Aggie said, 'Done. What about the kitchen?' They froze what leftovers they could and disposed the rest. 'Tucson's feeding us this weekend,' Sarah said. 'It comes out even.'

Krantz promised to put the trash out Sunday night. Then he was calling: 'Heads up, the van's here.'

'I hope we thought of everything,' Sarah said.

'We're not going clear off the planet,' Will said, piling duffels in the driveway. 'We can buy a candy bar wherever we go.'

'Hey, yeah,' Denny said. 'Let's do that.'

Two heavily armed patrolmen jumped out to help load bags into the biggest SUV the department owned. Then they were all belted in and whirling off to . . . where?

'Couldn't find what we needed downtown,' the man riding shotgun said. 'Conventions had 'em all sewed up the next two days. So you're going to the Hilton East. You'll have your choice of watching mountains on one side or looking down on . . . nothing much on the other,' he said, smiling

225

into Denny's beaming face. 'You like that, huh? Should be a lively scene. Town's full and the weather's perfect.'

'Any chance there's a pool?'

'Probably more than one,' he said. 'Here's the brochure.'

She grabbed it and began calling out gleefully the amenities she found: wi-fi, full-service gym, in-room movies. Nobody in the vehicle was inclined to rain on Denny's parade, so the group rolled up to the back door of the towering hotel looking cheerful.

The two men in the front of the vehicle, suddenly dead serious, said, 'Sit still till we come back for you. Then please be prepared to move fast and silently.' They jumped out of their seats carrying the assault rifles they took off an over-head rack. They were joined by four equally well-armed officers who piled out of vehicles that pulled up close on either side.

The escort faced outward to do a quick check of the surrounding area, then alternated facing in, out and in again to make an aisle like a black-clad, armed-to-the-teeth wedding procession for their charges to walk through. Will went first. Then Denny, Aggie and Sarah all followed the beckoning hands of their guards. An inside team was holding the elevator. They were on the seventh floor and inside the suite with the door locked before Sarah had quite managed a deep breath.

Their jolly driver's helper, who had morphed into a ninja warrior when they arrived at the hotel, mellowed back again now into a kindly guardian who said his name was Josh and that he would take the first shift with them in the suite.

'My orders are to stay on this door,' he said. 'So I can't give you privacy in the sitting room but you're welcome to close the doors on the bedrooms if you need to say something private. Order anything you want from room service anytime they're open. When it comes I'll ask you to step into the bedrooms. I won't taste your food but I do vet the waiter. He won't see you and you won't see him.' He beamed at them like a satisfied teacher on the first day of school. 'Any questions?'

Denny said, 'Can I go swimming?'

Josh said, 'No, the pool's outside.'

'You get a vacation from swimming, be happy,' Aggie said. Her face said, *Don't nag.*

Denny took a deep breath and said, 'OK.'

Josh smiled at her and said, 'It's dinnertime. Aren't you hungry?'

'Hey, I can always eat. Is everybody else ready?'

At Denny's urging they ordered a different dish for each of them with extra plates so they could all sample everything. The big platters of food, combined with the fatigue they had all been trying to ignore, reduced them all to brainless lumps of protoplasm. Ten minutes after they sent the food away, the four of them were nodding over a thriller on the TV set. When Will began to snore they turned it off and went to bed.

Sarah woke in the gray dawn, out of a dream of being stalked by an unseen menace through a forest of oleander bushes. Will was beside her, sleeping peacefully. She lay still for a few seconds, enjoying the comfort and safety. When she couldn't wait any longer she slid out carefully, trying not to wake him, and was padding toward the door when he said softly behind her, 'What's up?'

'Just need the bathroom,' she said. 'Go back to sleep.' But when she came out he was standing by the bed in his underwear, pulling on his jeans. 'What, you can't go back to sleep?'

'Already slept ten hours. Most I've had in one stretch in years. You want some coffee?'

'I don't think room service is awake yet.'

'No, but there's a coffee set-up out there in the sitting room. Relax here and I'll see what I can do.'

She got back in bed and thought, maybe just ten more minutes . . . Half an hour later she woke to the sound of Will coming through the door with cups and a carafe. 'Hang on,' he said, putting them down on her bedside table, 'I think I saw a paper under the door.' He was back in a minute with napkins and the morning paper.

'God, you're a ball of fire this morning.'

'This isn't all – I got info too. There's a new man out there this morning. His name is Alvin and he was born to please. There may not be a pool indoors but he says there's a great gym, running machines, weights – the whole nine yards. Soon as the extra guard gets here Denny and I can do a half-Iron Man – won't she like that? There's no limit; we can do another one Saturday. Also I talked to the news-stand in the lobby and ordered us a pile of Metropolitan papers for Sunday. You and Aggie can catch up on the news

228

in New York and LA and London. How does that sound?'

'Almost too much fun to imagine,' Sarah said. 'From now on I think you should forget about diet and exercise and just make sure you get plenty of sleep.'

At home, Will was rarely idle. He loved his tidy workshop and spent most of his free time keeping their house and grounds shipshape. Cooped up for a weekend, Sarah saw, he dreaded the boredom. To cope with it he would concentrate on keeping everybody else amused.

'Humor him,' she told Aggie, who was gaping at his suggestion that he would try to get a patrolman to walk the halls with her if she felt in need of a hike. 'He's suffering separation anxiety from his toolshed.'

Will and Denny got a stiff workout after breakfast. As soon as they were gone with the officer who came to guard them in the gym, Sarah settled her mother in a comfortable chair with a good light, saying, 'I hope you brought a good book.'

'*Doctor Zhivago*,' Aggie said. 'Been meaning to read it since you were little.'

With all her family occupied, Sarah pulled a chair in front of a window in her own bedroom and began to stare out of it at the distant Rincon mountains, where nothing much was going on. A wisp of early morning cloud evaporated as the sun rose higher, leaving a featureless pale blue sky above the hazy peaks.

From time to time her lips moved and she made a note in the small tablet on her lap.

Will and Denny came back about one, drained

of excess energy and showered to squeaky clean-liness. They all played a noisy word game during lunch. Then Will, who never read fiction, borrowed a thriller from Sarah and read for ten minutes before falling asleep. Aggie and Denny took turns reading and napping.

Sarah continued to stare out the window. Slowly, her notes covered one page and then another.

On Saturday morning their guard said, 'Dispatch says we had several men call in sick so he can't spare an extra guy for gym detail. Sorry.'

'Just as well,' Will said. 'That workout yesterday – I'm getting complaints from a couple of muscles I forgot I had.'

Sarah urged him to investigate the sports chan-nels on TV and he took her up on it, sharing the riches with their sitting-room guard.

'OK, Denny, time to get serious,' Sarah said and unboxed a thousand-piece puzzle she'd been saving in case Aggie had another stroke and they had to take turns sitting vigil. They worked at it sporadically for the rest of the day, crowing so mightily when they placed the last two pieces that the two sports fans stuck their heads in, alarmed.

A few minutes later Aggie turned the last page of *Doctor Zhivago* and said, 'There, I did it.'

'Good,' Sarah said. 'Did you enjoy it?'

'Mmm. Kind of like *Gone With the Wind* with snow.'

By Sunday morning, when the papers came, they all dived into them like the starved news junkies they normally were not. For a couple of hours the only noise in the suite was the rustle of newsprint. Then the hotel sent up a complimentary sampling of Sunday brunch. By noon Sarah felt bloated with food and sated with information.

Delaney called at one and asked, 'How are you doing out there in the boonies?'

'Just terrific,' Sarah said. 'Getting ready to Google a few items so we can finish the *New York Times* crossword.'

'Sunk as low as that, have you? I better get you out of there before you get too depraved for police work.'

'Don't tease me, boss. Are you saying this torture could end?'

'Yes. The teams covering your house are begging to be relocated to a gang war – they haven't had three days this dull since they got their shields. I spoke to the chief and he agrees that this can't go on forever. We'll put one man walking your perimeter and assign an hourly drive-by to the man on the beat. Watch it for a couple of days and re-assess.'

'So we can go home?'

'Soon as I can find a van and a driver. Can you be ready in an hour?'

'Would you believe ten minutes?' She hung up and shared the news. Whooping with joy, they all threw things helter-skelter into duffles.

At home they walked around the house, touching things, taking their spaces back. Sarah commandeered the laundry and washed piles of dirty clothes.

Dietz unlocked his toolshed and did not come

out for some time. 'Not that I don't trust the TPD to provide full security,' he told Sarah when he took her out to see, 'but just for the hell of it I got out my deer rifle.'

He showed her how he disarmed his Remington, raised the hinged floorplate and cleaned it, checked the bolt action and gave the bolt and trigger mechanism a fresh rub-down with one of the silicone-impregnated soft cloths he kept in the case. 'Then I re-armed it, see? Four bullets in the magazine and one chambered.' Fresh and gleaming, it lay on a towel on his work bench with a box of ammo nearby.

'Sooner or later,' he said, 'all these cops will have to leave. I expect you'll have nabbed the guy by then, but just in case, I like to be ready.'

'Beautiful, Will,' Sarah said. She kissed him. 'We'll be fine, won't we?'

'You bet.'

Aggie toured her tiny kitchen, opened cupboards and peered into the freezer. 'What do you all want to eat tonight?' she said and began naming off frozen leftovers. When she got to 'a cupful of penne with some kind of sauce,' Denny said, 'How about a pizza with everything?' and the affirmatives rang through the house.

Delaney called an hour later. 'Everything OK there? Nothing missing?'

'Perfect. I'll get the duty roster from Dispatch and send some thank-you notes – the guys on duty here did a great job.'

'Good. The chief's very anxious to call off the one remaining guard. Are you comfortable with that?'

232

'Absolutely. The department's been more than generous to us and we appreciate it, but Will and I can take it from here.'

'I think so too.'

'Can we have a meeting in the morning, please?'

'Already on my skej. You have some thoughts?'

'Thoughts, questions, even a few answers.'

'Yeah, I think everybody does. See you in the morning.'

Monday morning in the kitchen had an edgy feel – three silent adults getting back into their routines. Will and Sarah clipped on holsters and settled badges, and Aggie's lips moved silently as she checked two lists.

When the wall phone rang Sarah answered, said, 'Just a moment,' and told Denny, who had just wandered out in her pajamas, still half asleep, 'This is for you.'

Denny answered, blinking, her voice still gravelly. 'Hello?' And then, at little intervals, 'Yes. OK. Fine.' She hung the phone up, looking dazed.

'My swimming class is canceled for two days. The coach had to go out of town.' She slumped in her chair at the table, scowling. 'Five days with no swimming, drat! I'll be all flabby; I'll lose my edge.'

'Oh, nonsense,' Aggie said. 'Flabby – for heaven's sake, you're as lean as a greyhound. Enjoy the break. Read another book.'

'Tell you what,' Will said, settling his body camera and taser, 'I have three interviews scheduled this afternoon, all on the south side of town.

233

You want to do a ride-along? We can take a little detour on Valencia between calls and spot some cars.'

'Hey, yeah. Could we?'

'Sure. Bring a book to read while I'm working. And your car manual. We'll practice on Toyotas and Hondas today.'

'Oh, fab-a-docious. What time?'

'I'll pick you up right after lunch.'

'And you and I,' Aggie said, fixing her granddaughter with a stern eye, 'are not going to say one more word about swimming again until Wednesday.'

'Very well, dear Grandmother,' Denny said. 'Whatever you say.' She folded her hands demurely in her lap and batted her eyes, copying a pose she had learned from an illustrated copy of *Alice in Wonderland.* Aggie pointed one bony finger at her silently.

'Careful, Denny,' Sarah said. 'That's her threat pose. She used it to strike terror in me and my sister when we were growing up.'

'And what I got from that was one cop and one outlaw,' Aggie said. 'Shows you what I know about child-rearing.'

Eleven

'Let's start with what we know,' Delaney said. 'Somebody shot a bullet into Sarah's car. That's an assault on a peace officer, which Arizona law makes a class-two felony if it involves the use of a deadly weapon.'

'A smart lawyer might object that a .22 pump is hardly a deadly weapon,' Leo said. 'More like a plinker for tin cans and small varmints.'

'In my book it says "deadly weapon or dangerous instrument,"' Delaney said. 'Any rifle is going to qualify.'

'There's also the problem that she was off duty, though,' Ollie said. 'I looked up some stuff over the weekend,' he said, shrugging. 'We all ran in there Thursday with our holster covers off, ready to start a war with the bad guys who were shooting at Sarah. Then we stood around for a couple of hours while nothing happened. After I got home I started thinking, what was that all about? Nobody got hurt, the shooting seemed inept as hell. Is it possible this was just some kid who got his hands on his dad's old rifle?' He turned his hands up. 'Started me thinking about the gray areas.'

'No,' Delaney said. 'Forget gray areas. A peace officer has been assaulted, and in Arizona we don't let that go unpunished. As for being off duty, Sarah is not on street patrol, she's a Tucson police detective involved in several ongoing investigations. She doesn't go home and forget the whole thing till the next shift. We get called out, we go. One can argue that a police detective is never off duty.'

'Also, there's the lurking,' Oscar said. 'That's the part I hate. He stalked her; he waited in her yard. That behavior seems to fit the cartel, doesn't it? They go after people; they are relentless.'

'But they don't go after people with .22 caliber ammo,' Ray Menendez said, 'last I heard.'

'No, they don't,' Jason said. 'And they don't go alone and they don't fool around. Hate to say this to you, buddy,' he tilted his shining bald dome toward Sarah, 'but if that was the Sinaloa cartel shooting at you on Thursday, you'd be *dead*.'

'I tend to agree with that,' Delaney said. 'But I haven't heard from you yet, Sarah. You said you had some thoughts over the weekend.'

'Yes.' She held up her tablet, showed a page of single-spaced typing, and flipped to several more pages, equally full. 'I told Will when he got there that night that I felt something was hinky. Don't get me wrong, my niece was in the car when the shot went through it and my mother was a few feet away in the backyard, so I was very glad to see that SWAT team come swarming in. And when you guys turned up as well, trust me, you all looked like heroes to me.'

'Oh, now . . .' Feet shuffled, Leo coughed and Ollie made a small hissing noise he'd learned from his eight-year-old son. But the self-deprecation didn't last long because they all knew how she felt about getting attacked in her own yard. On the street, they dealt with homicide, assault, rape, without flinching – all part of the job. But that was work. Home was where you got the respite that helped you keep your head on straight. Home was not to be messed with.

'But three days in that hotel . . .' She made a face and they all chuckled. 'I had plenty of time to think, so I did. And what I've got on my first page of notes,' she held it up, 'matches what

236

you all said just now, almost exactly. The gun was wrong, the ammo was wrong, the single shooter was wrong. The poor aim was utterly ridiculous.'

'The second page says this' – she read from the tablet – 'Hinky or not, though, I can't make it unhappen. Somebody stood in my yard, waiting, till I turned in my driveway and offered the perfect shot. Then he fired one bullet that made a loud noise and messed up a city-owned vehicle but didn't come close to hitting me or my niece.' She waited a few seconds, then scrolled down and carried on reading. 'I want to rule out the kid on a shooting spree who doesn't even know my name. A kid on a shooting spree doesn't stand patiently in a hedge of prickly leaves in hundred-degree heat, waiting to get a shot at a homeowner he doesn't even know. How could this naughty kid even be sure I was due home?'

'If he's from the neighborhood . . .' Ray said.

'If there was a troublesome kid like that in my neighborhood, I'd know about him,' Sarah said, looking up from her tablet. 'You know how it is: people hear there's a cop moving in and right away they're on your doorstep asking you to keep an eye on so-and-so. My one hesitation about moving into the Blenman-Elm neighborhood was that there weren't many kids around near Denny's age. I know them all now and nobody's ever complained to me about any of them.'

'OK,' Delaney said. 'I've been thinking about it too and I agree with you. Forget the kid. What other thoughts did you have during those three long days?'

237

'That we were being played,' Sarah said.

Jason Peete said softly, 'Bingo.'

Around the table, heads nodded and the faces of her teammates showed relief. 'Been waiting for you to say it,' Ollie said. 'I think so too. It's the only way all this conflicting evidence makes sense.'

'To make us think the cartel was going after Sarah, right?' Oscar said. 'I've been wondering about that myself.'

'It's pretty lame, though, isn't it?' Ray said. 'I mean, I like it, but how could anybody think we'd be stupid enough to believe one shot from a .22 pump—'

'We were stupid enough to believe it for a couple of hours on Thursday night,' Delaney said. 'You want to do the math on what that little game of hide-and-seek cost the department?'

Looking stricken, Sarah said, 'Hey, boss, I—'

'No offense, Sarah, you did the right thing calling for help and our response was by the book. We're not going to change protocols over one screwy incident. But think about this: we might be a little slower to send the SWAT team to the next alarm from Sarah's house. So maybe it wasn't so lame.'

Sarah felt a shiver, and looking down saw goosebumps forming on her arms. *Damn!* She waited three seconds to be sure her voice was steady when she said, 'So we need to catch this bugger before he makes his next move.'

'Fine,' Ollie said. 'I'll be glad to go after him myself, barefoot and unarmed in the dark if necessary. Just tell me who he is.'

'Well,' Sarah said, 'I have some thoughts about that. May I read you some more notes?'

'Go ahead,' Delaney said.

She picked up the tablet again. 'Lois Johnson kept saying Calvin's killing looked like a cartel hit to her. I said to her once that there were things about this murder that didn't seem to fit that scenario – that the victim had no resistance wounds on his hands and arms and the door wasn't forced. All the evidence at the scene said the murderer knocked on the door and the victim let him in. She said something like, "Well, sure, in a clown outfit, why not? He would have presented as part of the entertainment. A marcher asking for a drink of water." And Lois had all the clout in the room, so I let it go.

'But ever since then I keep going over it again in my head, that the evidence in the house said that after this attacker shot the friendly home-owner in the ear he beat his head to a bloody pulp.' Sarah put the tablet down and watched the faces blinking at her around the table. '*After.* You hear what I'm saying? After Calvin Springer was dead he got his cheekbones broken and his tooth knocked out of his jaw.'

'That's right,' Delaney said. 'The ME was wondering why there wasn't more blood from such a beating and you said something about not liking the idea that the killer kept on beating on the guy after he was dead.'

'Yes. It's been bothering me ever since. You've all been to a lot of homicide scenes. You get to know what to look for, don't you? So think about it – did this one look like the work of a professional hit team? All surgical and clean, get the job done and get out? No, it did not. A big fight, and the window broken – to me, it had all the earmarks of one man in a bloody rage.'

Seeing she had everybody's full attention, Sarah leaned back in her chair. 'Lois Johnson and her accountants spend their careers trying to put guys in jail for money laundering. Nothing wrong with that, but now that we know Calvin Springer was really Bill McGinty I don't think we should let her influence what we believe about who murdered him.'

'OK,' Delaney said. 'Go ahead; what do you believe about it?'

'That in the last few minutes before this killer took off his clown suit and walked away, he wasn't working for money. He was intent on revenge, close up and personal.'

'Oh, Sarah,' Jason said, 'I see where you're going with this and I am so ready to walk that path with you.'

'You put my feet on it,' Sarah said, 'by saying you thought there were things he was leaving out.'

'Things who was leaving out of what?' Leo said. 'Are you two talking in code?'

'I'm sorry,' Sarah said. 'We're remembering a conversation we had after we interviewed Jack Ames. Jason felt he was leaving something out of his story about old times on the boats in the Baja. Ever since then we've both been kind of turning over rocks in our minds—'

'Oh, please,' Jason said. 'Not that again.'

Everybody laughed but not for long. They were

240

all excited now, wearing the intent expressions of a team on the hunt, still puzzled but sure they were closing on the quarry.

'Finish your story,' Delaney said. 'Who needs revenge?'

'Jack Ames,' Sarah said.

'For what?'

'For the brutal killing of his foxy girlfriend, Poppy McGinty.'

'She's his girlfriend now? I read your entry in the case report after that interview and I thought you said they were just good friends.'

'I didn't say that. Jack Ames said that and I reported it, but Jason and I both thought he was blowing smoke.'

'Then you should have put that in the case report.'

'I guess I should have. It was just a feeling and I was looking for some evidence to back it up.'

'Don't do that. Never again, you hear? You're a detective who's interviewed many people and your feelings *are* evidence.'

'OK, my bad. But follow me through this, will you? We had what seemed for a while like a red-hot theory, that since McGinty was hooked up with the cartel he probably killed Calvin Springer. That's all gone up in smoke now. So why don't we consider that maybe the drug dealers weren't involved at all?

'Mabel – the widow Conway, remember her? Ollie, you thought she was a reasonable woman, didn't you?'

'Solid as a rock,' Ollie said.

'Certainly not one to go spinning romantic fantasies, right? But she was sure Jack was in love with Poppy McGinty. She told Fred she was worried about it. And Fred, being the male buddy, saw it too but said leave it alone, Jack's a grown-up. But if she was right, Jack Ames lost two women he loved within three years. That's a lot of pain and anger to absorb and keep to yourself. Jason, you didn't believe what Jack said about his feelings for Poppy, did you?'

'Sure didn't. He was tappin' up a storm by the time he made that speech. He couldn't sit still anymore.'

'OK. I felt the same way. I think that Jack Ames never got over the pain of losing Poppy. Now suppose Mabel was right about something else. Suppose that years later, that day at the Mercado, Fred actually did see Bill McGinty? If he did, the chances are Jack saw him too. He'd always believed McGinty killed his wife. Then he saw the guy where he least expected to, right here in Tucson. It must have brought all the pain back to him. If I'm right, the Fourth of July parade offered him his first chance to punish the no-good husband who killed the woman he loved.'

'I don't know, Sarah,' Leo Tobin said. 'That's a pretty far-fetched story. But say for the hell of it we buy your revenge idea – we agree Jack Ames was probably the man in the clown suit who killed old Calvin because he turned out to be old Bill. Why would that make Jack Ames come into *your* yard and shoot up *your* car?'

'Well,' Sarah said, looking at the ceiling light,

'maybe I jerked his chain a little too hard the last time we talked.' She told them about her last conversation with Jack Ames.

'I don't think you jerked too hard,' Jason said. 'I'd say it worked exactly the way we hoped it would. He decided you were getting a little too close for comfort so he'd see if he couldn't plant a little doubt in everybody's mind.'

'You think,' Delaney said, 'that when that drug war started in Agua Prieta he thought an attack on Sarah might get us to look across the border?'

'Yes,' Jason said. 'He must be able to shoot better than that. I think he was hoping to mislead us.'

'What worries me a little about that idea,' Ollie said in what Sarah thought might be the best example of understatement she'd heard this year, 'is it might have seemed clever to him while he was mad at Sarah but as soon as he calmed down he might have started thinking he should have used a better convincer.'

'Yeah,' Ray said. 'And then, you know, shooting at Sarah probably felt pretty good to him. Maybe so good he'd like to try it again with bigger ammo.'

'Or closer up,' Delaney said. 'He's proved he can kill close up.'

'So,' Sarah said, 'now that you all finally bought the idea, are you going to sit here and scare me to death or shall we figure out how to get this guy?'

'Aside from having no proof that any of this story is true,' Delaney said, 'I'm ready to plan.

243

What physical evidence have we got? One bullet?'

'And one bone button,' Leo said, 'that looks like it belongs on an old raincoat.'

'But that button can't belong to the shooter, do you think?' Oscar said. 'Why would anybody wear a raincoat when it's a hundred and three in the shade?'

'To hide his rifle while he walks to his car,' Jason said.

'And keep himself from being scratched all over by an oleander bush,' Leo said. 'This guy's a planner, isn't he?'

'Yes. A very sweaty planner if he wore his raincoat in my yard that afternoon,' Sarah said. 'Let's ask Sandy if she found evidence of DNA in the swabs she took off the corner post.'

'Even if she did, what have we got to compare it to?' Delaney said. 'The whole universe in NCIC, I suppose. But Jack Ames isn't going to have a file in there, is he? He's just been doing good deeds out in Marana, according to you.'

'And murdering Calvin Springer, according to me,' Sarah said. 'But you're right – we may not have that evidence filed yet either. Where are they, the DNA tests on the clown costume?'

'Don't know,' Delaney said. 'Ask Sandy about that, too, while you're at it. Here, use my phone; put it on speaker so we'll all know.'

'The swabs from your yard are safely stored in the cooler here,' Sandy said. 'They're in a kit. It's all labeled, don't you worry – we won't lose it.'

'But you haven't done any testing on it yet? You don't know if the samples will yield any DNA?'

'No. They're listed – they've been assigned a number. When the number comes up we'll start the procedures. That's how it works.'

'How about the clown suit? Has anybody started on that yet?'

'The clown suit?'

'Yeah, the one we found in the dumpster. With the mask, you know, and the shoe?'

'I don't know, offhand. I'm not the only scientist in this section; there's five of us full-time and a couple of—'

'Sandy,' Sarah said, 'we have an urgent need for that information. What would it take to get those two items tested today?'

'You kidding?' Sandy said. 'Do you know how long that queue is right now?'

'No idea.'

'Somewhere between five and six hundred cases. As usual.'

'OK. But I did hear somebody say the test can be completed in about forty-eight hours if it gets top priority.'

'Which is about as likely right now as a heavy snowfall on East Speedway Boulevard. If the president of the United States got shot there this afternoon we would do that if there was any doubt about the identity of the shooter. It would require all other work to be put aside while we ran that one test. I do not want to be around for the uproar that would cause. Some of the cases we're working on now have been waiting over a year just to start. A hundred or so lawyers phone this section every month to ask about progress. Forget it, Sarah. DNA is a complicated, expensive process, and one of the things it takes is a lot of time.'

'I hear you,' Sarah said. 'Just thought I'd ask.' She hung up, sat back and asked her superior, 'What's the next option?'

'Hardball,' he said. 'If you're pretty sure your mojo is working. Are you?'

'You said to report my feelings. I strongly believe my feelings about Jack Ames will be verified by the evidence in hand but I can't prove it unless we test the evidence.'

'Fair enough.' Delaney's pale eyes rested on Jason. 'You started this witch-hunt, apparently. You still think you were right?'

'He was tap-dancing around *something*. And I think she's nailed what it was.'

'OK. Then you all need to get out of here while I call the chief and do a little soft shoe of my own.'

His cheeks were flaming brightly by the time he reassembled his team. The chief had triggered his allergies by quoting from the price chart for DNA tests and pointing out the way they multiplied when they displaced ongoing tests.

'I asked him if he would rather face the prospect of another attack like the one in your yard last week and he admitted the test was a bargain by comparison. So we're on, they'll start immediately – simultaneous tests of the clown suit and the swabs from your yard. Then he reminded me that the department emergency funds are down to almost nothing and we have been told not to ask the city for relief. Till people start building houses again, the city of Tucson is broke. I tried to get a word in about all the cartel money we're going to share with ICE but his final words to me were, "This had better be a very good hunch or we are fucked."'

Sarah sat up straight in the brittle silence that followed. When she thought her voice would work, she said, 'Forty-eight hours?'

'I think so. You will know more about that soon because your next task is to go to the DNA testing lab and check to be certain they know exactly which items we want tested. We don't want any stupid mistakes to screw up this expensive procedure now, do we? No. So go, make sure, view the items, check the listing – whatever it takes to assure me we have the right goddam blood and sweat in those machines.'

She wasn't going to win any popularity contests at the lab either, she saw when she got there and asked for Sandy. A handsome young man in scrubs looked at her as if she'd ordered spiders on toast to go.

'Not a good day to talk to Sandy, if you haven't heard,' he said. 'She just took her major funk back to the freezer. She'll be out soon, though. Nobody stays long in the freezer.'

'I can talk to someone else, if – oh, here she comes.'

Gloved and gowned in plastic, Sandy pushed a cart loaded with carefully wrapped and labeled packages. Her brooding expression grew even darker when she saw Sarah.

'You people really know how to play dirty, don't you?' She parked her cart by her workbench. 'You proud of yourself, going around us to the chief, causing all this extra work?'

'I'm sorry about that part. Are these my—' Sarah leaned to look at the labels.

'Don't touch anything!' Sandy said, jumping between Sarah and the cart. 'What are you doing here, anyway? You come to gloat?'

'Of course not. Sandy, can we please call a truce? I came because my boss insisted. He says I have to verify that the tests you're about to run are the ones we asked for.'

'He thinks I'm too dumb to take the right samples out of the freezer? I have a master's degree in organic chemistry, goddamn it! What has he got?'

'Probably a terrible headache. Delaney took such a beating from the chief of police about asking to jump the queue that he now says if there is any mistake in what we test we will all face a firing squad.'

'God, isn't this a swell place to work? Everybody mad at everybody else, just because we're trying to do our jobs.' Sandy was not a natural grudge-holder, though. She was coming around. 'These are your items, see? The clown suit and the mask. I must admit I'm hot for that mask – around the mouth is always the *best*. And here we have the sweat off the corner post and the button off the coat. A coat, in July? But we'll test it anyway; it's what we do when we're asked.'

'And we're all so grateful when you do what we ask.'

'Uh-huh. Some people manage to ask politely, without bullying. We have to back all the current tests out of the machines now and then clean the machines. It's going to be a couple of hours before we can start on your stuff.'

'So we should expect a report sometime Wednesday morning?'

'If all goes well. Have you ever noticed how rarely that happens?'

Denny was incandescent when Will brought her home Monday night. 'I can ID all Toyotas without fail,' she bragged. 'And most Hondas. The Toyota Prius is almost too easy to be fun. Don't you think, though, that most older model cars are easier to identify than new ones? Why have our rides all started to look alike?'

'We all started demanding better mileage,' Sarah said, 'so the tail fins had to go. Right, Will?'

'And the big trunks and most of the chrome. Everything's lighter and more aerodynamic now.' He grinned at Denny. 'Tell her about the chaser's dream car.'

'Oh, yeah – toward the end of the hunt we saw a totally beat-to-the-socks Dodge Dart. I wish you could have seen it! It had this long broad hood with twin, um, air scoops – is that what they're for? And it was kind of electric blue but had one greenish door and one kind of pukey-gray one that was wired shut. Looked like it had escaped from a junkyard but there it was, keeping up in traffic, no problem. The owner must be some kind of a magical mechanic.'

'Easy to follow, huh?'

'I would know that car anywhere! Just for the fun of it we turned off once and lost it, got back on the street and found it again within ten minutes.'

'Denny wanted to do it again,' Will said. 'She really had the blood up today – all she needed was a deerstalker cap. But I saw some signs we might be kind of spooking the driver by then so we quit.'

'That sounds like fun. Excuse me a minute.' In her bedroom with the door closed, Sarah looked up a number in her notes and dialed it.

'Mabel?' she said when the hoarse voice answered. 'That old car of Jack's you were telling me about the other day . . . could you describe it for me?'

'Describe it? It's a, let's see, a blue Dodge Dart that looks about a hundred years old but never seems to get any older.'

'Did you say it has mismatched doors?'

'Yes. One green and one gray. Why?'

'Oh, this is just a silly thing that I shouldn't even be bothering you about. One of my team members came back off a job and described an old car he saw on the street. And I know it was wicked of me,' she giggled a little, hoping she sounded light-hearted, 'but I bet him five dollars I could ID the make and model.'

'Listen, if you find ways to get some fun out of that hard job of yours, all I can say is good for you.'

'Well . . . thanks for being so understanding. How are you doing?'

'Pretty well. I've decided to ditch quilting and try ballroom dancing – what do you think?'

'Excellent idea. My mother loves it. The hard part is getting her boyfriend to go along.'

'Ah. I'm not ready for a boyfriend yet, if I ever will be. But I've got a couple of women friends who want to try it too, and we've agreed to take turns being the lead.'

She put her head back in the kitchen and said, 'Will, I've got a drawer stuck, can you help me?'

Back in their bedroom she told him about her conversation with Mabel, adding, 'I think you and Denny just had fun tracking the man we spent the whole weekend hiding from.'

'Holy shit.' Will turned toward the wall and breathed into the plaster for a long minute. When he turned back, he said, 'If I'd had any idea whose car that was, I never would have—'

'I know. Did you see the driver? Can you describe him?'

'Thin number-five male in an old hat that shaded most of his face. I wasn't much interested in him – we were both looking at the car.' The nerve was twitching in his cheek – the tic he got after he was shot. She'd thought it was gone for good. 'Why didn't I know about his fishing car? But then why would you tell me all about your interviews? I certainly don't do that.'

'Praise be.'

Stone-faced, he contemplated the shutters closed against the afternoon sun. Finally, 'You don't know for sure yet, do you, that Jack Ames is the shooter?'

'No. Not till the DNA test comes back.'

251

'But you do know for sure whoever shot your car got a look at Denny?'

'She claimed she saw him so he may have caught a glimpse of her.' Then she had to ask. 'How about today?'

'Today she was glued to the window, grinning all over her face. He wasn't aware of us at first. And he's probably used to getting some extra attention in that car. By the end, though, he was starting to do a few evasive maneuvers to see if we were following. He might have got a good look at her before we backed off.'

They looked at each other in the gloom of the shuttered bedroom, two grave faces in search of relief that neither could offer.

'We just have to get through tomorrow,' Sarah said. 'The day after that is Wednesday. Sometime Wednesday, we'll know.'

'If there's a match—'

'If there's a match we'll pick him up right away and that's the end of it.'

Sorting through bad options, Will came to, 'But if there isn't—'

'Back to Shit City. Up to our eyeballs. Don't even think about it. Those alleles are going to *match*, Will.'

The nerve stopped jumping. He had made up his mind about something. He leaned closer and said, 'OK with you if I bring my deer rifle in the house? There's no cop out there now, walking the perimeter. I'll keep it under the bed on my side.'

'All right. Wait until after we eat, OK? Then I'll tell Mom and Denny where it is. We can't have any secrets about loaded guns in the house.'

She went back to the kitchen. Handing her a bowl of potatoes, Aggie said, 'Well, did you get it sliding all right?'

'What?' Sarah said. 'Oh, the drawer. Yes, it's working fine now. Trust Mr Fixit.'

'I always do,' Aggie said.

Twelve

Tuesday morning, Sarah checked her watch twice before ten o'clock. Her computer kept telling her the time was right. It was her mind that was out of step. It kept racing out of the building and flying four miles north to where the gleaming stainless-steel containers of the DNA lab percolated toward her answer.

She knew better than to get invested like this in an outcome. Facts were facts; you took the ones you could find and worked with them. Trying to get the evidence to prove your theory was a fool's game. Hadn't she learned that long ago?

But this Tuesday she could not listen to the voice of experience. She wanted Jack Ames identified as the bad guy and put away so that Denny was safe, and she was ready to throw rocks at objective truth if it offered any other answer.

At that, Tuesday was a cake-walk compared to Wednesday. She had passed a restless night worrying about whether to let Denny go back to swimming class and woke Will at dawn to discuss it. He said he understood her concern but he thought they should all get back to their routines and stick to them.

'You don't know for sure what that DNA test is going to show. We could be at this hunt for some time yet. Our best chance of keeping calm is to go about our business and stay ready for anything.'

Sarah closed her eyes and took a deep breath. When she opened them, she said, 'I know you're right. Do you think I ought to tell her what we think?'

'And make her as nervous as we are? What's the use of that?'

'Same with Aggie, I guess.'

'Absolutely.'

They presented a cheerful front at breakfast, Sarah thought, but Aggie was a little too brisk and never quite met her eyes.

She knows something's up. Would it be kinder to tell her? But the day seemed to have its own momentum; they talked about Aggie's grocery list, Denny came into the kitchen yawning, Sarah blew a kiss and went to work.

She got through the morning by concentrating ferociously on a case that was hitting one road-block after another on its way to court. By noon, desperate for word from the lab and longing to call Sandy but not quite able to summon the nerve, she called Aggie instead.

'So,' she said, 'is Denny getting ready to go to swim class?'

'Already standing on the front step in her gym clothes,' Aggie said. 'The meet's at Sunshine Swim School today so they're leaving early. They have to drive miles east on Speedway, almost out of town. She'll be really tired tonight.'

'Good news for you, though, Ma. You get a nice long afternoon to yourself. You should take a nap.'

'I believe I will. Something about this long hot summer is making me tired.'

Sarah closed her phone, thinking, I know what's making you tired and it's not the weather. Everybody in the big house on Bentley Street was wound tight, waiting for the truth to show its face. And not talking about it was making it worse.

She went back to work. What else could you do? The Bergman case was due in court in a few days. The file had to be brought up to date, the physical evidence checked one last time. *Anyway, if I wasn't busy I'd jump out of my skin. What's holding up those people at the lab?*

She knew the practice meet at Sunshine ended at three o'clock and figured it would take about an hour for the van to load up and get everybody back to Catalina Terrace. Denny was catching a ride home with one of the other mothers today and Sarah was hoping to have good news to tell her tonight. But the clock on her desk scrolled on past three-fifteen with no call from Sandy. A problem with one of the tests? When her phone chirped at three twenty-three she almost dropped it trying to pick it up and answer.

255

But it wasn't Sandy. It was a text message from Denny and all it showed was the number three.

For two seconds she froze in her seat while her brain protested, wait now, this was just a game to pass the time. Wasn't it?

But then her memory showed her Will saying, 'No fooling around, now, we must never use this number unless we're serious.' She saw the three of them making that pact, shaking hands.

Then she was out of her chair, tapping her phone to bring up the tracking app. She paused by Ollie's workspace till she had a clear image of the icon, moving slowly southwest on Grant. She poked his shoulder and held the phone in front of him as he looked up.

Pointing to the moving icon on her phone, she said, 'This is Denny, coming toward us on Grant. I'm pretty sure she's on a swim-team bus and I know she's in trouble but I don't know what kind. I'm going to go find her now. Will you round up the team and follow me soon as you can? Text me when you're on the road.'

Her phone rang as she grabbed her day-pack and trotted toward the stairs. When she answered, Will said, 'I got a number three from Denny – did you?'

'Yes. I've got the icon on-screen. The way it's moving I think she must still be in the swim-team van.'

'I got it up now. Hang on, let me watch a minute.' A silence, then, 'Not changing lanes, coming on steady. I think you're right: she's probably still in the van. You asked for help yet?'

256

'All my guys are coming behind me. Probably ten minutes back. Where are you?'

'Coming up Country Club, just passed Speedway. You?'

'On Elm Street, turning onto Tucson. You'll see them first. Hold on, I'm getting a text.'

Ollie typed, 'All exit sta now u want SWAT?'

She told Will, 'Ollie's offering a SWAT team but I think four cars off the street will do better, don't you?'

'Yes, it's too long a wait for a SWAT outfit. Four beat cars can do a good box.' There was a silence full of sweat and then he said, 'Hang on, I think I see the van.' Sarah waited, feeling her heart beat till he said, 'Yes, the swim-team van just passed me. Still going nice and steady on Grant and that Dodge Dart is right behind it. I'm turning to follow them now.'

'The blue Dodge you followed on I-10?'

'Yes. He's following the van.'

'Can you see Denny on the van?'

'No. There's one small window in the back and I can just see the tops of three small heads. I'm dropping back a little – I don't want to scare off Mr Dodge. They'll be heading up to Hedrick, right?'

'Yes. Probably turning on Tucson. Soon as I'm sure I'll call Dispatch to ask for a box on Tucson north of Grant. What do you think about cross-streets – Water, Spring?'

'Copper's got the best space.'

The van turned off Grant onto Tucson with the old blue Dodge close behind. Sarah said, 'OK, turning onto Tucson now. I'm calling Dispatch.'

He was silent while she called. Then he asked, 'You see your guys yet?'

'They're meeting me at the turn. It's just ahead . . . and there they come, crossing Jackson.' She texted Ollie, 'Box Dodge Dart @ Tucson/Copper.'

Then Dispatch called and said, 'Four cars boxed around Copper and Tucson, waiting for your signal.' She wouldn't see them till she called, but she remembered how it felt to be in the cars, waiting, hoping the prey kept coming.

When she saw the sign for Flower Street, Sarah said 'Go!' into her hand-mike. Eight cars swarmed the intersection of Tucson and Copper just as the Dodge entered it. When she saw they had the blue Dodge stopped inside a rectangle of flashing light strips, Sarah called Ollie and said, 'Will you go stop the swim-team van?'

Two minutes later, Will Dietz climbed onto the team vehicle, which was stopped by the curb just past Glenn. He found Ollie standing guard over a startled coach and driver and five thoroughly spooked middle-school swimmers, all face down on the floor.

After sundown, Sarah and her family sat out on the patio in the dim glow from two house lights, nothing but a bug light turned on outside. The heat had eased a little. Doves made sad sounds in the trees. Sarah had been home long enough to enjoy a plate of warmed-over hash and a cold glass of Shiraz. Relaxed in the canvas recliner, she finally got to hear Denny's side of the story.

'We won our meet so we were pretty happy

getting on the van,' Denny said. 'But the street was full of cars and we could see we'd be forever getting home. Coach kept saying, "At least we get to go back on Grant. A change of scenery will help." But at rush hour, who can tell the difference? The MGs were bored, of course, so they decided—'

'Wait,' Aggie said. 'What are MGs?'

'Mean Girls. You saw them in swim class, remember? Pulling sneaky stunts on this one little waify girl named Brady who only has one ratty swimsuit. On the bus today they got really awful, mocking every move she made.'

'Are they still doing that?' Aggie looked at Sarah. 'I thought we agreed somebody should make them stop.'

'We did,' Sarah said. 'I guess we've all been waiting for somebody else to do the job.'

'Yeah, well, I was about ready to today,' Denny said. 'I couldn't take it anymore. But I looked around to see where the next light was so I could judge how long till I jumped up—'

Aggie said, 'Jumped up for what?'

'To clobber Snotty Patty with my fanny pack.'

'Good Heavens, child.'

'Grandma, usually I agree it's not right to hit people but nobody else has done *anything*. Brady was almost crying, and the closer she got to tears the more the MGs liked it! Patty had the back of her hand on her forehead and was going on like, "Ooh, it makes me so saaad," and her pals were just breaking up over that. But Coach Joan pretended she couldn't see them – she was being all polite and sweet, setting a good example the

259

way she does. I decided maybe Patty could follow her example better if I broke her nose first. But when I looked around out the back window I saw that crazy car.'

'The Chaser's Delight.' Will's voice came dryly out of the deep gloom by the sumac bush. 'So helpful that he drove his fishing car.' Rocking contentedly in his old wooden yard-sale chair, he sipped a beer and watched the moon rise over the bug light.

'Why did he do that, I wonder?' Sarah said. 'Make himself so easy to spot?'

'I think he's a quiet polite type and that car helps him get in the mood for mischief,' Will said.

Sarah said, 'Did you know right away what you were looking at, Denny?'

'Oh, I knew the car all right but I wasn't sure he was following the van. I thought, he's got just as much right on this street as we have, let's not get crazy. But there's so much construction on Grant now . . . Our driver decided to detour around some of it and when we turned off onto Water Street for a while the blue Dart stuck right with us. A few blocks later we got back onto Grant and he was still there. That's when I sent you guys the message.' Despite the hot night, she shivered. 'Did you get it right away?'

'Yes,' Sarah said. 'But it took a few seconds for me to make myself believe it. You made my day, Will, when I called you and you said you were already on it.'

'Well, we said we'd never use it to play games and I knew Denny wouldn't go back on that.'

'I got scared, though,' Denny said, 'when we drove on and on and nothing happened. I guess it wasn't so long but it felt long.'

'We about set a new land record for rapid response, actually. That's some crew you got there, Sarah.'

'We've been over some jumps together so we trust each other. The box went really well, didn't it? But I suppose it didn't feel so cut and dried to you, Denny.'

'Well, I got so nervous, hoping I did the right thing. So when Patty started again with one of her Brady imitations, I was so strung out I really couldn't stand the distraction so I jumped up and swung my fanny pack at her and yelled, "If you don't cut that out I'll break your face!" And just then the van sort of lurched into the curb and stopped, and Ollie jumped on the bus with that cannon in his hands and yelled, "Everybody down on the floor!"'

'After that everything was kind of a blur for a while.'

'For me too,' Sarah said. 'There's so much to do during an arrest like that and we hadn't exactly sorted out who was in charge. So I went ahead and read Ames his Miranda rights – somebody had to – and bless those street cops, they all just followed my lead. The arrest van got there fast so I was feeling kind of on a roll till I got that phone call from Sandy.'

Denny said, 'No kidding. She called you in the middle of all that?'

'Yup. I'd forgotten all about her and I was letting all my calls go to voicemail while we booked Jack Ames. I activated the phone to tell the station we were coming in with a prisoner because Ames had called a lawyer and was starting to object to everything so I didn't want any hang-ups with the fingerprints and blood tests.

'But the minute my phone went live there she was, waiting. Just furious, yelling at me, "You're in such a freaking hurry for these results so we all work overtime to finish them and now you can't be bothered to answer your phone. What the hell is it with you?"'

Will said, 'Was that the DNA report?'

'Yeah, the one I'd been waiting for all day. She was so mad I was afraid for a while she might hang up without giving it to me. "Even for a detective," she said to me, "you are exceptionally pushy and inconsiderate, do you know that?"'

'Why Sarah,' Aggie said, 'that's so unfair.'

'I thought so too. But I really wanted those test results so I poured apologies and praise over Sandy like syrup on a waffle. And when she finally calmed down she gave me just what I needed to settle all the arguments.'

'He's the killer, no question?'

'No question – a perfect match. It's sad, in a way. He's a really nice man, most of the time.'

'Except when he's shooting somebody in the ear.'

'Well, just that one time.'

'Isn't it wonderful, though,' Will said, 'how proof can shorten the work day?'

'You can't help but love it. Soon as he heard what we had, Ames quit protesting and just started justifying everything he did. It was almost comical – I couldn't get him to stop then. He was really proud of himself for wearing the clown suit.'

'Well, that was clever.'

'Yes, it helped him get in and out both. But even though we'd Mirandized him I was trying not to hear any more – didn't want him to say later he was coerced. I said, "Wait, you better talk to that lawyer before you say any more," but he said, "No, I want you to understand that I had to punish that monster for what he did to Poppy." I said, "You didn't have to shoot at my car, though, did you?" He said, "Well, I'm sorry about that, but I was trying to throw you off my trail." But just then Delaney came and shut the discussion down. He said, "Let's let him cool off in a cell overnight and charge him tomorrow."'

'So even after a major arrest, you actually got home before dark,' Aggie said. 'Would you like another piece of cake?'

In bed that night, Will said, 'When you write your report of this day's work, might be just as well if you leave my name out of it, hmm?'

'Um. I could make that work, I guess. If you think it's best.' She had been wondering how to suggest it.

'Did you get a chance to ask Ames why he was chasing Denny?'

'We had a minute together while we waited for the intake officer at the jail but I was trying not to talk to him by then. We'll be doing a full-scale interview tomorrow before we book him and

Delaney didn't want to take the edge off that. But by then Ames wanted to talk; I guess he was beginning to feel the loneliness of the cell. He looked at me and said, "I wasn't going to hurt her. Just grab her for a few minutes and then let her go."'

'Of course he would say that.'

'Sure. I said, "Why?" And he said, "I wanted you to understand what despair feels like."'

'Man, he's got a nerve, saying that to a cop.'

'Yes. Well, people don't know, do they?' She slid closer and said, 'Hold me, will you?'

He wrapped his hard arms around her; they both made nesting sounds, and slept.

Denny went back to swim class the next day. She was quiet at dinner – they all were, exhausted from yesterday's stress, not wanting to talk about it anymore and too tired to think of anything else.

But when Sarah asked her, 'How was swimming today?' Denny erupted unexpectedly into giggles.

'It was good,' she said. 'Quiet.'

Sarah raised her eyebrows. 'Quiet but amusing?'

'Well . . . swimming was just OK. But I over-heard something before class.'

All three adults were watching her now.

'That wingnut named Cheryl – she's one of the MGs, you know? I heard her in the shower whispering to Patty. She said, "What was that all about on the way home yesterday?" And Patty said, "Did you know Denny comes from a whole family of vigilantes? Be careful around her, she's got this nutty thing about *justice*. If she sees you do anything she doesn't approve of she calls her cop friends and starts beating up on people, and they come with *guns* to see if she needs any help."'

'Denny, now come on,' Sarah said. 'Are you sure she said that?'

'She did, honest. And nobody made fun of Brady today.' Denny folded her napkin and giggled some more. Her braces flashed in the late summer sunshine. 'I feel sort of like the Caped Crusader.'

Sarah saw the delight in Will's eyes and sent him a small headshake. 'Denny,' she said, 'we are cops. We are not vigilantes.'

'Oh, I know that, Aunt Sarah. But you should see how nice it is when Brady gets to swim in peace. She's finally getting a decent kick in the butterfly.'

'That *is* nice, but—'

'Also,' Aggie said, 'if the adults in her life had done the right thing, Denny would not have been stuck there alone with all that bad behavior.'

'You're right, Ma – you have kind of a thing for justice too, don't you? But right now I'm trying to make sure Denny doesn't get the idea that she can make her own law and fix whatever's wrong with the world by beaning people with her fanny pack.'

'Why would she ever think that,' Will said, 'when we just showed her she can fix everything with her phone?'